"The train d___ women, ___ ___ said

She'd anticipated a showdown with their wagon leader if her disguise was ever discovered. Well, the time had arrived. And she wasn't going to let him intimidate her into backing down.

"You're darn right it doesn't," Jeb said. "And for many good reasons."

Kerry looked Jeb Hunter squarely in the eye. "I'd be interested in hearing those reasons, Captain. But right now I'm more concerned with getting some dry clothes and trying to figure out how we're going to get my wagon out of the middle of the river!"

She turned her back on him and marched up the bank. Jeb Hunter felt his gut twist. A woman. Damnation, what a development. A lone woman on his train. And not just any woman—one who wouldn't listen to orders and who had a stubborn streak as wide as Kansas...!

Dear Reader,

If your mother didn't tell *you* about Harlequin Historical, this Mother's Day might be a good time to let *her* in on the secret. The gift of romance can enhance anyone's life, and our May books promise to be a spectacular introduction. Critics have described Ana Seymour's romances as "spirited," "heartwarming" and "impossible to put down." This author is sure to please with her latest title, *Jeb Hunter's Bride*, the story of a feisty adventuress whose journey west heals the haunted soul of a handsome wagon train leader.

And don't miss *The Wilder Wedding*, by up-and-coming author Lyn Stone, the story of a sensible heiress who believes she is dying and, determined to live for the moment, proposes to a dashing and dangerous private investigator. Rae Muir returns with *Twice a Bride*, the second book of her captivating WEDDING TRAIL series. In this authentic Western, a trail scout's daughter marries a rugged hunter to fulfill her father's dying wish—only her father doesn't die....

Rounding out the month is *Lion's Lady* by award-winning author Suzanne Barclay. In this latest title featuring the stormy Sutherland clan, Lion Sutherland must choose between his duty to his clan and his undying passion for the woman he betrayed.

Whatever your tastes in reading, you'll be sure to find a romantic journey back to the past between the covers of a Harlequin Historical. Happy Mother's Day!

Sincerely,

Tracy Farrell
Senior Editor

Please address questions and book requests to:
Silhouette Reader Service
U.S.: 3010 Walden Ave., P.O. Box 1325, Buffalo, NY 14269
Canadian: P.O. Box 609, Fort Erie, Ont. L2A 5X3

JEB HUNTER'S
BRIDE

ANA
SEYMOUR

Harlequin Books

TORONTO • NEW YORK • LONDON
AMSTERDAM • PARIS • SYDNEY • HAMBURG
STOCKHOLM • ATHENS • TOKYO • MILAN
MADRID • WARSAW • BUDAPEST • AUCKLAND

ISBN 0-373-29012-8

JEB HUNTER'S BRIDE

Books by Ana Seymour

Harlequin Historicals

The Bandit's Bride #116
Angel of the Lake #173
Brides for Sale #238
Moonrise #290
Frontier Bride #318
Gabriel's Lady #337
Lucky Bride #350
Outlaw Wife #377
Jeb Hunter's Bride #412

ANA SEYMOUR

has been a Western fan since her childhood—the days of shoot-'em-up movie matinees and television programs. She has followed the course of the Western myth in books and films ever since, and says she was delighted when cowboys started going off into the sunset with their ladies rather than their horses. Ms. Seymour lives with her two daughters near one of Minnesota's ten thousand lakes.

For my aunt and uncle,
Betsy and Richard McCosh, in celebration of the
50th anniversary of their very own Western romance.

Prologue

Independence, Missouri
April 1857

Kerry closed her eyes as the scissors sliced through her long black hair. "Do it quick, Paddy, before I change my mind."

"I wish you *would* change your mind," her brother grumbled. "And stop calling me Paddy." The shears clicked ruthlessly as shimmery cascades of hair fell to the ground around them.

"It's the name our father called you. Out of respect for his memory, if nothing more, you should use it."

Patrick Gallivan sighed. "Kerry, you were twelve when we came here—you remember the Old Country almost as well as Papa did. But I was only six. I'm American—I don't want an Irish name."

"You're Irish, too." Kerry's eyes were still shut. "Is it too horrible to look at?"

Patrick stepped back and reviewed his handiwork. "Well, you don't look like a man, if that's what you're asking. I don't know how you expect to fool anyone.''

Kerry opened her eyes and slowly bent over the silver filigree mirror that had been her mother's back in Duncannon. ''Oh dear'' was all she could say.

Patrick put down the scissors with a snort of disgust. ''I knew you'd be sorry, Kerry. What a dumb idea.''

Kerry glared at her thirteen-year-old brother. ''I suppose you'd rather go back to New York and stack boxes of fish for the rest of your life.''

Patrick shuddered. ''I never even want to *see* another fish.''

''Then you'd better help me with this. Because otherwise there's no way the association will let us stay with the wagon train. Single females are not allowed.''

Patrick's face softened. ''You're not a single female, Kerry. You have a male protector—me.''

Kerry swallowed the lump that had lodged in her throat the minute she had seen her shorn head, and reached for her brother's hand. ''You *are* my protector, Pad...Patrick, but I don't think the association leaders will see it that way.''

''The lawyer in St. Louis said that the contract Papa signed was''—he stopped and screwed up his mouth as he tried to remember the legal terms—''transferable in perpetuity to his heirs.''

''Yes, but he also said the members can vote to remove *any* wagon considered undesirable for the welfare of the group.''

For a moment neither said anything. They'd had enough of feeling undesirable since leaving Ireland.

Instead of the golden land of promise they'd expected, New York City had proved remarkably hostile toward the small band of immigrants who had arrived in the fall of 1853 with little money and fewer prospects. It was no wonder that in the squalor of the overcrowded immigrant neighborhood Sean Gallivan had been immediately homesick for the green hills of his homeland. No wonder that he'd dreamed of reaching California, where a man could still live and support his family from the fruits of the land.

Finally Patrick grinned. "Well, if they do have the right to kick us off the wagon train, I guess we'll just have to be sure they don't want to. We'll have to show them what a fine couple of lads we are." His voice held the same brave determination that had helped Kerry keep going over the past horrible month. Her little brother was growing up, she'd thought more than once as they dealt together with her father's sudden death. He was growing up just in time to face a world that sometimes seemed too harsh for even the strongest spirit.

Kerry smiled back at him. "So...do I look like a *fine* lad?" she asked with an exaggerated brogue that made the word sound like "foine." Standing up from the table in the tiny boardinghouse room they'd shared since arriving in Independence two days ago, she put her hands on her hips and stalked across the room with giant steps. She was wearing a pair of Patrick's trousers, which came well above her ankles, and a jacket of her father's that hung on her narrow shoulders like a potato sack.

Her brother watched her thoughtfully. "You don't

have to walk like a rooster. Just move normally…only don't, you know, sway your hips.''

Kerry's eyes widened. "I never sway my hips."

"Yes, you do." He grinned mischievously. "When
the Flanagan brothers used to come around, you
would sway them even more."

Kerry tugged at the hem of her father's coat to
cover more of the tight pants. "That shows how much
you know, little brother. I *hated* the Flanagan brothers.''

"Not Mickey…" Patrick teased in a singsong tone.

Kerry gave a huff. "I don't have time to listen to
your nonsense. Tomorrow we face the head of the
association, and if we can't convince him that we're
capable of driving a rig to California, we're in big
trouble. So, truly now, how do I look?''

"You'll have to wear boots to cover those bare
ankles.''

"I'm going to wear yours. You can almost fit into
Papa's by now, the way your feet are growing.''

"Mine are too big for you," he protested.

"I'll make do.''

Patrick shook his head, still studying her. "I don't
know, sis. We'll have to hope that this Captain Hunter
is half-blind.''

"I don't think we want our trail guide to be half-
blind," Kerry observed dryly, flopping down on the
narrow cot that was the room's only bed. Their funds
were growing distressingly low, so they had taken the
poorest room they could find, and Patrick had slept
on the floor for the past two nights. Today they would
hire a temporary wagon to take them, along with their
father's tools, which they had brought from New

York, to Westport Landing. There they would join the encampment gathering along the banks of the Missouri River. The fully outfitted Conestoga their father had arranged through painstaking correspondence over the past few months should be waiting there for them.

Patrick laughed. "Well, not blind, maybe, just a little near-sighted. And you'll have to try to keep out of his way as much as possible."

Impatiently she tore off the oversize coat, revealing curves that would instantly give the lie to her deception. She threw the coat on the bed, then ran her hands threw her newly shorn hair. "All I want is to get to California." With a last look in the mirror, she sighed. "I plan to stay out of everyone's way—especially Captain Hunter's. I hope the man never even knows I'm alive."

Chapter One

Westport Landing, Kansas
April 1857

Jeb Hunter rode along the double row of wagons, nodding an occasional greeting to his newest band of pilgrims. The wagons always looked so fresh and pretty at this stage—their hickory-stretched covers flapping proudly in the gentle Kansas breeze. It was the largest group he had taken yet. From a trickle of daring pioneers a decade ago, the western flow had grown to a mighty river, so that by now at midseason the trail outposts—Fort Kearney, Fort Laramie and the like—were bustling cities with thousands of wagons passing through. But the numbers hadn't lessened the danger, nor lowered the toll. Each time Jeb went across, the crosses marking trail deaths had multiplied like seeds scattered in the wind.

"Afternoon, Mr. Todd, Miz Todd," Jeb called, flicking his finger against the brim of his leather hat. The Todds were exactly the kind of people he liked to have in his party. Frank Todd was coolheaded, strong and a good shot. And he only had a wife to watch out for—no children, no mother or sister-in-law to lessen the odds. One man protecting one woman, the way things were meant to be. Every time Jeb took on a big family with helpless females and children he felt the familiar knot in his stomach. It wasn't as bad as it used to be. There had been times after he'd lost Melanie that the knot had gotten so big and tough, it would actually make him sick. He'd have to stop along the trail and puke out whatever had gone into his stomach over the past few hours. But nowadays he could usually swallow down the knot and get his mind back to other matters.

Frank Todd hollered back to him. "Will we be ready to roll on schedule tomorrow, Captain?"

Jeb nodded and reined his horse to pull closer to the Todds' wagon. "We're waiting on two more outfits, and they're both due in this afternoon."

"One will be those Irish boys, isn't that right?" Eulalie Todd asked. At Jeb's nod she continued, "Those poor boys with their father dropping dead so sudden like. It's a wonder they still want to make the trip."

Jeb frowned. "Their father already had his equipment all purchased. He did a good job of it, too. It's a fine wagon. But I'm not too comfortable myself with the thought of the two of them tackling it alone. If we could talk them out of it, I'd be a mite relieved."

"Don't we want all the wagons we can get?" Frank asked.

"Not necessarily. We already have nearly fifty, and anything more than that can get difficult to manage."

"Do you want me to talk to the boys when they get here?" Frank had been elected representative for the paying members of the association, which meant that Jeb could use him as an arbiter if there was a disagreement among the settlers. They also were carrying Jeb's personal supplies and food. Once they started rolling, he would camp with them each night and share their cookfire.

"No, I'll handle it. Legally, they're signed on, and their wagon's already been delivered here from Boone's place. So if they're up to it, I guess we'll take them."

Frank nodded his approval. "You tell them to call on Eulalie and me if they need some extra help."

Jeb smiled. "The papers say Gallivan's children are thirteen and nineteen years old. Thirteen's barely out of knee britches, but I'm hoping that the nineteen-year-old will turn out to be a burly fellow who can pull his own weight."

"Well now, I'd say nineteen's a fine age to be starting a new life out West," Eulalie Todd offered. "Most lads are in their prime by then. But they'll be grieving still. You tell them to come on over and see Eulalie if they get to feeling poorly. I'll feed them a nice hot bowl of turnip soup." Her voice became wistful. "Back home we'd have the house full up of neighbor children every time I made my turnip soup." She looked over her shoulder as if she might see all the way across the prairie to the neat brick house she had left behind in St. Louis.

"I'll do that, ma'am." Jeb turned to her with the deep smile that lit his face only seldom these days. "And I'll plan on polishing off a bowl or two of that soup myself.'' He winked at her, then tipped his hat once again and rode away.

Patrick eyed their new wagon with a look of dismay. ''How are we supposed to fit everything in there, sis? Papa's tools alone will take up half the space.''

Kerry was thinking the same thing. She had that sick feeling in her stomach that had become so familiar since the day three weeks ago when she and Patrick had returned to their hotel room back in St. Louis to find their father slumped over the edge of his bed, still and cold. She took a deep breath. ''We'll take out all these supplies and put the toolboxes in first, then pile things on top of them. It'll be tight, but I think we can do it.''

''And where do we sleep? On top of the roof?'' Patrick's voice gave signs of beginning its descent into manhood, but at the moment it was shrill, sarcastic and annoying.

''We'll sleep on the roof if we have to in order to get all this to California. If Papa could bring these things all the way from Ireland, I can sure as shooting get them to California.''

Her brother leaped nimbly into the back of the wagon. ''We could just take the metal pieces and leave some of the wooden things behind. I can make new ones myself when we get to California.''

This last was said with a deliberately casual air that told Kerry her brother knew perfectly well that his woodworking was not even close to the master craftsman level that had been passed along in the Gallivan family for generations. Patrick was good with his hands, but he had not had time to develop his father's skill. But Kerry would never be the one to tell him this. "It was Papa's dream to start a new life in California, Patrick. To start over on rich, new land and with the things he brought from home. Now that he's gone, we're going to do it for him. We'll find the room." Kerry bit down hard on her lip. This was not the time to give way to grief, or to discouragement. "Maybe we don't need all these supplies the Boone store sent. There are only two of us to feed now instead of three."

"That's right. Papa certainly won't be eating anything this trip." Patrick's face brightened. "Maybe we could sell some of this food back to Boone's and it would give us a little cash."

Kerry tamped down her annoyance at her brother's light tone. She knew that Patrick missed their father every bit as much as she did, but his youthful high spirits gave him the edge on dealing with his death. With each passing day, it seemed to be easier and easier for her brother to talk about him, to consign him to a place in the heart and mind reserved only for memories. Kerry had not reached that point. She still felt as if any minute she would turn the corner and see his dear, weathered face. When the realization hit that this would never happen again, she'd feel as if a hand was clutching at her throat, threatening to squeeze away her breath. Sean Gallivan was dead. After all his dreams, all his planning, all his saving, he would never see his dream fulfilled in the promised land of California. But she would.

"We'll ask Captain Hunter when he shows up. In

the meantime, let's start moving some of these barrels out so we can get organized.''

"I thought the captain was supposed to be here to welcome us."

Kerry pulled herself up beside her brother. There was scarcely room for the two of them inside the narrow bed of the wagon, which was already crammed full with the supplies her father had ordered. Patrick was right. There was no room left for the beloved woodworking tools that had been made by their great-grandfather—two heavy boxes of them that had already journeyed across an ocean and a third of a continent.

"Captain Hunter has many duties. I'm sure he'll be along directly."

Kerry was in no hurry for the meeting with the wagon train captain, knowing that the encounter would be the first true test of her disguise. This morning when they'd left Independence, Patrick had settled the roominghouse bill himself and the man at the livery stable had hardly given her a glance. And she was becoming more comfortable in her brother's trousers. But she couldn't hope to escape scrutiny forever.

She worried about her face. Before packing her mirror, she had taken a long look at herself. The short hair didn't change the fact that her face was distinctly feminine—the lips full and red, the bright blue eyes heavily lashed. Her face was bronzed by the sun, not lily-white like that of the true ladies she had seen parading up and down Park Avenue back in New York. But her cheeks were smooth as polished marble. No one who came close would believe that they belonged to a man. Once they'd left the city this morning she'd rubbed dirt all over her face, much to her brother's amusement.

"Hallo there!" A voice reached them from the front of the wagon.

Patrick jumped down and leaned around the edge. "We're back here."

From the dark shelter of the wagon, Kerry peered out at the man who was pulling up his horse next to her brother. Her first impression was that he was big. Even mounted in his saddle, she could tell that he was much taller than the immigrant lads she had spent time with back in New York. Fully half a foot taller than Mickey Flanagan, she'd wager.

"Mr. Gallivan?" the man asked, bending to look inside the wagon.

Kerry's stomach tightened. "My father's dead," she said gruffly, remembering at the last minute to keep her voice low.

The man looked disconcerted. He rubbed a hand along a whiskery chin. "Ah...I know that. I'm sorry. We've been in touch with your lawyer, of course. But I was addressing you, sir. I'd be happy to call you by your first name, if you prefer, but I don't know what it is. I'm Jeb Hunter," he added.

Kerry sat back on her haunches and willed herself to stay calm. Of course, *she* was Mr. Gallivan now. And she'd have to do a better job of keeping her wits about her if she wanted her ruse to succeed.

Her brother calmly reached a hand toward the new-comer. "Pleased to meet you, Captain. I'm Patrick, and that's Kerry. Skipping the 'mister' part would be fine with my...ah...brother."

"Kerry?" the captain asked, still trying to see into the dim interior.

"Ah...Ker...ah...Kiernan." Patrick corrected firmly.

Captain Hunter cocked his head. "Irish name, right? Well, are you two gentlemen finding everything to be satisfactory?"

Patrick looked at his sister to reply.

Kerry took a deep breath and spoke carefully in the deep voice she'd been practicing. "We seem to have a few more supplies than we can fit, Captain Hunter."

Jeb grinned. "Old Albert Boone knows how to pack them in, that's for sure. But I think you'll find that they've given you just enough to cover your needs. The wagon may look crowded now, but you'll get used to it."

Kerry risked leaning a little into the sunlight. In spite of her resolution to stay away from Captain Hunter, he would have to see her face sometime, and it might as well be now. "The problem, Captain, is that we've brought a few items along with us from New York that have to go in our wagon."

She noticed that he started a little when he saw her, and she quickly pointed behind him, hoping to distract his attention. Jeb gave her one more hard glance, then turned back toward the rented wagon. With a low whistle he swung a long leg over his horse and jumped to the ground. "What in the name of Jupiter is all that?"

He didn't sound pleased. Kerry swallowed. "There's some farm equipment, and the two boxes are my father's tools." The defensive tone made her voice creep higher.

Jeb stalked over to the freight wagon and looked at the jumbled contents with disbelief.

Once again Patrick took charge. "My brother and I are going to start our own ranch in California. My father brought those things with him when he came from Ireland."

Jeb turned around and looked from Patrick back over to Kerry, who had once again retreated into the shadows. He shook his head. "There's no way you'll be able to take all this with you. Your father should have understood that it would be impossible. I'm sorry, lads." He lowered his head and once again tried to peer inside the dark recesses of the wagon. "Listen, I know your father's death must have been a terrible shock to you two. If you want to head on back to New York, I'll be sure you get your money back from the association and from Boone's, too."

Kerry's cheeks flushed hot. She had been told one time too often over the past few days that she ought to consider giving up. Vaulting over the lip of the wagon she landed hard on the ground and turned to face Jeb Hunter with her hands on her hips. "Captain Hunter, my brother and I are going to California, and we have a contract that says you have to take us."

He took a couple steps toward her. His eyes were an odd hazel color, the corners crinkled from years of riding outdoors in the prairie sun. He had a strong face that matched the raw strength of his tall body. Her anger died as swiftly as it had arisen. "We won't give you any trouble," she added softly. "I promise."

Jeb looked at her curiously, then over at Patrick, and back once again to the loaded freight wagon. "That stuff came all the way from Ireland?" Jeb snatched his hat off and ran a hand back through his unruly, light brown hair.

"All the way from Ireland," Kerry said firmly. "And now it's going all the way to California."

Jeb looked uncertain. The expression didn't sit naturally on his face. He stretched his neck to look around toward the front of the wagon where the team of four oxen grazed placidly. "The more weight your oxen pull, the more water they'll need." Jeb put on his hat and pushed it to the back of his head. "Water can get mighty precious along the trail."

Kerry had begun to relax. Though he had given her some strange glances, it appeared Captain Hunter was not going to question her identity as the *son* of Sean Gallivan. "I've noticed that many of the families are bringing along a milk cow. Will their cows need water, Captain?"

He gave a reluctant smile. "I reckon they will."

Kerry nodded. "Then you can just consider the extra equipment to be our milk cow."

Jeb pulled himself back on his horse in an easy, natural motion that did something queer to Kerry's insides. "I'll make a bargain with you. Cut this stuff in half." He gestured to the freight wagon. "Leave the plow, one of those toolboxes, whatever else you can. There'll be a representative from Boone's out later on this afternoon to take back any leftover supplies. He'll probably give you some money for whatever you have to leave behind."

"Captain Hunter, my brother and I have already had to leave the body of our father behind in St. Louis. I intend to take whatever else I can of him to California." Kerry realized that her voice had trembled slightly. Furiously she bit painfully into her lower lip. But her emotion had apparently not affected Jeb Hunter.

"I'm sorry. At least half that pile stays here...or you and your entire wagon stay. Take your choice. We leave at dawn, boys. I'll leave you alone to make your decision."

When Kerry made no reply, Patrick said, "Thank you, Captain. We'll be ready to go at dawn."

Jeb took a last look over at the freight wagon. "Just remember we've got two sets of mountains to cross before you get to the California. My best advice to you is to travel as light as possible."

Then he wheeled his horse and rode off, sending up a cloud of dust that stung Kerry's eyes.

"Maybe he's right, Kerry," Patrick said after a moment. "We don't really need all those things. I can get new tools when we get out there, and then I'll make whatever else we need."

Kerry had a sudden vision of her brother as a small boy sitting at their father's side, earnestly copying each move of Sean Gallivan's sure, swift hands. She blinked hard and let the tears well up to wash away the dust. "We're going to build Papa's ranch in California, Patrick. It's going to be every bit as rich and beautiful as he dreamed. And," she added fiercely, "we're going to do it with his grandfather's tools."

They had worked through the night. The settlers' representative, Frank Todd, had ridden up at dusk to invite them to a campfire and farewell party, but they had politely declined and continued shifting and shoving and unloading and reloading until the inside of their wagon was more intricately arranged than a Chinese puzzle. It had been almost dawn before Kerry had been satisfied that everything was packed. The two big toolboxes were covered with supplies, impossible to see from any angle. Everything was on board except for a box from the Boone store labeled Meat Cakes.

"I think I'd have trouble getting one of these things down anyway," she'd told her brother.

"They're not so bad," he'd replied, munching on one. "At least they're not fish."

When their father had become fanatical about his plans for the journey to California, they'd saved money by eating the broken and sometimes half-spoiled pieces of fish Patrick had been able to bring home each day from the docks. Now just a fishy odor was enough to make them both queasy.

The man from Boone's outfitters had come and gone the previous evening, so the box of meat cakes sat in the grass alongside the wagon. "We have an hour or so until dawn," Kerry said finally. "We could probably sleep."

"I'm too wide-awake," Patrick replied, sitting down beside her at the little campfire they'd kept burning through the night. "It's hard to believe that we're finally on our way. So much has happened...."

His voice trailed off. "It's not fair, is it?" Kerry mused. "He should be here."

Patrick nodded as they both stared at the glowing embers. After several minutes he said, "You go ahead and sleep if you want, sis. We have a long day ahead."

"No. This is restful right here. A few moments of

peace before everyone else is awake. Maybe we'll be able to sleep along the way.''

Patrick grinned. ''Show me a square foot of space inside the wagon where I can curl up and then I'll think about napping.''

Kerry sighed. ''There'll be more space as we use up the supplies along the way.''

''You boys must be eager to get started.'' Jeb Hunter's voice came out of the darkness behind them. ''You're the first ones up.''

''We haven't been…'' Patrick began, then stopped as Kerry elbowed his side. ''Ah…we're ready and waiting.''

''I hope you got enough rest. The first couple of days are usually grueling.'' Jeb glanced over at their wagon. ''I see you got your wagon loaded. Did you sell the rest of your stuff back to Boone's?''

''Yup. No problem,'' Kerry replied quickly without so much as a stammer. What was one more lie among the many she would be forced to tell to maintain her masquerade?

Captain Hunter was studying them keenly in the firelight. Kerry didn't like the speculative look in his eyes when he glanced her way. She bent over to put a log on the fire, hiding her face. ''Like my brother said, we're ready to go.''

Jeb sauntered casually over and peeked in the back of the wagon. ''It looks pretty full up in there.''

Kerry gave a noncommittal murmur in reply.

He walked back over to the fire and stood towering over them. ''Just so you understand. Sometimes the trail gets too tough—we have to lighten the load, leave things behind. You'll find the way littered with family heirlooms, tools, furniture, all kinds of 'essentials' that somehow just don't seem that essential anymore a thousand miles out from Westport Landing.''

Kerry wanted to look him directly in the face, but she had to remember that her disguise was more important at this point than her pride. She kept her eyes lowered. ''I understand what you're saying, Captain. I can assure you that my brother and I will do whatever it takes to reach California.''

''Well, I admire your attitude, Kiernan. That's the kind of spirit we need along the trail.'' Jeb lapsed into silence as he once again studied the two Irish boys. He'd been disappointed when he first saw the elder Gallivan brother. The lad was slight, almost sickly thin, and looked not much older than his little brother. But the young Irishman had stood up to Jeb well enough—both brothers had, for that matter. Perhaps they would also stand up to the rigors of the trail. ''How well can you boys shoot?'' he asked them.

Patrick and Kerry looked at each other. ''We're willing to learn,'' Patrick said finally. ''There's a fine new rifle with the supplies Papa bought.''

''You've never been hunting, never shot a gun?'' Jeb asked, incredulous.

''There are very few buffalo wandering around the streets of Manhattan, Captain,'' Kerry retorted, watching him from under her thick eyelashes.

Jeb chuckled, but shifted uneasily. He could swear that the boy raised his hackles in a way that he'd only experienced with women. It was an odd sensation. Perhaps it had something to do with the fact that the lad was so femininely slender. And then there was that face, so perfect it looked as if it had been chiseled directly off one of the marble statues he'd seen once in a book.

"Well, you'll have to learn to shoot out here—both of you. Maybe one of the other men will give you some lessons. Have you met your neighbors yet?" When both boys shook their heads he continued. "Up in front of you will be Scott Haskell. He's an argonaut and is traveling alone."

"An argonaut?" Patrick asked.

"A prospector. That's what they're calling them—after Jason and the Argonauts. You know—the never-ending search for the Golden Fleece." There was a disdainful note to his voice.

"I thought the Gold Rush was pretty much over," Kerry said.

"There'll always be a gold rush somewhere as long as men think that money is the secret to a happy life." Jeb had learned otherwise a long time ago, but it wasn't a lesson he shared easily. "Anyway, the outfit behind you belongs to the Burnetts—a young couple from Virginia and their two young'uns. Nice folks."

Patrick jumped up from his place by the fire, looking as if he was ready to start this instant. "Do we stay in the same order for the whole trip?" he asked their guide.

"We keep the same order usually, unless there's a reason to switch. But each day the lead wagon goes to the rear."

"How come?"

Jeb smiled. "It's so that every outfit gets a chance at one blessed, dust-free day." When Patrick looked confused, he added, "You'll understand what I mean after an hour or two on the trail."

He wished them luck on their first day, then left to begin a last-minute check on the other wagons.

By the time the first licks of dawn began appearing across the prairie, most of the camp was awake, bustling with energy and the same kind of suppressed excitement that Kerry could see in her brother's face. She herself was wishing she could find a place to get away from everything and sleep for about a week. The long night of loading had taken a toll, as had the past few weeks of grief, strain and worry. Promising herself a good night's sleep once they were out on the trail, she dabbed some water on her tired eyes, then rubbed more dirt across her cheeks.

Actually, she told herself, she should be feeling great. She'd successfully accomplished what she'd promised to herself as she'd stood watching her father's body being lowered into the ground in a cheap pine box. This morning they started west. The wagon train captain had accepted them. Once they left Westport, there was no turning back. Even if her disguise was discovered, they'd have to let her continue on with them. The most difficult obstacle had been met and conquered. She should be feeling on top of the world, but as visions of her father's twinkling blue eyes covered the blur in her own, she couldn't seem to feel anything but tired.

"Wagons, ho!" She turned around at the sound of a childish shout, then blinked to try to clear her vision. She must be more tired than she realized, because she was suddenly seeing double.

"Forward, ho!" shouted vision number two. Kerry gave a small laugh at her own confusion. The pair were twins, of course.

"Good morning," she said as the two identically clad youngsters ran up to her, stopping abruptly a safe five feet away. "Who are you two ladies?"

The little girls giggled and the one on the right said, "I'm Polly, she's Molly."

Kerry masked a wince at the thought of a mother who would name her daughters like two rhyming parrots. "Pleased to meet you. I'm…Kerr…Kiernan. Kiernan Gallivan." She'd entirely forgotten to lower her voice, but the girls didn't appear to question her masculinity.

"We're Burnetts," Polly added. "We're gonna be your neighbors, Ma says, and we have to be nice to you, 'cause you and your brother lost your pa."

After too much false sympathy from strangers, Kerry found the girl's directness disarming. Once again the unshed tears stung her throat. "Yes, we did," she said softly. "How old are you two?"

"I'm older." Polly continued to be the spokesperson for the duo. "Five minutes. But we're both ten."

Kerry turned her eyes to Molly, whose smile was just a little more tentative than her sister's. "Well now, ten's a wonderful age, isn't it, just starting to be grown-up."

Molly looked down at her scuffed shoes. "Pa says we get to drive the wagon," she contributed in a voice Kerry could hardly hear.

"That sounds about right. My brother's thirteen and he's been driving for at least three years."

"But he's a boy," Polly pointed out. "That's different."

"Not always. It doesn't have to be different."

"You talk kind of funny."

Kerry didn't know if the girl was referring to her high pitch or her slight accent, but decided to stay with the safer topic. "That's because I grew up in another country. Have you ever heard of Ireland?"

Both girls nodded and Polly said, "In school. On the train we won't have any school and maybe not for a long time, but my Ma will teach us."

"That's good, Polly. Learning's important."

"That's what Ma says."

"It sounds as if your mother's a smart lady," Kerry replied with a smile.

"I told you girls not to bother the neighbors till we all get started." A pretty blonde who didn't look old enough to be anyone's mother was walking toward them from the next wagon. The smile on her face diluted the reproachful tone of her words.

"She talked to us first, Ma."

"They're not a bother, ma'am." Now Kerry made an effort to keep her voice low.

The woman came up behind her daughters and draped an arm lightly around each. "I'm Dorothy Burnett. And you must be one of the Gallivan boys."

"I'm Kiernan, ma'am. Pleased to meet you." Kerry took a step back toward her own wagon, hoping the woman would not offer a hand to shake. Her slender hands were the one part of her that was impossible to disguise.

"And I see you've already met Polly and Molly." With a little laugh and the air of someone who'd made the explanation many times in the past, she continued, "Their real names are Priscilla Jo and Margaret Mary, but their father put the nicknames on when they were just babes and somehow they've stuck."

Kerry grinned. "Polly and Molly it is, then. You girls will have to help me out on which is which for a while."

"They've been known to trick people in the past," Dorothy said, laughing, "so be careful."

Kerry was drawn to the woman's warmth. It was nice to have another young woman along as a companion, and for a moment she felt a pang knowing that, thanks to her masquerade, she and Dorothy would not be able to become confidantes. It would be comforting to confide her secret to someone. "That's all right, girls," she said a touch wistfully, smiling down at the twins. "I've been known to trick people myself on occasion."

Chapter Two

Jeb Hunter had been right about the dust. It didn't take even the hour or two he had predicted for Kerry and Patrick to realize that moving along in the middle of a train of nearly fifty wagons was a grimy business. The first part of the trail out from Westport was level, easy going—the "sea of grass" her father had told them about during those long evenings of planning back in New York. But the endless procession of wagons had worn the actual trail down to bare ground, and each wagon churned up its own little dirt cyclone as they rolled along. Following the example of some of the more experienced travelers, Kerry and Patrick tied bandannas over their faces to keep out the worst of it.

"I guess I won't have to rub dirt on my cheeks any more," Kerry joked to her brother as they sat side by side on the wagon seat. "There's enough natural accumulation of the stuff to disguise the President of the United States."

"I wish papa had bought us horses instead of these

stupid beasts,'' her brother grumbled. ''Then I could ride out into the fresh air like Captain Hunter.''

All morning they'd watched their wagon master riding from one wagon to the next, checking equipment, giving advice and generally elevating spirits as his flock took their scary first step beyond civilization.

''Horses don't stand up well enough pulling a heavy load. Papa said it had to be mules or oxen, and oxen were cheaper.''

''If he'd bought mules, I could at least have ridden some of the time.''

Jeb Hunter was riding toward them. ''I'll not have you criticize Papa's decisions, Patrick,'' Kerry said absently, her eyes on their guide. It was his extraordinary, almost golden eyes that drew her frequent glances, she'd decided, but she had to admit that the face that went along with the eyes was ruggedly handsome. He had creases along each cheek that made his expression look severe except when he smiled. He didn't seem to be a man who smiled often.

''Are you listening to me, sis?'' her brother asked.

''What?''

''I asked if you thought we might switch the oxen for mules when we reach the changing station.''

Jeb pulled up to them, and at the very last minute Kerry remembered to tug down the brim of her big felt hat. ''How are you boys getting along?'' he called.

''Fine,'' Kerry mumbled. What was wrong with her? She must be even more tired than she thought. Captain Hunter had asked them a simple question, and she'd felt it inside her like a jolt. He was a fine figure of a man, that was for sure, but she had no business getting jittery around him like a maid at her first dance.

"I wish my papa had bought mules," Patrick complained, drawing the captain's eyes away from her. Kerry let out a long breath.

"You've got good animals there, Patrick. You might be thankful to have oxen when your arms start aching from those reins. They're much easier to handle."

"My arms don't ache, and I'd give anything to be able to ride out like you do."

Jeb smiled. "One of these days after everyone's settled you can ride the rounds with me on the back of my horse. Or, even better, you can ride Storm by yourself for a spell and I'll climb on up there with your brother."

Patrick darted a glance at his sister, whose eyes had widened in dismay. "Ah...that's all right," he answered. "I don't mind it so very much."

Jeb seemed a little puzzled at the boy's quick refusal. "Well, the offer's open. And, of course, you can always get out and walk along out in the grass. You and your brother can take turns driving and walking to get a little time out of the dust."

Kerry found her eyes wandering to the way Captain Hunter's strong thighs gripped the side of his horse. With a puff of irritation, she forced her thoughts back to the trip. "Do you really think the oxen are a better choice, Captain Hunter?" She was hoping that the captain's opinion would validate her father's careful preparations.

"There're folk who take both sides," Jeb answered, "but I might go for the oxen for just one reason."

"What's that?" Patrick asked.

Jeb hesitated a moment, then said. "It's a long way to California, and things don't always go as we plan. If we find ourselves up against it, an ox makes a sight tastier meal than a mule."

Patrick and Kerry looked down in dismay at the four black hulks that plodded along in front of them. As Captain Hunter tipped his hat and started back to the Burnetts' wagon, Patrick turned to his sister and said with a weak grin, "At least it's not fish."

They stopped for nooning early in deference to the first-time nerves and muscle aches of the new pioneers. Kerry was relieved to climb down from the wagon and stretch her back. She felt as if she had spent the morning inside a butter churn. Patrick so far seemed unaffected by the jolting. He'd been up and down from the wagon a dozen times already, sometimes walking alongside, sometimes running out into the long grass to get a look at the line of wagons stretching out as far as the eye could see.

As Kerry took out two apples and some jerky for their lunch, her brother came walking sedately back to the wagon with a visitor. Kerry recognized the man as their neighbor to the front—the argonaut, Captain Hunter had called him. She tugged on her hat and tensed her shoulders. She'd be glad when she'd met everyone on the train and had been generally accepted as a male.

In spite of her nervousness, the introductions went smoothly once again. Kerry let out a breath of relief and allowed herself to study Scott Haskell from underneath her hat. He was not as handsome as their trail guide, but his face was pleasant, instantly likable.

"I wanted to come back and meet you boys last night," he was saying, "but I didn't get in until late."

"It wouldn't have mattered how late you came," Patrick replied cheerfully. "We were up all night trying to get the wagon packed up."

Haskell's bushy blond eyebrows shot up. "All night! You boys must be even more tired than I am after working all day yesterday at Iron Joe's."

"Iron Joe's?" Patrick asked.

"The blacksmith, lad. I was a blacksmith up in Pittsburgh, and I earned my team of mules by shoeing just about every other blamed mule on this train."

"Are you going to be a blacksmith in California, Mr. Haskell?"

"Call me Scott, lad. And you too, Kiernan." He gave Kerry what started out to be a quick glance, then seemed to catch himself and let his eyes rest on her face.

"So *are* you?" Patrick persisted.

"What was that, boy?"

"Are you going to be a blacksmith out West?"

Finally he shifted his gaze back to Patrick. "No, sirree. No more smoky bellows for me. No more iron filings itching my hide like a swarm of marsh flies. I'm planning to be rich, Patrick, my lad. The only kind of metal I'm going to be dealing with anymore is gold—pure, yellow gold."

"Golly." Patrick was looking up at Scott Haskell as if he had just crossed the Missouri River on his bare feet.

Kerry felt a twinge of impatience. All she needed was for Patrick to get fancy ideas about gold prospecting instead of working with her to set up the ranch. Once they reached California she would need her brother's help more than ever. "We wish you luck, Mr. Haskell, I'm sure," she said briskly. "But first of all we have to get there. And we should probably be tending to our lunch before Captain Hunter calls for us to get moving again."

He turned that disconcerting gaze on her once more, and this time a secret little smile played around his lips. "You're absolutely right, young man. I'm going to head back to my wagon this minute. But I'll be looking forward to getting to know you *boys* better at the meeting tonight."

Kerry remembered that Captain Hunter had told them that there would be a formal meeting that evening to discuss any problems that might have arisen during their first day. "We'll be there," she said wearily. And after the meeting, she would finally get some sleep.

This was the sixth spring that Jeb had set out with a new band of travelers. Every year there were two or three outfits that headed back by the time they reached Fort Kearney. He usually could predict which ones they would be after the first day on the trail.

This trip it would definitely be the Wagners. The man's wife had not stopped complaining the entire day. And perhaps the Pendletons. They had come all the way from England, but both looked as if the journey was beginning to be too much for them. He wasn't sure about the Irish boys. They certainly had the spirit for it, but it was a tough thing to leave behind a father barely cold in his grave and head out across a continent. He'd found himself thinking about them frequently during this first long day.

He had to spread his attention around—there were always adjustments to be made at the beginning and these people had paid equally for his help. But he'd swung back to the Gallivan wagon as often as he could. Young Patrick was refreshingly enthusiastic and observant. He'd even exclaimed over the different clouds of dust tossed up by the mule teams versus the oxen. The older boy had less to say, but there was a determined expression on his handsome face that intrigued Jeb. When he'd tried to engage the young Irishman in conversation, the lad's answers had been curt and uncommunicative. But somehow Jeb sensed a great vitality behind those vivid blue eyes.

He watched the two brothers as they made their way to the edge of the circle of settlers who had gathered by the big fire Jeb had built a short ways out in the prairie. He had not circled the wagons this first day. That could wait until they were into Indian country.

In the early-spring twilight he could see the faces of his charges. Good folk, generally—steady and determined. He scanned the crowd, but his eyes kept turning back to the striking faces of the two Irish lads.

"Patrick, Kiernan! Come on up front," he called to them finally. "We never got a chance to introduce you to everyone."

Patrick looked at his sister, then gave her elbow a comforting squeeze. Kerry closed her eyes briefly. She was exhausted. But she had wanted to get through with introductions. It might as well be now. With her hat tugged down and concentrating on not swaying her hips, she stalked around the circle to the front. "These are the Gallivan brothers," Jeb was saying, "and I hope all you folks will do your best to make them feel welcome."

Jeb didn't dwell on the presentation. There were a lot of issues to cover, and everyone was tired, so he nodded to Kerry and Patrick to take a seat and started in on the meeting.

Kerry sank heavily to the ground. The few minutes of standing in front of the crowd had used up the last bit of strength she had. She had fully expected that any minute someone—a sharp-eyed child, probably—would point to her and cry out, "Why, that's a girl." But no one had raised a voice. She was now officially Kiernan, one of the "Gallivan brothers." And she could sleep a little easier tonight.

After the meeting, Scott Haskell stepped into place beside her as she made her way back up the line to their wagon. Patrick, not yet out of energy, had run ahead of her. The sky had darkened and was slowly becoming spangled with stars. Her father had said that they would have spectacular nights out on the prairie, but the real thing was far beyond his descriptions.

"It looks like our good weather is going to hold," Haskell observed, matching his pace to hers.

Kerry's face was hidden by the darkness, so she relaxed as she answered sleepily, "The sky's unbelievable. I never knew stars could be so bright."

"We're lucky. Some trains start out in spring rains that don't stop for days. They end up eating mud the rest of the trip."

"My brother and I are prepared to eat anything we have to as long as we get to California."

Haskell chuckled. "You are two mighty determined lads. How old are you, anyway, Kiernan?"

"Nineteen."

Haskell nodded. "You're not too big a fellow, are you?" he asked casually.

"Ah...no. Folks aren't so tall where I come from."

"Patrick looks as if he'll be a strapping gent someday. He's already almost as tall as you are." Haskell's blond hair glinted in the starlight, and he had that same secret smile on his face that had made Kerry uneasy when they'd met earlier in the day.

"I guess he'll be bigger than I. Our father was a tall man." She was finding the conversation a little odd. Scott Haskell had barely met them. What did he care about her brother's height—or hers?

He looked at her steadily in the darkness for a long moment. Then he gave a little nod and switched subjects. "I understand you're headed for the Sonoma valley."

Kerry shrugged her shoulders to ease out the tension. "Yes. Where are you headed, Mr. Haskell?"

"Scott, please," he said with a smile.

"Scott."

"I reckon I'll look around a bit—see where the veins are running richest. Probably south of San Francisco somewheres."

Kerry started to reply when suddenly her foot, clumsy in Patrick's oversize boot, hit a large rock that had been camouflaged by the darkness. She fell off balance directly toward her companion. Scott turned quickly and caught her with strong, sure hands at each shoulder. "I'm sorry," Kerry faltered, embarrassed. She righted herself, grimacing as her ankle gave a nasty twinge.

"Are you all right?" Scott asked.

"Yes, just…I'm sorry." She took a step away from his grasp, giving a little gasp as her foot hit the ground. The twinge was turning into a definite throb. "I seem to have twisted an ankle."

Scott reached out and took her slender hands. He pulled them toward him and turned them over slowly studying them in the starlight. Then he looked into her eyes. "Perhaps those heavy boots are too much for what must be delicate little feet…*Miss* Gallivan."

Under the smears of dirt on her face, Kerry blanched. "I…what do you mean?"

Scott smiled. "Don't worry, lass. Your secret is safe with me, though I can't imagine how anyone on this train can actually believe that you're a male."

Kerry pulled her hands away from him. "When did you know?" she asked dully.

"The minute I saw those beautiful blue eyes," Scott answered cheerfully. "I couldn't believe that God would be so cruel as to waste them on a man." As her features became more dejected he added gently, "Your face is well disguised by the dirt and floppy hat, lass, but I saw your hands. Those slender wrists couldn't belong to a man."

Kerry moved another step backward, only to be reminded once again of the pain in her leg. "The lawyer in St. Louis told us that they wouldn't take a lone woman," she explained, a little breathless with nerves at her sudden discovery and the pain.

"And you wanted to come anyway."

"Yes. My brother and I have to get to California."

Scott nodded, suddenly serious. "You're a brave lass, Kiernan. Is it Kiernan?"

"Kerry."

"Ah. That's better. You're a brave lass, Kerry, and, as I said, I won't be turning you in. In fact, I hope you'll consider me a friend."

His eyes were kind and his hand gentle as he gave her shoulder a little squeeze. "If you will keep my secret, Mr. Haskell, I will definitely consider you a friend."

"Good." He cocked his head. "But you'll have to learn to call me Scott."

She smiled, then sighed. "I guess I'd better, Scott, because I'm already going to take advantage of your friendship."

"Just ask."

Giving her foot a rueful glance, she told him, "I'm afraid I'm going to need some assistance getting back to my wagon."

Scott frowned. "You *are* really hurt, then. Damnation, what luck. I wonder if anyone in the group is trained in medicine?"

Kerry put both her hands up in protest. "No, please. I'll be fine. If you'll just help me to my wagon, I'm sure by tomorrow this'll be back to normal."

Scott hesitated. "You don't want anyone looking at you too closely. Is that it?"

Kerry tightened her jaw against the pain that was beginning to radiate in rings up her leg. Scott grasped her elbows as she swayed. Her hands clutched at his forearms. "Will you help me? Please?" It was not a plea that came easy to her, but at the moment the pain was overriding her usual sense of independence.

Scott bent his head to see her eyes in the starlight, then without a word scooped her up in his brawny arms.

"You don't have to carry me," she protested.

Scott shook his head. "You weigh no more than a feather, lass. I could carry you from here to California without breaking a sweat."

The ache pulsating upward from her foot obliterated all sense of embarrassment she might have felt at this unexpected intimacy with a man she had barely met. "Thank you," she murmured. Then added in a tired voice, "Tomorrow I'll be back on my feet."

But the next day there was no way Kerry would be able to walk and take a turn away from the dust. Her foot had swollen so that even Patrick's large boot would not fit over it. Patrick had bound it in rags over which Kerry had painfully pulled on a large wool sock.

Scott appeared at breakfast to ask about her injury. He offered to make a bed for her in the back of his much roomier wagon, but she refused, accepting only his offer of help in climbing up onto her wagon seat.

Kerry told no one else of her mishap, but there seemed to be some mysterious network of communication among the wagons, and before they were a half hour out on the trail, Jeb Hunter rode back to them, his forehead creased with worry.

Without preliminaries he said, "I understand you hurt your leg last night, Kiernan."

She nodded, keeping her face down under the big

hat. After her discovery by Haskell, her confidence in her disguise had disappeared. "Just an ankle twist—nothing serious," she mumbled.

Jeb shook his head. An injury already—the very first day out. He hoped it wasn't an omen. "Are you sure it's not broken? We won't exactly be running into any doctors between here and Fort Kearney. I guess I'd better have a look at it."

Kerry tensed, and Patrick, riding alongside her in the box, gave her a reassuring pat on the knee. "My brother will be fine," he said. "Honestly. You don't have to worry about it."

Jeb hesitated. The boys' independence was admirable, but the health of his band was his responsibility. He'd seen broken legs fester and turn rotten. "I'll just check it over to be sure," he said in a tone that left no room for argument. "I'll come around when we stop for the nooning. In the meantime, Patrick, why don't you take over the reins and let Kiernan climb in the back to lie down—get that leg propped up."

"There's no room back there to lie—" Patrick began, then stopped as he saw the slight shake of his sister's head. "All right, Captain. We'll do just as you say."

"Good lad." Hunter wheeled his horse and headed back along the train.

"Now what?" Patrick asked after a moment.

Kerry had turned her head and was watching the guide's retreating form with an indignant expression. She was starting to get a little tired of Captain Hunter's high-handed ways. Her father had paid good money to hire his services, as had the other people on the train, yet he acted as if he were the one who had the final say in everything.

"I'm not sure I like that man. He thinks he's the boss."

"Well, he is the boss in a way," Patrick said reasonably. "Everyone on the train has to do what he says."

Kerry turned around on the seat to face her brother. "We're paying *him*, remember?"

"But he's responsible for all of us."

"Well, he's not responsible for…" She sputtered a moment, letting her temper build. "For my feet!" she concluded, looking down at her bandaged leg.

Patrick shook his head. "I think he's going to want to look at your ankle—one way or another."

Kerry thought for a minute. "As soon as we stop for lunch, I want you to run up and fetch Mr. Haskell—Scott. Tell him I need to take him up on his offer."

Patrick frowned. "What offer?"

"Of help. If my foot's already been looked at by an expert, Captain Hunter can't insist on treating it."

"Mr. Haskell's an expert?"

Kerry's chin lifted and her smile held a touch of defiance. "He shoes horses, doesn't he?"

Scott had agreed to help deflect the attention of the wagon train captain from Kerry's obviously feminine legs, but only with the condition that she let him really check on the state of her ankle.

"I'm telling you, it's nothing," she said, her dirt-smeared face growing red. She'd been without a mother since she was a child and had grown up in a household with two males. She wasn't used to *anyone* seeing a portion of her body that should in all decency be covered up.

"Sorry, lass," Scott answered with a charming grin as he climbed up on the side rail to lift her down from the wagon seat. "If I'm to help out with this little deception of yours, I've got to do it with a clean conscience. What if your ankle's actually broken?"

"It can't be broken," Kerry answered firmly. "I can't afford for it to be."

Scott chuckled and bobbled her a bit in his arms as he awkwardly stepped backward down to the ground. "It wouldn't dare," he clarified.

"That's right."

His chuckle turned into a laugh. Against the hard surface of his chest, Kerry felt warm and comforted—the way she felt when she used to crawl up into her father's broad lap as a child. She put the thought out of her head. She hadn't needed the comfort of her father's lap for some years now, and she certainly didn't need the warmth of a man's arms. She was just feeling a little weak because of her injury and because the throbbing had kept her awake for yet another sleepless night.

"Well, we'll just take a quick look, lass. On a strictly professional basis, I assure you." Now his blue eyes smiled at her. "In my capacity as your...ah...*veterinarian.*"

Patrick had finished watering the oxen and came up behind them. "Is my brother going to be all right?"

"How about you lift down one of those boxes for your *sister* to sit on, lad," Scott answered.

Patrick's eyes widened and he turned to Kerry. "He knows?"

Kerry nodded. "It seems that my disguise was not convincing to Mr. Haskell. But he has promised to keep our secret."

"Criminy, Kerry. I told you this wasn't going to work. It's not going to work, is it, Mr. Haskell?" Patrick kicked the wagon wheel with his boot.

"It's Scott," he said, still holding Kerry lightly in his arms, then added gently, "the box, lad." Patrick pulled a packing crate from the back of the wagon and positioned it where Scott could easily set Kerry. After she was situated, Scott stepped back and continued, "I can't answer you for certain, Patrick, but no one else has questioned your sister's identity. She's a smart lass. She may be able to pull it off."

"As long as Jeb Hunter doesn't insist on seeing my ankle," Kerry added grimly, stretching her leg out in front of her. Her foot, bandaged with strips of cloth she had torn from a petticoat last night, stuck awkwardly out the end of her too short, borrowed trousers.

"Maybe he won't even come around," Patrick suggested hopefully, but before he had even finished the words, all three lifted their heads at the sound of a horse riding toward them. The wagon master was approaching their wagon, his eyes on Kerry.

Scott pushed back the brim of his hat, then stood awaiting Jeb Hunter's arrival with crossed arms. "Afternoon, Captain," he said in a loud voice, drawing the trail guide's gaze.

Kerry twirled around on the box so that her bad leg was partially out of view.

"Afternoon," Jeb answered gruffly, pulling his horse to a stop a few feet away. "I came to see the lad's bad ankle."

He dismounted and walked toward them, but Scott took a step closer, cutting off his approach. "He says it's fine."

Kerry watched as the two men came to a stop opposite each other. Something in their demeanor made their positions look more like a confrontation than a conversation.

"I know," Hunter said, with just a brush of irritation in his voice. "But I'm going to check it out just to be sure."

He started to take a step around Scott, who reached out and put a hand on his arm. "I've looked at it myself," he said. "There's no need for you to bother."

"Scott's an expert," Patrick chimed in.

Jeb Hunter looked down at Scott's restraining hand. "An expert?"

Scott removed his hand and spoke in conciliatory tones. "I've worked with this kind of injury before," Scott said. "Ankle sprains and the like. I think Kiernan's going to be just fine if he keeps off it for three or four days."

For the first time since her injury, Kerry was oblivious to the pain as she watched the exchange between the two men. They were not destined to be friends, that was clear. And it looked as if it would take little to set off a spark of animosity between them. "I wish everyone would stop talking about me and my blasted foot," she said, making her voice as forceful as she could in its low range. "Mr. Haskell says it's fine, and it's practically stopped hurting. So I'd like to just forget the whole incident.''

Jeb Hunter looked over at her and frowned. ''Did you get it properly bandaged?''

''Yes. As we said, Mr. Haskell is something of an expert.''

He took a step backward and turned his glance back to Scott. ''The lad seems to take your word for it, Haskell, and it was nice of you to help out. But in the future I'd appreciate it if you remembered that I'm the one responsible for the health of the people on this train.''

Scott gave a bland smile. ''Sure, Captain. We all know that you're the boss man.''

Hunter seemed to hesitate for a moment, trying to decide if Scott's comment had carried hidden sarcasm, but he evidently decided not to press the issue. ''Fine. We'll be getting started again here in about twenty minutes.'' He nodded to Patrick, then turned with a last caution to Kerry. ''Stay off that foot, then, Kiernan.''

When he mounted up and rode away Kerry discovered that she'd been holding in a deep breath. She let it out slowly. ''Well, that's one crisis past.''

Scott dropped to one knee beside her. ''But I'm still going to look at your foot, lass.''

She winced in pain and embarrassment as he deftly pushed the trousers up her slender leg and began to unwind the cloth strips. Her ankle was puffy and grayish blue. Scott gave a low whistle, then looked up at her with a wink. ''Now I've heard of a nicely turned ankle before....''

Kerry laughed and found herself relaxing in spite

of herself under the influence of Scott Haskell's charm. By the time he had gingerly felt along each side of her ankle, declared that there appeared to be no broken bones and rebandaged it, she had lost all her self-consciousness and was enjoying his banter. Though his detection of her secret had undermined her confidence in her disguise, it felt good to know that she had at least one ally on the train besides Patrick. She was determined to get to California on her own and wasn't looking for help from any quarter. But it didn't hurt to know that once in a while she could let down her guard and be assured of a friendly face.

Chapter Three

By four days later she'd begun looking forward to Scott Haskell's friendly face. The morning after he had first bandaged her ankle, he had shown up just after dawn with a load of firewood, his own coffeepot already full of water and a can of coffee. Kerry had awakened from another restless night to decide that it wasn't worth the effort to prepare anything warm to combat the chill of the spring morning. But she was happy to sit peacefully, leaning against the back of the wagon wheel, while Scott bustled around their small camp and prepared a nice breakfast of fried bacon and strong coffee.

The noon stop had been brief, and the travelers had eaten a cold lunch, but that night, Scott had appeared once again to work with Patrick on fixing supper.

By the next day, Kerry could hobble around on her own, but Scott had adamantly refused to let her move, taking over the cooking chores, directing Patrick with good-natured teasing, as naturally as if he had been an older brother. But his occasional unguarded glances at Kerry were not always brotherly, much to her amazement. She recognized the male admiration in his gaze, and found it incredible that he could find anything attractive in her, dressed as she was in her odd male attire and already grimy from the trail.

Everyone else on the train seemed to take her male status for granted. The well-meaning neighbors who had stopped by after hearing about her injury treated her with that breezy indifference often extended to an inconsequential young man who had yet to make his mark in life. There was no deference, nor anything in their manner to suggest the stilted courtesy prescribed by society for a single young woman. She found it liberating.

It was only with Scott that she felt back in her feminine role. He was looking at her that way now from the other side of the campfire. The two were alone. Patrick had joined some of the other youngsters at another wagon. "I've appreciated your help these past few days, Scott," Kerry said finally, when the silence had stretched out long enough to be awkward.

Scott grinned. "I'm a born romantic, Kerry. Always ready to help a damsel in distress."

Kerry chuckled and held out her arms to flop the sleeves of her father's jacket. "Damsel is a bit too elegant to describe me, I'm afraid."

Scott's face grew serious. "I'd have trouble finding the right words to describe you, Kerry. I look at your beautiful face and into those big blue eyes and it makes my heart stop cold."

Kerry flushed and leaned back a little, moving her face out of the circle of firelight. "I thought only Irishmen knew how to talk blarney."

Scott stayed serious another moment, then smiled.

"I'm sorry. It must sound like that. I've spoken too soon. Forgive me, lass."

Kerry shook her head in confusion. "No, I didn't mean… There's nothing to forgive. You're…you've been so nice to us."

Scott waggled his eyebrows mockingly. "And as with all beautiful females, you're wondering if my motives are pure."

Kerry giggled. She'd never met a man who could put her so at ease. She had a feeling that Scott's easy charm would be appealing under any circumstances. It was in marked contrast to the taciturn manner of the wagon master, who had been by to ask about her foot several times, but had never stayed more than the time it took to get an answer on the subject. While she was relieved that he didn't again ask to look at the injury and that she would not have to undergo a close scrutiny that might risk revealing her secret, she found herself a little annoyed by Jeb Hunter's brusque manner.

"I'm not too concerned about your motives, Scott," she answered her new friend. "Patrick and I are both grateful to have you around."

"He's a fine boy. You can be proud of him."

"I am. We'll make a good team in California."

"That's a tall order, Kerry—starting up a ranch with just the two of you."

Kerry's chin came up. "Not too tall, though. We'll make it work. I can do anything a man can do." She gave a rueful glance down at her foot. "When I have two good legs, that is."

Scott narrowed his eyes to see her face in the dim light. "Perhaps you won't be alone by then. I've heard that young women don't stay unmarried for long in the West.''

Kerry grinned. "But I'm not a young woman, remember? And I'm not interested in having a man in my life telling me what to do."

Scott barked out a laugh. "I guess that states it plain enough."

A shower of sparks rose from the fire as a log broke in two and slid off the top of the pile toward Kerry. Scott was on his feet in an instant, moving to her side and shoving the log back with his boot. Kerry had started to push herself backward, but he reached down and stopped her with a hand on her shoulder. "You don't have to move, lass. I'll just rebuild this."

He knelt beside her, his leg touching hers, and, using a smaller, unlit log, maneuvered the burning ones into a more stable pyramid. "That ought to do it," he said, pushing himself backward to sit beside her. Their legs still touched, and neither one pulled away.

Kerry drew in a deep breath of warm air that smelled of dry meadow and smoke. "It's a perfect night," she said dreamily, looking up at the black velvet sky.

Scott leaned back on his hands and looked upward, then turned his head to study her. "Yes, it is," he answered finally. "When I set out on this journey, I had no idea just how perfect it was going to turn out to be."

His voice had grown unmistakably husky, and Kerry turned toward him in surprise. Their gaze held for a long minute, then Scott reached out a hand and gently pushed back a lock of hair that had fallen over her forehead.

His fingers were rough on her smooth skin, but she didn't mind. They moved a little into her hair, a gentle caress. "I like your hair short," Scott murmured. For once she was not wearing her big felt hat. She made no effort to resist his touch. The warm contact blended with the peacefulness of the night to make her relaxed and happy. He leaned closer until she could see the stubble of his whiskers. Perhaps he was going to kiss her, she thought in a kind of haze. Darkness had closed around them like a protective cloak. She wouldn't mind if he did, she decided sleepily, and her eyes drifted closed.

"Good evening!" came a deep voice from just beyond the light of the fire.

Kerry and Scott pulled apart abruptly. Scott scowled into the darkness. "Hunter," he acknowledged in an uncharacteristically gruff tone.

Kerry's cheeks were burning, though she didn't know exactly why. She and Scott had not been doing anything wrong, but she felt like a child caught stealing cookies.

Jeb Hunter moved to the other side of the fire and crouched down. "How's the foot today, Kiernan?" he asked. There was an edge to his voice.

Kerry straightened up farther and slid her leg away from contact with Scott's. "It's fine," she said with a dry mouth. Her voice came out much too high. Forcing it to a lower register, she repeated, "The ankle's nearly healed, I think."

The captain nodded, then looked from her to Scott and back again. He seemed at a loss as to what to say. After a moment the silence became awkward, and Kerry said, "Would you like a cup of coffee, Captain?"

Scott made a slight grimace of annoyance at her invitation, but he recovered quickly. "Your duties must be about done for the day, Hunter."

Jeb gave a faint smile. "My duties won't be done until I get you and everyone else on this train to California, Haskell."

"Done enough for a cup of coffee, at least." Scott got to his feet and went to fetch a tin mug from the canvas sack that held the Gallivans' dishes.

Scott Haskell acted as if the wagon belonged to him rather than the two Irish lads, Jeb noticed, and tried to decide why the thought irritated him. He knew that part of the reason was simply that the affable young Haskell had declared his intentions of becoming a prospector. Jeb had left California and taken up his job as trail guide partly because he never again wanted to have anything to do with the gold rush fever. Whenever prospectors joined up with one of his wagon trains, he found himself wanting to shake them until that eager, hopeful look disappeared from their eyes.

Scott returned to the fire, poured a cup of coffee and handed it to Jeb, who was still crouching at the other side of the fire. "Have a seat, Hunter," Scott urged, now evidently resigned to the wagon master's interruption of his private moment with Kerry.

Jeb hesitated, then sat back on the ground and reached for the cup. "Much obliged," he said tersely.

"Are we keeping on schedule, Captain?" Kerry asked, this time remembering to keep her voice low.

Jeb nodded. "We've been lucky so far—no rain.

The wagons have made good time over this nice dry trail."

"It's not too dry, is it? We'll have plenty of water along the way for the animals?" Scott asked.

Jeb shrugged. "No way to tell. It could be a problem. We usually hit spring rains at this point, but they can turn a nice trail into a muddy nightmare. And an easy river into a raging flood."

Kerry shivered a little in spite of the warmth of the evening. "Will we be crossing a river soon?" she asked.

Jeb shook his head. "Not for a few days anyway. We'll keep this side of the Kansas for a ways. We don't usually cross it this soon."

"We do cross it, then?"

"Yes, we have to, before we reach the Blue. But if things stay this dry, it'll be no problem to ford. Still, it's a good-sized river—that's one of the reasons I made sure everyone's load was light enough before we left."

He watched as the Irish lad cast a guilty look back at his wagon. Jeb suspected that the two Gallivans had not completely followed his orders about how much load they could carry. Well, time would tell. They wouldn't be the first outfit to have to abandon precious possessions along the way. He wished, though, that they had listened to him. He had an odd, protective feeling about the two newly orphaned lads. He'd like to get closer to them, but so far they had not seemed to welcome his presence or seek his advice. Now it appeared that they had found a different protector in Scott Haskell. "You'll be in front of the line tomorrow, Haskell,'' he told the prospector. ''Then the next day you'll move to the rear.''

Scott had resumed his seat next to Kerry, though not quite as close as before. He cocked his head and looked over at her. ''You know what, Hunter?'' he said. ''I'm going to move my wagon behind the Gallivans'. They can have my day at the front and their own, too. Then in two days we'll both move to the rear.''

Jeb stopped the coffee cup halfway to his mouth. ''Now why would you do that, Haskell?'' he asked, the irrational irritation surging once again.

Scott turned back to Jeb. ''I don't want to split off from the...ah...boys.'' At Jeb's surprised expression, he added, ''Kiernan still might need my help with that bad foot.''

''I thought you said the foot was better.'' Jeb's gaze went to Kerry.

''I...it is,'' she stammered. She, too, was surprised that Scott would give up a blessed, dust-free day just so that their wagons wouldn't be separated.

''Well, it doesn't matter. We're not switching the order of the wagons,'' Jeb said firmly.

Scott sat up straighter and said calmly, ''The move won't concern any wagons except the Gallivans' and mine. I don't see why it should be a problem.''

''It's not your job to see the problems, Haskell. It's mine. And I'm telling you we don't switch the order.''

There was a moment of silence as Scott and Jeb glared at one another across the fire. Once again Kerry had the impression of two rival bulls facing off for leadership of the herd. It made her distinctly uncomfortable. "That's okay, Scott," she said quickly. "You should take your day in front like everyone else."

Scott shook his head. "It's my wagon. I guess I can put it where I want."

Jeb set his cup down next to the fire and got to his feet. This time his voice was soft, deceptively silky. "It's your wagon, Haskell. But it's my train. And you'll put your wagon where I tell you to put it or I'll be asking you to leave."

Kerry could almost feel Scott bristling at her side. She reached out and put a hand on his arm. "Honestly, Scott," she said in a low voice. "I'll be fine."

Jeb's eyes followed the movement. There seemed to be some kind of unspoken communication between the prospector and the younger man that Jeb found unsettling. He couldn't put his finger on the reason. His gaze drifted to Kiernan Gallivan. In the dancing firelight, the lad's features looked almost pretty. He was a bit too delicate for the rigors of the West—that must be why Jeb felt such a need to protect them. Hell, he should be happy that the boys had Haskell to help them out. Jeb had enough to think about along the trail. He considered changing his mind about the order of the wagons, but decided against it. He'd learned from experience that making people understand that his orders were the law could mean the difference between life and death. "So we're all agreed then?" he asked after a moment.

Scott looked down at Kerry's hand and seemed to be considering his reply. Finally he said. "All right. We'll keep the wagons in order."

Jeb nodded. "Good." He waited for further comment, but when both Scott and Kerry were silent, he said in a stilted voice, "Thanks for the coffee, then." And without making a sound he disappeared into the darkness.

"He doesn't like me," Scott observed.

"Why do you say that?" Kerry asked. Her hand was still on his arm.

"I don't know. A man can just tell when another man would rather take a swing at him than shake hands."

"What possible reason could he have for not liking you?"

Scott shrugged. "Maybe he doesn't like gold prospectors," he said lightly.

"Well, now, that's a silly notion," Kerry said with a little laugh.

She started to move her hand away from his arm but he reached down and captured it with his own. "Maybe so, but he doesn't like me."

Kerry wrinkled her nose. "Well, I'm not so sure I like him very much."

Scott laughed. "He's not the friendliest fellow, is he?"

"No. And he's...high-handed."

He released her hand, holding his own up in a gesture of surrender. "I'll take note. You don't like forceful men."

He said it in a teasing tone, but Kerry did not return his smile. "I don't know," she said slowly, considering his words. "I'm not sure I like men much at all. Or rather, I like them okay but I'd just as soon not have to have anything to do with them. Except for Patrick, of course. I plan to do fine on my own."

Scott looked at her oddly. "If you ask me, that's one prediction that's not likely to come true." Then before she could start to bristle, he added, "Not that you wouldn't do fine on your own, lass. It's just that I don't think the men you encounter will want to let you."

"Why not?"

Scott let out a puff of exasperation. "Lord, Kerry. You may try to cover up in men's togs and throw dirt on your face, but any male under the age of ninety who sees the real you is going to be attracted."

It was the blarney again. But somehow Scott Haskell sounded more sincere than the boys back in New York City. Perhaps there was some truth to it after all, she thought with amazement. Growing up without a mother, she'd never had anyone to talk with about the effect a woman can have on a man. And her father had certainly never mentioned that she was pretty or that she might have an allure that could attract masculine attention. She wasn't at all sure that she liked the idea.

"Well, at least I won't have to worry about that this trip. No one even knows that I'm a girl."

"Except me."

The fire was beginning to die, and Kerry had trouble seeing Scott's face in the dim light, but his voice held a resonance that was as palpable as his earlier caress on her hair. "Yes, of course. Except you." She cleared her throat and rubbed her arms briskly. "It's starting to get chilly out, don't you think?"

Scott's smile was understanding. "I'm anything but chilly, lass, but it *is* getting late. Do you want me to help you with anything more tonight?"

Kerry pushed herself to her feet without putting weight on her bad ankle. "No, I'm just going to curl up and go to sleep." She pointed over at the wagon where Patrick had earlier thrown their bedrolls.

"I'd feel better if you and your brother slept inside the wagon."

"There's no room."

"One of these nights it's going to rain, and then you'll have to find the room somehow."

Kerry sighed. "Well, it's not going to rain tonight." She swept an arm up at the cloudless sky. "So I guess we'll just cross that bridge when we come to it."

Scott hesitated, then said. "There's plenty of space in my wagon, lass." When her finely arched eyebrows lifted in surprise, he added with a grin, "I just mean...if it should start to rain and you need to take shelter fast."

Kerry smiled in return. "Thank you for the offer, Scott, but Patrick and I will work out something. You've already gone to too much trouble for us. For me."

Scott's voice grew soft again. "Heck, Kerry. That's what neighbors are for." He laid his palm against her cheek for an instant in a gesture that was anything but neighborly, then nodded and turned to walk to his own wagon.

"Captain Hunter?"

Jeb whirled around, startled by the voice. His years on the trail had sharpened his senses and usually made him alert to everything going on around him, but he hadn't heard the boy approach. "Oh hello, Patrick. How's your brother's foot getting along?"

He expected he'd get the same story he'd been told by Kiernan himself last night at the Gallivan campfire, but it seemed the natural question to ask.

"He's getting around all right now. In fact, my...brother said I could come ride with you for part of the way today if the offer's still open."

Jeb felt a spurt of pleasure. Patrick was an earnest young lad, a little too serious for his age. He'd worked hard along the trail without a single complaint. Jeb wondered fleetingly if he and Melanie would have had such a son. The twist in his insides was so familiar by now that it passed almost without notice. Almost.

"I'd be happy to have you ride with me, Patrick. You'll have to sit at the back of my saddle, you know."

"I know."

The boy's black hair and blue eyes were nearly identical to his brother's, but whereas on Kiernan they looked almost pretty, Patrick showed the promise of turning into a handsome, virile young man. The contrast between the two brothers was marked.

"If you want I can ride with your brother for a while and you can sit on my horse by yourself. We'd keep it alongside your wagon," he added, to reassure the boy that he wouldn't be completely on his own.

Patrick eyed the gray roan stallion with longing, but he said, "No, I'd rather sit behind you."

Jeb shrugged. "All right. It's probably better. That way I can keep track of things up and down the train. You're sure your brother won't need any help?"

"I'm sure. Anyway, the Burnett twins are going to ride with her today."

Jeb frowned in confusion. "Ride with who?"

Patrick's face paled. "Ride with *him*, I mean. With my brother."

"Oh." Jeb nodded. "Well, good. If he needs anything, they can fetch Mrs. Burnett."

"Yup," Patrick said, his skin returning to its normal color.

There was something a little odd about the Gallivan brothers, Jeb decided, as he mounted his horse, then reached down a long arm to pull Patrick up behind him. And yet he was drawn to them nevertheless. Perhaps it was because he identified with their recent bereavement. It was still so soon after their father's death. They needed time to recover. It was the natural way with grief. With most grief.

He felt the boy's arms clasp around his waist and put his big hand over Patrick's smaller one for a moment of reassurance. "Ready?" he asked.

"Yes, sir." The childish, eager voice made Jeb smile in spite of his dark thoughts as he signalled his horse to move. Patrick was young. It wouldn't take long for time to work its healing power on the boy's grief. Unlike Jeb's own. He had refused to let his loss grow any less vivid with the passing years. He didn't intend to ever allow time to numb the wound. He didn't deserve to heal.

Kerry was thoroughly enjoying herself for the first time in what seemed like weeks. Once Polly and Molly had become completely comfortable in her company, their conversation had become delightfully unreserved. It appeared that the shyer twin, Molly, had developed a crush on Patrick, and her irrepressible older sister had already learned to use the fact as a weapon.

"Molly has a boyfriend," she told Kerry, her little mouth making a round expression of excitement.

"I don't either," Molly argued with a scowl.

"Do, too."

"Do not!"

"Do, too!"

Kerry sat up on the high wagon seat with a sister on each side. She laid the reins in her lap for a minute and put her arms around each. "Here, now. Let's not have a fight. It's not polite to tease about boys, Polly," she chided gently.

Polly was undaunted. "It's your brother," she told Kerry in dramatic tones, sending a glance of defiance at her sister, who gave a wail.

Kerry hid a smile. "That's all right, Molly. There's nothing wrong with feeling a fondness for a boy. Most girls do at some point or another."

Molly looked up into Kerry's face, blinking hard. "You won't tell him?" she asked in a painful whisper.

Kerry shook her head. "Not a word. I promise. And don't you go telling either, Polly," she cautioned. The wagon lurched over a rut in the trail and she picked up the reins again. "Now, were you girls going to teach me that ballad your mother was singing at the campfire last night?"

All at once the quarrel and Patrick were forgotten as the girls vied to teach their new friend a favorite family song. Kerry leaned against the backboard of the seat and enjoyed their antics, trying to remember when she herself had been ten. Had she ever been as carefree as the Burnett twins? Her mother had died giving birth to Patrick when Kerry was six. It had broken Sean Gallivan's heart, and most of Kerry's memories concerned her attempts to try to make up to him for his loss. It seemed that no matter how hard she tried, it had never been enough. She could never make up for her mother's absence.

The sisters had lapsed into an argument again about the order of the verses, but there was less vehemence than when the dispute had involved a matter of the heart. "How would it be if we sang it once each way? That way I'll be sure to learn the whole thing." Kerry's suggestion was all it took to settle the matter. The two little girls squabbled, as was natural for two siblings so close in age, but they were good-natured children, and Kerry found it relaxing to be with them. She had not given a thought to her disguise all morning.

But her relaxed state came to an abrupt end as she saw Jeb Hunter riding toward them with Patrick bouncing along behind. At her side, she could feel Molly straighten up on the seat, and Kerry found herself doing the same. She pulled reflexively on the brim of her hat.

"You have helpers along today, Kiernan, I see," Jeb called out to her. His voice was much lighter than it had been around the campfire last night. The tone made him sound younger. His face looked younger, too, as he gave her one of his rare smiles. Kerry caught her breath at the difference in his expression.

"I certainly do," she answered carefully, keeping

her voice extra low. She hoped Polly and Molly wouldn't pay attention to her sudden change in register. "And you have a helper of your own."

Jeb turned around in the saddle to give Patrick a fond look. "He'd make a good guide himself one of these days."

Kerry's smile dropped as she said quickly, "Not likely. We're going to be ranchers, remember? And Patrick's going to do carpentry like our father."

Jeb didn't appear to notice the vehemence of her remark. "He's got sharp eyes. He's been pointing out things along the trail that I missed myself."

Patrick was beaming at the praise. "It's been great, Ker…Kiernan," he exclaimed. "I wish I could ride every day."

"You don't want to be a bother to Captain Hunter, Patrick," Kerry said softly.

"He's no bother. I've enjoyed the company." Jeb pulled his horse around and matched its stride to the slow plodding of the oxen. "I just brought him back because we're stopping for lunch and I thought you might need his help. In fact, I thought I'd join you for the meal myself."

Kerry's gaze went to the wagon in front of them. She knew that the minute the wagons rolled to a halt, Scott would be back to get the noon meal for her as he had since her accident. But she couldn't very well turn down the captain's request for an invitation.

"Certainly, Captain Hunter," she said trying to mask her misgivings. "You're welcome to stay."

Chapter Four

They rode along for another few minutes before the wagons in front started drawing to a halt one by one. "The head wagon must have reached Silver Creek," Jeb explained. "I told them we'd stop there."

Almost instantly the twins' mother appeared to collect her girls. Kerry noticed that the polite smile Captain Hunter turned on Dorothy Burnett was not any different than the one he used with Frank Todd or the motherly Eulalie Todd or anyone else on the train. Scott, on the other hand, who joined them immediately, as Kerry had predicted, flashed the pretty blonde a charming grin and cocked his head in a greeting that showed appreciation of her as a young, attractive woman. Jeb Hunter didn't seem to like women all that much, Kerry decided. Or perhaps he saw himself in such a lofty position on the train that he felt above flirting with a pretty girl. Of course, either way, it was a matter of indifference to her.

"I've brought lunch," Scott said, hoisting a heavy iron kettle. "Boone's finest molasses baked beans. A whole tin of them," he added, looking from Kerry up on the wagon seat down to Dorothy and Jeb and Patrick, who had dismounted from Jeb's horse. "Plenty to go around."

His tone held no indication that he was annoyed by Jeb's presence, but Kerry already knew him well enough to sense a certain tenseness in him that was not natural to the easygoing Scott. She didn't analyze why she felt it was her job to be sure that he and Jeb Hunter would not antagonize each other. She had been responsible for taking care of the males in her own family for so many years, it just seemed to come as second nature. "Captain Hunter is going to stay for lunch," she said, sending Scott a bright smile and silent thank-you for his forbearance. Her gesture was rewarded by an immediate warming of Scott's expression.

Jeb watched the interplay between Kiernan and the affable prospector with renewed confusion. There was definitely a communication between the two young men that went a step beyond neighborly. If he hadn't seen the unmistakable look in Scott's eyes when he'd been greeting Dorothy Burnett, he'd be almost worried that Haskell had unnatural designs on the young Irishman. A silly notion, he decided. After all, he'd felt some kind of pull himself toward both boys—a protective, paternal instinct.

Nevertheless, he felt a bit awkward and out of place as the prospector assumed control of things as if he were part of the family. "Will you and the girls eat with us, Mrs. Burnett?" Scott asked Dorothy with another charming smile.

"Can we, Mama?" Polly asked as she scrambled down from the wagon.

"I suspect your papa will want us to eat back with him, honey. He missed not having his kittens with him this morning."

The girls were obviously disappointed at the refusal, but neither one pouted or asked again to have their way. With good-natured smiles they waved goodbye to Kerry and followed their mother back to their own wagon.

Scott had set the kettle on the ground and was building a small fire to heat the beans. "You can light it now, Patrick," he said, straightening up and brushing off his hands. Then he turned to the wagon where Kerry was still perched up on the seat. He put his foot up on the sideboard. "Let me help you down," he said to her.

Kerry looked over at Jeb. "I can manage myself, now, Scott."

Ignoring her protest, he hoisted himself toward her and lifted her off the seat. In a minute they were on the ground, but not before Scott had said in a low voice in her ear, "But I *like* helping you, sweetheart."

No one else could possibly have heard him, but Kerry's face flamed. It was the first time he had used such an endearment, and it occurred to her that he'd decided to use it to somehow stake a claim on her right in Jeb Hunter's presence. The thought irritated her. She pushed away from him the minute he set her on the ground and limped over to the fire. "I'll do that," she snapped at Patrick, taking the box of matches from him and crouching down by the fire.

Her brother looked at her in surprise. "Are you all right?"

She nodded, concentrating on lighting the curling

edges of the branches Scott had placed under the logs for tinder. She kept her head down, still feeling the heat in her cheeks. "You go fetch some water," she told Patrick. "It'll be time to move before we know it and we'll still be sitting here hungry."

With another doubtful look at his sister, Patrick grabbed the bucket that hung from one side of the wagon and headed toward the river. Jeb stood watching the exchange. "There's no hurry," he said. "The animals need a good long rest on a day this hot. We'll start up again later this afternoon when it begins to cool down a bit."

His voice had taken on a comforting tone, almost like an adult dealing with a cranky child, and Kerry realized that she was sounding churlish. She was at a loss to know what had set her off so. Scott had had no business calling her sweetheart, but it wasn't a capital offense. And the captain had done nothing to deserve her ill humor. She raised her head and smiled at him. "It was kind of you to take Patrick today. Quite a treat. He always wanted to ride in New York City, but of course there was very little opportunity."

"A city's not the best place for a boy to grow up," Jeb answered, returning her smile. "He'll like the West. And I enjoyed having him with me. He can ride with me anytime."

Kerry chuckled. "You'd better not say that or you'll never be rid of him, Captain. He's none too happy sitting up on the wagon with me."

"I mean it. Storm's a big animal—it's no problem to have Patrick along. You're welcome to give it a try, too, when your ankle's better."

Kerry found herself drawn to Jeb Hunter's rare

smile. It transformed his face from the authoritative wagon train captain to a man who would take the time to give pleasure to a young boy. The fire caught and blazed with a sudden flare of heat. She backed away, noticing out of the corner of her eye that Scott was watching her exchange with the captain with a slight scowl.

With a sigh, she reached to set the pot of beans on the fire. She felt a little like the jugglers she used to see sometimes on the streets of New York—trying to keep two quite different men happy. And she didn't think it would get any better as they continued across the country. As much as she had hoped to make this trip without notice from anyone, the discovery of her secret, coupled with her accident, had provided her with a protector in Scott Haskell. And as much as she wanted to keep out of the way of their captain, she was already realizing that the long days on the trail became a little more interesting every time Jeb Hunter rode up to their wagon.

It had become the custom for Jeb and Patrick to ride together at least part of every day. The sight of the brawny wagon captain with the Irish lad bouncing along behind him on the big roan stallion had become a common sight up and down the train. And each day, Jeb found himself spending a little more time at the Gallivan wagon, staying for one more cup of coffee, listening to one more of Kiernan's amusing tales of the scrappy life he and his brother had led back in New York City.

There was a special warmth between the two brothers that drew in their visitors, rather than excluding.

Scott Haskell evidently noticed it, too. The aspiring gold hunter was often present at the Gallivan wagon when Jeb showed up there, and he never seemed overly happy at the wagon captain's arrival, though Jeb wasn't sure why. It should do no harm to have two men concerned with the boys' welfare. Yet sometimes Jeb felt almost as if he and Haskell were rival suitors vying for the hand of a pretty girl.

Jeb became more fond of Patrick each day and more fascinated with the older boy. Kiernan's ankle was almost healed by now, and he was again able to move around to the neighboring wagons at the camp each night. The young man always seemed to have an encouraging word for everyone. He'd sat for hours one night listening to Eulalie Todd's reminiscences about St. Louis. And he regularly took the twins off for a walk or some other adventure to give Dorothy and John Burnett a few moments' respite from their offspring's constant activity. Jeb, himself, looked forward to his conversations with the young Irishman, whose questions about the trail and about what they could expect in California were intelligent and animated.

As he felt himself drawn to the Gallivan wagon for the fifth evening in a row, Jeb decided that the attraction must be that Kiernan Gallivan's interest was flattering. He'd lived alone for so many years that he'd forgotten what it could be like to sit with someone and talk over his day.

As usual, Scott was also present at the Gallivan campfire when Jeb arrived, and all four Burnetts had joined them for some trail songs that were being enthusiastically led by Polly and Molly. Molly had got-

ten over her shyness with Patrick and now unabash-
edly made her fondness for the boy obvious to the
entire group, always choosing the seat next to him
and sitting as close as she dared. Even her sister's
occasional taunts on the subject had not dimmed her
youthful infatuation.

Jeb accepted the cup of coffee Kiernan offered him
and settled down to enjoy the companionship. He'd
led six trains across the country, but he'd never before
let himself get close to the wagon train members.
He'd always told himself that it wasn't good to get
too close. It was too hard to be a leader to people
who were your friends. And he'd preferred his loneliness. He didn't want to see happy couples, families
eagerly planning their promising futures together. He
didn't want to think about how he'd done that very
same thing with Melanie.

"I hate to break up the gathering," Jeb said loudly
as the group finished up a long ballad. "But we have
a tough day ahead of us tomorrow. It would be a good
idea if we all got to sleep." Tomorrow they would
cross to the north side of the Kansas River, which
they'd been following since they left Westport. It
would be the first major test of the settlers' stamina.

"Can I ride with you, Captain?" Patrick asked eagerly.

Jeb shook his head. "Sorry, Patrick. I'll have to be
helping folks across the river all day. I'm afraid Storm
will have enough work without an extra passenger.
Besides, I want both you and your brother in your
wagon when we ford."

"Do you expect problems with the crossing?"
Kerry asked.

"Nothing in particular. With the dry weather holding, the river's down. But crossing a river the size of the Kansas is always a tricky proposition. You'll find out tomorrow why I insisted that you and your brother lighten up your load."

Kerry swallowed down a lump of guilt. She and Patrick had packed and repacked their heavy supplies until they finally were able to jam them together in such a way as to leave a tiny bit of space for them to put bedrolls at night. But she knew that the wagon captain had no idea of just how full their wagon was. She thought for a minute about telling him, but changed her mind. After all, he'd said that the river was not as high as usual. And the four oxen they'd been given by the Boone store had proved to be reliable, if plodding, beasts. They'd make it across all right, she decided.

Patrick was watching her with an anxious expression as if he, too, had his mind on their overloaded wagon. She stood and went to stand behind him, putting her hands reassuringly on his shoulders. "It should be an exciting day, then," she said in a deliberately cheery voice.

Patrick twisted his neck to look up at her. "Do you think..." he began doubtfully.

She dug her hands into his shoulders to stop his question. "I think everything's going to be just fine," she said.

The others around the fire were all getting to their feet. John Burnett, a thin, serious man who said little but watched over his wife and two daughters with the care of a mother bear, reached to take Polly and Molly's hands to walk with them in the darkness. "Is it safe for everyone to ride across in the wagons, Captain?'' he asked. ''Perhaps I should carry my girls across one by one.''

Jeb shook his head reassuringly. ''As I said, the river's low. As long as we keep order and everyone follows instructions, we should all get across safe and sound without any problems. Without even getting our feet wet.''

John nodded his approval to Jeb, then said a formal good-night to Scott, Patrick and Kerry, before he turned to start back toward his wagon with Polly and Molly skipping along at his side.

''We'll see everyone in the morning,'' Dorothy added with a disarming smile that was in marked contrast to her husband's stiffness.

Jeb waited a moment to see if Haskell would take his leave, but when the prospector seemed in no hurry to depart, he said his own good-nights and headed down the line of wagons.

Scott waited until he had disappeared in the darkness, then turned to Kerry. ''I don't like to think of you having to handle those animals across a river.''

''I've managed to handle them well enough across the prairie,'' she answered with a little thrust of her full lip. ''I don't see how it will be so different.''

Scott took a step closer, then glanced over at Patrick, who had stood along with everyone else but had not moved away from the fire. ''Patrick, my boy, why don't you go give the animals a final check? Let me talk to your sister a minute.''

Patrick looked a little surprised to be dismissed in such a fashion, but then he gave a good-natured grin. ''You can talk to her, but you can't exactly do any sparking, can you? She's a boy, remember? It wouldn't look too good.''

"Patrick!" Kerry exclaimed. She didn't know if she was more distressed by the knowledge that her baby brother would think about such things or that he might be right in his assumption that Scott's request for time alone with her had romantic overtones.

"Well, it's true, Kerry. He goes moony-eyed when he looks at you, just like Mickey Flanagan used to."

Scott ran his hand over the bristly blond whiskers of his chin and looked as if he didn't know whether to laugh or scold. "Go on, boy," he said finally. "Nobody's going to do any sparking here. I just need to talk to Kerry."

Patrick skipped off to the back of the wagon and Scott turned to Kerry again. "Now don't raise those independent hackles of yours at me again, lass, but neither you nor the boy has the strength to hold that team if it should run into trouble during the crossing. I'd like to take my rig across and then come back and ride across with you."

Kerry realized that the offer, just like everything else Scott had done for them since their first day on the trail, was meant to be helpful. But once again she felt resentment over the assumption that she wouldn't be able to do the job just because she was a woman. She'd promised her father that they would make his dream come true. And if she had to break her arms holding the team to do it, she would do so. "We'll manage," she said, her lips tight.

By now Scott knew better than to argue. "All right," he said with a sigh. "But you be sure that

Patrick's sitting right up there with you to help out if you need it.''

"I don't know where else he'd be if he wants to get across. He's never learned how to swim.'' She said the words lightly, but the faint misgiving she'd had when she thought about the weight of their load grew a bit stronger.

"If you change your mind, you know I'd be happy to help you.'' Scott's expression had changed in the dying firelight. All at once it looked as if he wanted to do some of the ''sparking'' Patrick had mentioned.

Kerry took a step back. "I won't change my mind. Now we'd better get a good night's sleep, as Captain Hunter suggested.''

He watched her for another long moment, then reached down and captured her hand. "All right," he said softly, turning her hand in his and planting a kiss gently on the palm. "Sleep well, lass.''

Before Kerry could recover her voice, he had faded into the darkness.

The Kansas River flowed in an even, inexorable path across the prairie like molasses poured from a jug. Broad and tranquil most of the time, it woke up now and then to swirl around a bend, dancing over rocks and fallen tree trunks in a sudden spurt of energy, only to flatten out again on the other side.

Jeb had picked one of the traditional fording places. The grass on each side was completely worn away from the mulling about of caravan after caravan of wagons. If the spring rains had been normal, the banks would have been treacherously slippery with mud and Jeb might have considered continuing on to find a less popular crossing farther upriver. But the dry spell was still holding, and the train had made excellent time up to this point. So he'd decided that they might as well get the crossing out of the way.

It always took a full day out of their trip. He never let more than two wagons cross at the same time, since he wanted to keep watch and be able to come to their aid at the first sign of any trouble. To get fifty across would take hours.

He was up before dawn, eating a breakfast of biscuits and a cold cup of last night's coffee. There was no time to waste on a fire today. He'd already warned Frank Todd that he'd like to have him cross over first, test the route. Jeb would ride alongside, feeling his way. He'd crossed here before, but the river was constantly changing.

He mounted Storm and made his way back, checking to see that the owners of the first few wagons were awake and preparing for the crossing. He had told the ones farther back that they could sleep longer today. Their turn wouldn't come for hours. The Gallivan wagon and Scott Haskell's were far back in the line, having each taken their turn at the front only a few days before. But in spite of the early hour, Jeb could see Patrick fetching water for his oxen. He couldn't resist the impulse to ride back and say good-morning to the boy.

"I'll miss you up here behind me, son," he called as he approached.

Patrick grinned up at him and gave a slap to the side of one of the hulking black beasts. "I wish we could trade these in for a horse. Then I could ride with you all the time."

"And let your brother do all the work driving the wagon?" Jeb chided gently.

The boy's smile dimmed. "Well, no. I guess not."

"You can ride with me again tomorrow, after the crossing."

"Are they ready to start?" Now his handsome little face took on an eager expression. "Can I just ride down to the riverbank with you, Captain? I want to watch them go into the water."

Jeb smiled. He remembered the first time he'd seen a river crossing. He'd felt much the same excitement he was seeing on Patrick's face. Melly had been petrified, he remembered. She'd clenched his hand so tightly that her nails had dug into his skin, leaving a scar that had lasted for months. He'd looked for that scar recently, but couldn't find it anymore. It didn't matter. The scars he carried inside would never fade. The sudden memory put an effective end to his upbeat mood. He shifted in the saddle. "Is your brother awake?"

"No." The eager light in Patrick's eyes faded as he became aware of the dimming of Jeb's expression.

"You'd best stay here, then, until he does. The Todds will be starting across in a few minutes, but there'll be plenty of time for you to see wagons crossing. It's going to go on all day."

"So I can come down as soon as my brother is awake?"

Jeb tried to resurrect his smile. "Yes. Just be sure that you stay out of the way of the wagons when they start rolling down the bank. It's steep, and this will be the first good test of the brakes on some of these rigs."

"I'll be careful."

"Good boy," Jeb said with a nod. Then he rode back toward the front of the train, his face once again solemn.

As it turned out, most of the members of the train were almost as interested as Patrick in their first river crossing. By the time Jeb had crossed back and forth himself several times and was satisfied with the route, the banks had filled with spectators to witness the Todds' big wagon taking the first plunge.

Kerry and Patrick had walked down with Scott and the Burnetts. There was a festive mood to the day. A change from what had already become the numbing sameness of plodding along mile after mile of dusty prairie.

"For lunch we could bring a picnic here to the bank," Kerry suggested gaily, causing Scott to laugh.

"Isn't this trip a sort of five-month long picnic?" he asked. "We've been eating outdoors for every meal."

Kerry refused to be discouraged. "Yes, but today's different. We could have a little party. I'll make some lemonade."

Most wagons had started out with plenty of sugar, but the precious supply of lemons would only last a few more days. Then, except for the wealthier parties who had purchased some of the expensive flavoring extracts, they would have to be content with the flavor of whatever water they encountered along the way, however brackish.

"And we could open a package of sugar biscuits

and the tin of licorice drops,'' Patrick added with enthusiasm.

"Yea, a picnic!'' Polly shouted, jumping to her feet, followed inevitably by her sister. The two had been sitting still for long enough.

"Picnic!'' Molly echoed.''

Dorothy Burnett smiled indulgently. "It looks as if we're going to have a picnic today, my friends.'' She stood, more decorously than her daughters, and shook out her skirts. "I'll mosey back to the wagon and see what goodies I can come up with.''

Kerry also pushed herself up from the ground. "I'll go, too.''

When Scott and John Burnett began to stand as well, Dorothy waved a hand at them. "You other men stay here and mind the children on the bank. Then you can all come along back to the wagons in about half an hour to carry our picnic.''

Dorothy always made Kerry feel comfortable. It hadn't seemed to matter that the friendly woman thought that she was a man. She chatted with Kerry as naturally as if they'd been lifelong friends.

The two made their way up the bank and toward the row of waiting wagons, but a shout made Kerry look back over her shoulder. A wagon had come to a halt just a few feet into the river and Jeb Hunter was riding around it, trying to determine what had caused it to get stuck. He swung off one side of his saddle, hanging practically upside down toward the water. The movement strained the fabric of his clothes tight across his broad back and, Kerry noticed with a guilty flush, across his muscular buttocks. Out of the corner of her eye, she saw that Dorothy Burnett's eyes were also trained on their wagon captain. And Dorothy was a married woman! Kerry thought with surprise.

"We're lucky to have Captain Hunter," Dorothy said casually, making no mention of the gleam of feminine interest that Kerry had seen in her eyes.

"I suppose," Kerry answered uncertainly.

Dorothy halted and turned to look at her. "No supposing about it. He's one of the best, you know. They say he's never lost a wagon and never lost a life in all his crossings."

"Well, he does seem to be conscientious about his task."

"More than conscientious. At Boone's store I heard them say that Jeb Hunter would kill himself before he let something go wrong on one of his trains."

"Sometimes he could do it a little more graciously," Kerry said, thinking of the way he'd ordered Scott around more than once in her presence.

They'd reached the Gallivan wagon where Dorothy branched off to continue back to her own. She gave a little snort as she ended the conversation by saying over her shoulder, "I don't care if he's gracious as long as he gets my family safely across the country."

By late afternoon, most of the wagons had struggled across the broad expanse of water. On the other side, the usually organized camp was in disarray as wagons were parked every which way. Many had supplies lying on the ground around them, drying out from the soaking they'd received.

Patrick and the Burnett twins had been hopping

around for the past hour awaiting their respective turns to cross. Kerry was less eager. The closer the wagon edged to the water, the heavier it felt to her. She knew that there had been minor problems throughout the day with wagons getting stuck in the silt of the river bottom, and she hoped the extra weight of theirs wouldn't cause that problem. She had a feeling Jeb Hunter would be furious if he found out that she had not obeyed his orders about the size of their load.

As if her thoughts had conjured him up, he suddenly appeared next to their wagon. His clothes were totally soaked, but he didn't appear the least bit tired after an entire day of hard labor. "Have you had anything to eat all day, Captain?" The words were out of her mouth before she even thought about them. It was probably not a very masculine question for her to ask.

But Jeb seemed not to notice the lapse. "I'll eat tonight," he said with a dismissive wave. He appeared to be totally focused on his task. "Are you boys ready to cross? You've tied everything down?"

Patrick answered, his voice shrill with anticipation. "We've done everything you said, Captain. Don't worry about us—we're packed up tight as a boat."

Jeb nodded his approval. "Good. Now just don't get too fancy on those reins. Let the animals feel their way. Hold it steady." He looked from Patrick to Kerry, hesitated a minute, then asked, "You're sure you don't want one of the bigger men to ride up there with you?"

"We can hold them, Captain," Kerry said stiffly.

"All right." Jeb wheeled his horse around. "You and Haskell are next."

Kerry's hands were white where they wrapped tightly around the reins. *Please, don't get stuck,* she prayed silently to the four mute beasts in front of her. She and Patrick watched as Scott's wagon reached the edge of the bank, then gave a lurch from side to side as it started over the lip. They could see the wooden brakes hitting the back wheel rims as the rig slid down the small hill and entered the water. Kerry let out a breath she didn't know she'd been holding as their neighbor's wagon slowly righted itself on the more gentle slope of the river floor and continued deeper into the water.

Scott leaned around the edge of his canvas and grinned back at them. "Nothing to it!" he shouted.

"Nothing to it with a half-full wagon like yours," Kerry said under her breath.

Jeb was in the middle of the river. The water there reached to Storm's flanks, but the big animal stood stock-still against the current. "All right, Gallivans!" Jeb yelled, motioning them to start.

"Get your hand ready on the brake," Kerry told Patrick tersely.

"It is."

Frank Todd and some of the other men were serving as guides to urge any reluctant animals to make that first step over the bank. As Kerry signaled with the reins, Frank stepped up to their lead ox and gave it a hard slap on the rump. Clumsily the four animals struggled down the slope with the heavy wagon swaying behind them. Kerry gritted her teeth and held on.

"You're doing fine!" Jeb hollered his encouragement.

Scott's wagon had reached the deep, middle part of the river and appeared to be moving smoothly.

Kerry and Patrick bounced wildly as first the front wheels, then the rear, jolted over the edge of the hill. "Brakes, Patrick!" Kerry shouted, then felt a surge of relief as the wheels held and the entire rig slid into the water. Patrick released the brake. The wagon straightened out and continued slowly across the shallow, gravelly edge of the river.

Kerry sank back in the seat, suddenly weak from the release of tension. The bank on the other side was not as steep, and pulling up was not as tricky as sliding down. If the wagon had held up for the descent, they ought to make it all right.

The oxen plodded along passively in front of them, oblivious to the river swirling up around them, now covering their sturdy legs. They'd almost reached the middle, and the wagon slowed as the wheels bogged down in the silt of the river bottom. Finally, one of the lead animals refused to move altogether and the wagon stopped.

"Use your whip," Jeb shouted, turning his horse to ride their way.

Kerry sat up straight again and flapped the reins. Patrick grabbed the small bullwhip from its hook alongside the seat and snapped it over the animals without touching them. The cracks were startling, but none of the animals moved. "Just flick it on their backs," Kerry suggested. "I don't think it'll hurt them," she added at Patrick's doubtful expression.

Holding his slender arm up high, he cracked the

whip toward the back of the nearest ox. Instantly the animal lurched to one side, pulling the others off balance in their harness. The overloaded wagon shifted right, then tipped precariously to the left. Kerry heard a sickening crack as the left front wheel broke underneath them, then watched in horror as Patrick slid off the side of the seat and into the river.

Chapter Five

Jeb could tell even from a distance that the Gallivans' wagon was heavier than many that had crossed that day. Too heavy for a four-oxen team. And his worst fears were confirmed as he saw their animals balk once the load sank deep enough into the river mud. The veteran trail men who worked with Boone's outfitters knew exactly what four-, six- and eight-oxen wagons could handle. They certainly hadn't been the ones to overload the boys' wagon. Which must mean that the Gallivans themselves had not sent back the extra equipment as they had told him.

He'd already started his horse toward them, furious and worried at the same time, when their team suddenly spooked, sending the wagon pitching to one side and the younger Gallivan tumbling into the river.

Typically, the immediate panic at the threat to one of his charges clawed at his throat. And just as typically, he fought it back and steeled himself to act coolly. Storm was thoroughly used to the water after their long day, and the blessed animal did not appear to be at all fatigued. He surged forward in response to Jeb's urging, bringing them up to the Gallivan wagon in mere seconds. But by then the swift current had already carried Patrick's light body several yards downstream.

Jeb looked up at the wagon where Kiernan was standing in the listing wagon, his blue eyes wide with alarm. "He can't swim!" he screamed. Then, before Jeb could caution him to stay where he was, he put his foot up on the edge of the seat and jumped into the water toward his brother.

For a moment, Jeb was paralyzed by the boy's stupidity. Now instead of one boy to drag from the water, he'd have two. At least Kiernan knew enough to use the current rather than fight it, Jeb saw immediately, noting that the older boy was rapidly catching up to his brother. With a shake of his head and still fighting down that sick feeling of dread, Jeb pointed Storm downstream. Over on the bank he could see Frank Todd and the others running in the same direction. "What shall we do?" Frank yelled to him.

Jeb shook his head. The river was broad here without obstacles. If left unchecked the two boys could continue floating all the way back down to the Missouri. But the advantage was that there was nothing in the way to injure them. If they kept their heads, they should make it all right until he could get to them. It wouldn't be the first time he'd fetched a sopping passenger out of the river on a crossing. The tricky thing would be to fetch two of them at once. It was lucky the Gallivan boys were slight.

Thanking the Lord for his steady horse, Jeb moved over to the shallow gravel and spurred Storm into a gallop that took him past the floating boys. Then he pointed his mount once again into the middle, calculating the angle so that he would cut off their downriver progress. Kiernan had caught up to Patrick and the two boys were clinging to each other. He steered Storm directly toward them, then stopped. "Steady, boy," he told the animal. "Get ready for a jolt."

Hanging off the saddle from one leg, he leaned over the water and waited for the two boys to crash into them. There was a danger that the collision would knock both Storm and Jeb himself into the water as well, but there had not been time to formulate a better plan. The two bodies seemed to be rocketing toward them, faster than he had expected. He braced himself, then grabbed and lifted with all his strength just as they were about to hit. His actions diverted some of the force of the impact. Storm stumbled a little, but stayed on his feet. Jeb pulled himself upright in the saddle with the boys' weight pulling him in the opposite direction like weights on a balance scale.

Patrick was sputtering and panicky, pawing at Jeb to get a firm hold. Kiernan seemed more in control and grasped the horn of Storm's saddle to take some of the weight off Jeb. After a few seconds of struggle, Jeb was able to hoist the still choking Patrick around behind him to his accustomed seat. Then he turned his attention to Kiernan, who was draped stomach down across the front of the saddle, one hand still clutching the horn and the other on Jeb's left arm.

"Is he all right?" Kiernan gasped in a high-pitched voice. Then the Irish boy made a quarter turn bringing his now clean features not more than a foot from Jeb's face. And as he looked down at the body in his arms, Jeb's eyes opened in amazement to see the cloth of the boy's shirt clinging unmistakably to two most decidedly feminine breasts.

Kerry saw the astonishment in his face at once. She flopped back over on her stomach, hoping that she'd been wrong about the sudden revelation she'd seen in Jeb Hunter's eyes. But she knew that it was hopeless. Her soft, female body was sprawled most indelicately over one of Jeb's hard legs. Her slender hand still grasped the fabric of his jacket. Her own oversize jacket had been ripped off her and carried away by the river. She might as well be naked.

She waited for an explosion, but Jeb merely pulled her more squarely across the saddle and started toward the far bank. Her brother was still coughing, and after a moment, Jeb asked, "Are you all right, Patrick?" His voice was tight with anger.

"Yes." The coughs became muffled as Patrick struggled to control them.

Kerry wriggled around, trying to boost herself up from her uncomfortable position across the saddle horn. "Don't move!" Jeb barked at her.

"Our wagon..." Patrick began with a groan.

"Your wagon's got a broken wheel," Jeb snapped. "It was too damned heavy."

Both Patrick and Kerry remained silent the rest of the short trip across the river. When they reached the opposite bank, Jeb yanked Kerry's arm up and deposited her unceremoniously on the ground. Then he reached behind him and, a little more gently, swung Patrick down. Finally, he dismounted himself, his eyes never leaving Kerry, who stood shivering, her wet clothes clinging to every curve. She looked wistfully out at the river as if hoping that her jacket would come floating up to the bank so she could cover herself from Jeb Hunter's withering glare.

Scott Haskell came up from behind her. "Are you all right?" he asked gently, draping a blanket around her shoulders.

"Yes," she murmured, giving him a look of gratitude.

Other passengers had gathered around them, but Kerry was not too aware of their presence. Her attention kept coming back to Jeb Hunter's light brown eyes. Someone brought a blanket for Patrick. "I'm sorry," she whispered finally, trying to break the silence.

"It appears you have reason to be." The coldness in the wagon captain's voice sent another chill along her back.

"Now isn't the time for this, Hunter," Scott objected. "These two are freezing. They need to get warm and dry. Then you can talk."

"I suppose you knew about this, Haskell?" Jeb asked angrily, waggling a hand in the general direction of Kerry's front where her most obvious female characteristics had given her away.

"I knew that Kerry was a woman, if that's what you mean," Scott answered calmly. "I didn't see a need to make a point of the issue."

"Kerry, is it? So even the name was a lie?"

"The train doesn't take lone women," Kerry said. Now that her scare was over and she was feeling a little warmer under the blanket, she was more able to cope with Jeb Hunter's anger. She'd anticipated a showdown with their wagon leader if her disguise was ever discovered. Well, the time had arrived. And she'd be darned it she'd let him intimidate her into backing down.

"You're damn right it doesn't," Jeb said. "And for many good reasons."

Kerry pulled the blanket more firmly around her shoulders, took a step backward and looked Jeb Hunter squarely in the eye. "I'd be interested in hearing those reasons, Captain. But right now I'm more concerned with getting some dry clothes and trying to figure out how we're going to get my wagon out of the middle of the river. So if you'll excuse me..."

She turned her back on him and marched up the bank, looking tiny and bedraggled, the heavy blanket trailing along on the ground behind her. Jeb Hunter felt his gut twist. A woman. Damnation, what a development. A lone woman on his train. And not just any woman—one who wouldn't listen to orders and who had a stubborn streak as wide as Kansas. One whose campfire he'd looked forward to sharing night after night. One who somehow, inexplicably, had already managed to creep a small ways into the black hole that was his heart.

The breakdown of the Gallivan wagon meant that the crossing would not be completed that day. The few wagons still waiting on the far side formed their own little camp for the night. Most of the men on the train volunteered to help Jeb, Scott, John Burnett and Patrick with the monumental task of emptying the disabled wagon. When Kerry had waded into the river on her way to help, Jeb had rudely spun her around by the shoulders and sent her back on shore. "The *men* will handle this," he told her. "All I need is to have you stumble on that bad ankle. It would break for sure this time.''

Kerry had looked to Scott for support, but for once he nodded agreement with Jeb. ''You stay up on the bank, Kerry,'' he told her. ''You can organize the crates and supplies as we haul them up to you.''

So she'd stayed at the edge of the river, dry and warm, as a seemingly endless progression of her fellow wagon train members trekked back and forth ferrying every last box of her possessions to shore. It was a mortifying couple of hours, not helped by Jeb Hunter's glares every time he caught her eye. By now he'd realized exactly how much she and Patrick had crammed into their wagon. He hadn't yet commented on it, but she was sure that he would.

Finally, Frank and Scott led the Todds' six-oxen team into the water and hitched them to the Gallivan team. A group of men shoved the wagon from behind and after forty-five minutes of struggle, the broken vehicle was pushed and dragged up on the opposite bank.

Kerry watched helplessly, biting her lip and fighting off tears. She was too preoccupied to notice that Eulalie Todd and Dorothy Burnett were standing just behind her. The older woman put a comforting arm around her shoulders and said, ''It's not your fault, honey.''

The sympathy almost made the tears fall, but Kerry blinked them away. ''Yes, it is. The captain told me not to load the wagon so heavy, and I didn't listen to him.''

Eulalie hugged her close. ''The important thing is that you and your brother are all right. When you get to my age, you begin to realize that things are of no consequence—it's people who matter.''

"But I'm causing everyone so much trouble...."

Dorothy stepped to her other side and put her arm around her waist so that she was enfolded between the two women like a baby in a warm bunting. "You've helped out a lot of people on the train. They're happy to be able to return the favor, Kiernan. Or..." She faltered a little. "It's Kerry, is it?"

Kerry ducked her head and nodded. "I'm sorry I had to deceive everyone—especially you two. I wanted to tell you.''

She was surprised to hear mild-mannered Eulalie say in spirited tones, "Well, if they wouldn't make these ridiculous rules against women doing things they're perfectly capable of doing, you wouldn't have had to go to all that trouble.''

"We know why you did it, Kerry," Dorothy agreed. "And I must say I always thought you were much too helpful and good with the girls to be a male," she added with a laugh.

"I appreciate your friendship," she told the two women. "But I'm afraid our wagon leader isn't going to share your tolerance." She gave a great sigh. "And now he has good reason to be angry with me.''

The late-spring twilight had begun to darken and most of the men working on the Gallivan wagon had not yet had their supper. Jeb thanked them all for their work and told them that they would finish the repairs and bring the other wagons across in the morning. Kerry offered weak thank-yous as they began to disband to return to their own wagons, but most of them made no reply. Their stares were not hostile, exactly, but it was obvious that they weren't comfortable with her in her male clothing, now that she'd been revealed as a woman.

Patrick had been helping unload the boxes, but his usual boyish eagerness was missing. He looked small and crestfallen, and Kerry knew he was feeling almost as guilty as she was. All at once she wished they were back in New York City and had never heard of the Overland Trail or California. Maybe their father would still be alive if he hadn't set out on such an arduous journey. She knew the notion was crazy, but at the moment she was too despondent to be logical.

Scott came toward her carrying a plate of beans. "You haven't eaten, lass," he said. He, at least, was one male who was not looking at her as if she was some kind of a freak of nature. She offered him a smile in gratitude, but shook her head at the plate. "I don't want to eat anything."

Scott took her arm and led her over to a big log that had been placed on the edge of the riverbank. "You're too tired to know what you want, Kerry. But you need to eat. Sit," he said, pointing at the log.

It was easier to do as he told her, so she sat and made a token effort to swallow some of the nearly cold beans he urged on her. "Thank you," she mumbled.

Scott put one foot on the log beside her and leaned close. "I should warn you, lass. Jeb Hunter is furious with you."

The news didn't surprise Kerry in the least. "What's he planning to do about us?"

Scott shook his head. "I don't know, but he's out

for bear. It might be wise to stay out of his way if you can.''

''I'd be happy to, but I don't think he'll let it get by that easily. In the first place, I disobeyed his express order, and in the second place, our whole position on this train has been a lie from the beginning.''

Scott smiled ruefully. ''It doesn't sound too good, does it?''

Suddenly she decided that she couldn't swallow one more bite of the greasy beans. She handed the plate back to Scott and stood. ''I think I might as well get this over with.''

''Get what over with?'' Scott asked.

''The showdown. The scolding. Whatever it is our captain has in store for me. It's not going to do any good to wait until morning.''

Then she squared her shoulders and headed up toward the wagons to find Jeb Hunter.

Jeb was exhausted. River-crossing days were among the most difficult on the trail. It was almost as if he used up a little piece of himself with each wagon safely across. When something went wrong, it always made the day worse. In this case, they'd had the bad fortune to have the mishap occur at the end of the day when everyone would normally have been ready to settle in for an evening's rest. Instead, they'd had several more hours of hauling and shoving. All because of a stubborn female who'd lied to him from the minute he'd laid eyes on her.

His mood did nothing to ease the aching in his weary body. Eulalie Todd had tried to make him eat something, but he felt as if any kind of food would taste like sawdust at this point. He'd accepted Frank's offer of a long pull from his flask of whiskey and then had headed to his bedroll. It was another dry, mild night, which meant that once again he could sleep under the stars and leave the Todds alone in their wagon. Though he couldn't imagine that Frank would have much strength to make use of the privacy this night. He'd worked all day like a man half his age. Maybe Eulalie's motherly ministrations could revive him, Jeb thought with a tired smile as he shook his blankets out over a level, grassy spot. Normally he tried not to think much about those matters. He'd taken his ease now and then with a sympathetic bar girl at the end of the trail. But in general, his celibate life suited him. It was, after all, what he deserved. If he hadn't been such a greedy, restless fool, he'd still be living in California and going to bed each night beside Melly's sweet, warm body.

"Captain Hunter?" Kerry Gallivan's voice startled him in the darkness. He whirled around to face her.

"If I were you, I'd pick another time to talk with me," he said stiffly.

"You're angry. Of course, you have every right...."

Jeb took a step closer to her, his fist clenched with tension. "No, Miss Gallivan. I'm *furious*. And if you were only the male you claimed to be, I'd be tempted to give you the thrashing you so richly merit."

Kerry forced herself to stare straight into his wrathful eyes. "I'm sorry. I...we didn't have a lot of time to decide what to do after my father's death. It seemed like the only way...."

"And disobeying my orders about overloading your wagon was the only way, too?" he interrupted.

"Well, now," she said, sighing. "That was wrong. It's just that those tools have been in our family since..." Her voice trailed off forlornly, then she pulled herself up and said staunchly, "Go ahead and thrash me if you want, Captain."

In the moonlight her perfect features were startlingly beautiful, even now, with her jaw set in stubborn lines and her eyes half-wincing as if she really expected that he might hit her. Jeb felt the anger draining from him like water out of a sieve. Her words and the way she stood before him so defenseless had brought out his most irritating protective instincts. And, Lord, she was beautiful. How in the name of heaven had he ever thought that she was a man? Haskell had evidently seen through her disguise. What had been Jeb's problem? The anger began to build again, but this time it was directed along a more well-worn path—toward himself.

"Part of this is my fault," he acknowledged, his voice less tight. "A wagon captain's supposed to know what's going on with his passengers. He's supposed to know if they're sick or hurting, happy or sad, tired or strong." He ran a hand back through his disheveled hair. "And he sure as hell is supposed to know what sex they are."

He could see her painful swallow all along the length of her slender throat. Her slender, *feminine* throat. Damnation. "But I deceived you," she argued. "I went to great pains to be sure you didn't know, to be sure that no one knew. I felt it would be the only way we'd be able to get on the train."

"Haskell knew." Jeb wasn't sure exactly why that fact grated on him so.

She hesitated. "Well, there was the problem with my ankle, you know."

Ah, yes. Haskell had tended her ankle. The ankle that was attached to one of those shapely legs that Jeb had not been able to help noticing when she'd been sopping wet today with her man's trousers clinging to her like a second skin. Haskell had probably held her ankle in his hands, turning it, rubbing it, perhaps...

Kerry cleared her throat. "And Mr. Haskell has had more chance to spend time with us."

"When did you tell him?"

"I beg your pardon?"

"When did you tell Haskell the truth?"

Her thick black lashes swept down over the blue eyes. She looked as if she was reluctant to answer the question, as if she realized that the fact that Scott Haskell knew the truth was making her deception even more difficult for him. Finally she said, "I didn't tell him. He...more or less...guessed that first day."

"The first day," Jeb confirmed, his self-reproach mounting.

Kerry nodded, head down.

Jeb let out a long stream of air through his nose. Then he leaned down and pulled a towel out of his pack. His bout with the river had left him caked with mud. He'd need to wash before he could crawl into his blankets. When he'd straightened up, he told her, "I'm going to punish myself for my own stupidity by not berating you any further, Miss Gallivan. By not giving myself that pleasure."

Kerry's eyes filled with relief. "I promise I'll do everything you say from now on, Captain. Patrick and I will keep up and work hard. We'll find things to leave behind to make the load just right. And we won't question your orders...."

Jeb held up his hand with a look of surprise. "Wait a minute. Surely you understand?"

"Understand what?"

"Miss Gallivan, there's no way you and your brother are going to continue on to California. As soon as we reach Fort Kearney, we'll find an escort to take you back to St. Louis."

Kerry took a step backward, feeling almost as if she'd received that blow he'd threatened her with earlier. "Turn back now? You can't be serious?"

"I'm deadly serious. A single woman and a raw boy have no business on a wagon train."

Kerry couldn't believe her ears. "We've done fine up to now."

"Fine, right. Costing the entire train a day's travel by letting your wagon break down in the middle of the river."

Now Kerry's fists clenched at her sides. "Captain Hunter, my brother and I are going to California...."

Jeb stepped past her in the darkness and started to walk away toward the river. "Not on my train, you're not," he said, and was gone before she could make a reply.

Dorothy Burnett was waiting for her when she returned to her listing, disabled wagon.

"He says he's not going to let us stay with the

train," she told her neighbor in a dazed voice. She still couldn't believe what she'd heard.

"He's just angry, Kerry," Dorothy said, putting an arm around her shoulders. "In the morning he'll probably give you one of those superior male tongue-lashings and then everything will be fine."

Kerry shook her head. "That's not how it sounded to me."

Dorothy frowned. "Well, he can't just abandon you. No one would stand for it."

"He says he'll find us an escort back East when we reach Fort Kearney." Listlessly she picked up the coffeepot and dribbled water over the campfire to put it out for the night.

"That's crazy. If you've done all right up until now..."

"I know." Kerry sat down on an overturned bucket and dropped her head into her hands. "It doesn't make sense. I knew he'd be angry, but I thought once we were out on the trail, there would be no way he could refuse to take us."

"Maybe he can't. What do the papers say? Maybe you can force him to take you."

Kerry stuck her feet out in front of her. She was still in a pair of Patrick's trousers. Her own clothes were carefully buried at the bottom of one of the soggy trunks that were piled haphazardly around the wagon. She was not sure she could find them even if she wanted to, and after everything they'd been through today, her attire was the least of her concerns. "I don't want to *force* him. He's our leader. I can't make him into some kind of an enemy."

Dorothy kicked at the embers that had scattered

from the fire, lost in thought. Finally she said, "Well, then, make him into your friend."

"What do you mean?" Kerry asked.

"I mean, my dear Kerry, as long as everyone now knows that you're a woman, you might as well take full advantage of it. Hunter's flesh and blood. At least I think he is," she added with a chuckle. "Go talk to him. Bat those long black lashes if you have to. Didn't your mother ever tell you about how a woman can get what she wants from a man?"

Kerry's face flushed. "I was only six when my mother died. But I hope I know enough about those things to be above—"

Dorothy interrupted her with a quick hug. "I'm sorry, Kerry. You haven't had an easy road of it, have you? But don't get prickly on me. I wasn't implying anything immoral. I just meant that if you can manage to talk to Hunter on a friendly basis, he might find himself much more disposed to change his mind."

"Do you really think so?" Kerry looked dubious. She'd always looked down on the girls back in New York who used their looks and female manners to get what they wanted. Plus, whereas Scott Haskell's head might be turned by a pretty face, she had the feeling that Jeb Hunter was not so susceptible. She'd seen him polite and respectful to the women on the train, but she couldn't recall seeing him look at so much as one with that flirtatious smile that Scott seemed to use on every woman between ten and sixty.

Dorothy's eyes swept from Kerry's glossy black hair to her long, slender legs. "Kerry," she said firmly, "once we clean you up and put some decent clothing on you, I predict that our wagon captain is going to find it awfully hard to stay angry at you."

Chapter Six

Kerry knew that she should be tired enough to fall asleep standing up, but Dorothy's words were dancing inside her head and wouldn't let her alone to think about going to bed. She had bristled at her friend's insinuation that she use some kind of unspecified feminine wiles to get her way with Jeb Hunter.

It was true that Kerry had never had a mother to talk to about such things, but she was sure that if her mother had been alive to raise her, she would have cautioned her daughter against any such notion. But she'd vowed to do anything it took to get to California. And as Dorothy had said, it wasn't as if she was talking about doing anything...well, anything *bad*. It only made sense that if she could approach their captain in a friendly manner, he'd be more apt to listen to her calm and rational case for allowing them to stay with the train.

As she reasoned with herself, her feet seemed to already be taking her in the direction of the grove of trees where Jeb Hunter had laid out his bedroll. Her heart sped up its beat and her pace slowed as she approached. Perhaps he'd returned from washing and was already asleep. By the time she reached the edge of the grove, her hands had balled into fists and her lower lip was clamped firmly between her teeth. If he was asleep, she decided, she'd awaken him. She wouldn't be able to sleep until she'd tried to make him change his mind.

Jeb dried his arms briskly with the towel, rubbing away chill bumps on his wet skin. His body, at least, felt better after his bath. It had refreshed him and eased away the worst of the day's knots. His mind was still knotted, but he was used to dealing with that state of affairs.

He stood at the edge of the river, naked, letting the cool night air dry the rest of his body.

The camp had grown quiet. Across the river he could barely see the glowing embers of a couple of banked fires next to the wagons that hadn't been able to make the crossing. The majority of the wagons were on the far side, dry and repacked after their river adventure. They'd be ready to move out tomorrow as soon as the others made it across. And as soon as the Gallivan wagon was repaired.

The knot in his head threatened to tighten into a megrim. He'd begun having them after Melly's death, had endured them almost daily for over a year. But they came less often nowadays, partly because he knew how to keep himself away from issues that might bring one on. He'd taught himself to keep uninvolved, unemotional, unruffled, no matter what the circumstances.

But he'd broken that rule today. He'd been most

thoroughly ruffled by Miss *Kerry* Gallivan. And now he'd probably have to pay for his lapse with a headache.

He dried his face with the towel and rolled his neck from side to side. Sometimes it helped.

"Oh, my goodness!"

The exclamation made his neck straighten up with an audible snap. Reflexively, he reached down to cover his most exposed parts with the towel. Like some kind of nightmare, conjured from inside his aching head, there stood Kerry Gallivan.

"Excuse me, ah...Captain," she stammered. "I...ah...was looking for you."

Jeb recovered his composure quickly. Her embarrassment amused him, a tiny bit of revenge for all the trouble she'd caused him and would continue to cause him. "I thought we had finished our discussion for the evening, Miss Gallivan," he said calmly.

She looked away. "Please...ah...feel free to... ah...get dressed, Captain. I didn't mean to interrupt you."

"You didn't interrupt," he said. The surprise over, he was now definitely enjoying her discomfiture. "I'm finished with my bath. Don't let me stop you from yours, if that's what you had in mind."

He gestured toward the water with the hand holding his towel and hid a smile as he saw Kerry's averted eyes widen.

"No, I didn't come...I mean, I came to talk with you."

A hammer tripped at the back of his head. Jeb had had enough of the game. He threw the towel over his shoulder and reached for his pants. "I thought I warned you earlier that I'm not in the best frame of mind for a discussion. What we both need now is some sleep.''

Out of the corner of her eyes she could see that he was once again decently covered. At least the lower half of him. She turned toward him and said, ''I know, but the way we left things, I didn't think I'd be able to sleep. I can't accept what you told me, Captain. About turning back...''

''I'll listen to you in the morning, Miss Gallivan,'' he interrupted with a dismissive wave.

She'd been too direct, she realized at once. His eyes had narrowed and grown hard. He wasn't even going to listen to her. She tried to remember Dorothy's words about making him into a friend, but things just seemed to be frozen up inside her. ''Kerry!'' she blurted.

''Excuse me?''

''Could you please...'' She let out a deep breath. ''Call me Kerry instead of Miss Gallivan. Then it won't sound so much like you're mad at me.''

Jeb paused for a minute, his expression softening imperceptibly. ''But I *am* mad at you.''

Kerry bit her lip. ''I know. But I don't want you to be. I want us to be...friends.''

Jeb looked at her in disbelief. ''Friends? Miss Gallivan, I don't make friends with the people on my trains, with people whose very lives might depend on me. And if I did decide that I wanted a *friend*, you, my charming deceiver, would very likely be the *last* person on this particular train whom I would choose.''

He hadn't put on his shirt, and in the moonlight, Kerry was utterly aware of the sculpted muscles of his chest. His waist narrowed just at the top of buckskin trousers that molded along straight hips down to bulging thighs. Jeb Hunter was a powerful man, she thought for the hundredth time. Dorothy had been right—she would be wise to make him her friend, whether he wanted to be one or not. She just wished she were a little more certain of how to go about doing that. Dorothy had seemed to think it would be no trouble at all. But as she looked at Jeb's implacable expression, she wasn't so sure.

She tried to remember what Katie Flanagan would do back in New York. Katie Flanagan had had more beaux buzzing around her than bees at a honey pot, and if she hadn't had nine older brothers looking out for her, she'd have been married thrice over by now.

Kerry took a step closer to where Jeb was still standing on the edge of the bank. "What can I say to convince you that I'm sorry for...having to trick you?"

"Oh, I believe you're sorry, all right. What good does that do anyone?"

Maybe Captain Hunter would soften up if she let him kiss her on the cheek. But as soon as the thought entered her head, something trembly started happening down inside her. She clasped her hands together so the shaking couldn't make it all the way to the outside, and took another step closer. "Well, is there something I can *do* to make it up, then?" she asked, her voice grown small and squeaky.

Jeb stood looking at her for an interminable moment, his face totally unreadable. Then he said, "If I couldn't see that you're standing there shaking like an aspen leaf, girl, I might believe that you knew what you meant by that question. As it is, I'm going to save us both a lot of grief by sending you back to your wagon.''

Kerry squeezed her hands together more tightly. They *were* shaking, darn them. ''I'm willing to do anything it takes to get to California, Captain Hunter. I want you to agree to take us.''

''I don't take lone women on my trains, Miss Gallivan. *Any* kind of lone woman,'' he added. ''Now be a good girl and get back to your wagon to get some sleep. You'll have a busy day tomorrow reloading your wagon and deciding what you're going to throw away.''

His tone left no room for argument, but Kerry was not ready to give up. ''We'll talk about this again tomorrow when we're both rested,'' she said with an attempt at a smile.

''You can talk all you want, right up until the time we reach Fort Kearney. But it won't do you any good. At that point you'll be on your way back East.''

Kerry once again found her eyes drifting down to the captain's chest. Just because he was…strong, didn't mean he had to be a bully. She straightened up as indignation and a new resolution overcame her nervousness. Now that she knew that her overtures of ''friendship,'' whatever that might involve, were to be refused, she was feeling better. She was more comfortable fighting the captain with her wits and her will than with some kind of mysterious feminine wiles, which, for all she knew, she might not even possess.

''Back East?'' she said under her breath after he had nodded goodnight and headed up toward the trees. "We'll just have to see about that, Mr. Wagon Master."

Jeb's mood had not improved by the next morning. After his backbreaking day, he should have slept like the dead. Instead, he'd lain awake for hours, reliving the day. He'd close his eyes only to see Kerry Gallivan's face as she'd licked her full lips and nervously offered to do anything to make up for her deception. And he'd get that sensation again of drowning in her intense blue eyes. Then behind his closed lids he'd see water rushing past, and picture the few moments in the river when he'd feared losing two of his charges to the swift current. He'd drift halfway into sleep, but his dancing visions would change. Suddenly the eyes would be Melly's lifeless eyes, staring up at the ceiling of their cozy cabin as if doomed to relive the last dreadful moments of her life in some kind of horrible frozen eternity. He'd awaken with a start, sweating and terrified.

Kerry Gallivan was not Melly, he'd reassure himself. He'd *saved* Kerry. And her brother as well. He had nothing to reproach himself for. *This time* he'd been where he should be; he'd done the right thing. But, by God he'd not have to do it again. The sooner he got Kerry and Patrick Gallivan off his hands, the better.

Then he would lie back down and the cycle would start all over again. Close to dawn he gave up the effort entirely and got up. He'd get an early start on the day, and if they were lucky, the remaining wagons would be across and the Gallivan wagon fixed and reloaded by noon. They could still make four or five miles' progress today. Four or five miles closer to Fort Kearney where he would no longer have to worry about the late Sean Gallivan's misguided children, the younger of whom was at the moment making his way toward Jeb.

"How are you feeling today, Patrick?" he asked, trying not to take his sour humor out on the boy. "No ill effects from your dunking yesterday?"

Patrick looked younger, somehow. He'd lost a little of the cockiness Jeb had found secretly amusing. "Not from the dunking," he answered, "but I'm feeling pretty rotten about everything else."

Jeb waited for the boy to approach him. The Todds had not come out of their wagon yet, so Jeb had begun building the fire for morning coffee. "What aspect of it are you feeling rotten about?" he asked, being careful not to make his voice too sympathetic. He put most of the blame for the deception on the boy's sister, but Patrick had been involved and was old enough to know better. He didn't want to let him off too easily.

Patrick shrugged and mumbled, "I don't know."

Jeb could hear tears at the back of his throat, but he didn't relent. "Do you think it's the fact that you lied to me or that you and your sister disobeyed my orders about the wagon?"

Patrick looked up into his face, his eyes stricken with guilt. Intense blue eyes just like his sister's. "I told Kerry from the beginning that it was a dumb idea."

Jeb nodded. "Well, you were right. It's caused a lot of trouble, and it's going to cause a sight more before we can send you two home."

"Please don't send us back, Captain." The blue eyes misted over and one great tear hovered at the edge of his eyelid, threatening to spill down his cheek.

Jeb felt a tug on his insides. He reached out and clapped a gentle hand on the boy's bony shoulder. "I have to, Patrick. Your sister doesn't understand what a terrible place the West can be for a woman alone."

"Kerry's strong," Patrick began eagerly. "And our papa always said she was smarter than any of the men he knew."

"It doesn't matter Patrick, horrible things can still happen. Being smart doesn't help."

Patrick looked as if he had no idea what kind of horrible things Jeb might be referring to, and Jeb was not about to enlighten him. Though bright and quick to learn, he was still a child, and Jeb didn't want to be the one to put that childhood to an end.

"It's because you're so mad at us," Patrick said sadly.

Jeb pulled the youngster toward his side and gave him half a hug. "No, Patrick. I'm not mad at you. Not anymore. But I can't take you and your sister to California. I'm sorry."

Patrick's arms crept timidly around Jeb's waist. "Can I still go riding with you until we reach the fort?"

Jeb looked down at the small boy tucked under his arm. *This is what it would feel like to have a son,* he thought. This peculiar mixture of pride and uncertainty that turned your insides to mush. He ruffled Patrick's black hair. "You can ride with me as much as you want, Patrick. Until we reach the fort."

* * *

Kerry had slept poorly and was just getting up when Dorothy and the twins arrived at her jumbled campsite with a platter full of johnnycakes. "You have enough on your mind this morning, Kerry," Dorothy said. "I thought I'd bring you some breakfast."

Kerry smiled her gratitude. She'd needed to start the day with a kind word.

"Mama says they're going to kick you off the train, Kiernan," Polly said with a bit of pride in her voice at being in on the news.

"It's not Kiernan, it's Kerry," Molly reminded her sister shyly.

"Yeah, Kerry. 'Cause you're a girl after all, and Captain Hunter's not going to let you be on the train," Polly continued, without seeming to pass judgment on the situation. In the way of children, she was dealing with the plain facts, not the ramifications.

It was left to Dorothy to provide the sympathy. "Girls, don't bother Kerry about that right now. She had a hard day yesterday, and she has a lot of work to do today."

Polly put her hands on her hips and looked around at the jumble of crates and boxes. "This is just a *mess*," she said, shaking her head.

Her bluntness made Kerry laugh in spite of herself. "Yes, it is," she agreed. "A mess I'm responsible for, I guess."

"Do you want us to help you put it back?" Molly asked. Then she added with one of her shy smiles, "Will Patrick be helping?"

"We can all help, Kerry," Dorothy agreed. "John,

too. It never hurts to have another set of strong arms.''

''You've been so kind....'' Kerry began.

But Dorothy waved off her gratitude. ''And what about all the times you've taken these little chickadees off my hands?''

Kerry smiled at the twins. ''They're my pals.''

Polly's eyes were wide. ''But, Kerry, we didn't know you were a *girl*. Now we can *really* be pals, can't we?''

Kerry set the plate of johnnycakes on the little ledge that jutted out from the side of the wagon and went over to give each of the girls a hug. ''Yes, now we'll really be pals.''

''Until they make you go home,'' Polly added.

''Did you take my words to heart, Kerry? Have you talked with Captain Hunter yet?'' Dorothy asked.

''I'm afraid you were wrong about our captain being susceptible to the pleadings of a woman.''

Dorothy smiled. ''But I can tell by your expression that you're not giving up the fight.''

Kerry smiled back. Here was one benefit of having her secret out in the open. She could share with Dorothy some of the female camaraderie she had been longing for. ''Let me put it this way,'' she told Dorothy. ''The way I see it, a lot can happen between here and Fort Kearney.''

By noon the Gallivan wagon was repaired. Scott's blacksmithing expertise proved helpful in reshaping the metal parts that had been damaged in the accident. The wagon master had not stopped by, but Kerry and Patrick had taken it upon themselves to begin throwing away everything they could bear to part with in order to lighten their load.

"Everything but the tools," Kerry said.

"But the tools are the heaviest of all," Patrick protested. "Besides, none of these other people seem to think you need woodworking tools to start a homestead."

"None of these other people are lucky enough to have the heritage of their great-grandfather's tools. To carry on the tradition…"

Patrick stopped her by giving a frustrated kick to one of the heavy old boxes. "You know what, Kerry? Papa loved his tools. And you think you have to do everything just because it's what Papa would have done. But I don't even *like* working with wood."

"Patrick!"

"I don't. I'd rather be a gold prospector like Scott. Who wants to sit in a stuffy old room all day hunched over a piece of wood?"

"But Papa spent all those hours teaching you…."

"And I hated it. Every minute of it."

Kerry looked down at her brother and then over at the two boxes of tools. They'd been her great-grandfather's. But she had to admit that the boxes were in terrible shape, banged up and dirty. The tools inside were not in much better condition. If her father were here, she told herself, he'd be much more concerned with getting his family safely to California than with transporting his tools.

Forgive me, Papa, she prayed silently. Then she said to Patrick, "Open up the boxes and see if anyone up and down the line can use any of these things.

Maybe we'll make back a few of the friends we lost by causing this delay."

Patrick looked as if she had just told him to go buy himself an ice cream. He jumped on top of the largest toolbox and did a little dance, then jumped off the opposite side and bent over to pry open the lid. "No more fish and no more woodworking," he said happily. "California is going to be a great place."

After the excitement of the crossing, a kind of numbness seemed to set in among the caravanners. Jeb had told them that it would be another ten days of constant pushing across the prairie before they could expect to reach the fort, where they would take a couple of days of rest. Spring was pressing into summer, and the unending green landscape was dotted now with bright sprinkles of purple and blue and red—delicate wildflowers to remind them with tantalizing promise that there was life and beauty beyond the rolling sea of grass.

Patrick had resumed his rides with Jeb. With the resiliency typical of a child, it had not taken him long to recover from his frightening fall in the river or to stop feeling guilty about the events that led up to it. Kerry was finding it harder to forget. The captain no longer visited their campfire in the evening. He'd ride up to collect Patrick in the morning, nod a stiff greeting, then ride away again, and she wouldn't see much of either of them until the noon stop when he'd drop Patrick back at their wagon.

Kerry had continued to wear her male attire. She told herself it was the practicality of it, and that she didn't want to open trunks to unpack her own clothes.

But in her heart she knew that the reasons were more complicated. They had to do with that night along the riverbank with Jeb Hunter. Dorothy had told her to sway the captain with feminine wiles and she'd tried. The fact that Jeb had not only remained unswayed but had utterly rejected her made her wince with embarrassment every time she thought about it. She wouldn't make that mistake again.

Dorothy and Eulalie didn't seem to mind the fact that she was wearing trousers. And Scott was as attentive as ever, apparently indifferent to her mode of dress. It was only the other men on the train who now viewed her warily as she walked with Polly and Molly up and down the wagons. And she had to admit that she probably did look odd. She'd lost her father's big jacket, so there was nothing to cover up her trousers, which fit snugly along her thighs, cinched in at the waist with a piece of cord.

Five days after the river crossing, Jeb directed an early camp to take advantage of a perfect site between the river and a small wood. Even the adults on the train reacted like children let out of school, many of them wading into the river and letting the cold water wash away the dust of the past several days. As soon as they stopped and unhitched the animals, Patrick and Kerry had gone back to fetch the twins and all four had made their way down to the river.

"Mama says we can wade in the river in our shifts," Polly said, holding Kerry's hand and skipping along beside her.

"I don't want to," Molly protested, looking at Patrick out of the corner of her eyes.

"Everyone can swim how they want," Kerry declared. "It's a warm day and the breeze will soon dry our clothes if we get them wet."

Patrick spied a couple of his new friends, boys close to his age, who were already in the water. He gave a whoop and began to tear off his shirt. "I'm going in!" he yelled and took off running.

"Don't go in too far," Kerry called after him. She wished that his near drowning had taught him a little more respect for the power of the river. But she supposed she should be grateful that he wasn't a timid child. She could already tell that timidity did not serve one well in the West. And she and Patrick *were* going west. In spite of Jeb Hunter's continued total refusal to even discuss the matter with her.

The target of her thoughts was this moment walking along the bank, watching the antics of those who were playing at the edge of the water. He was smiling, which changed the whole look of his face. Kerry found her eyes drawn to him again and again as he grew nearer. Finally he glanced up and met her gaze. His smile faded.

"C'mon, Kerry," Polly begged, pulling her toward the water. "Let's go in."

She clasped one twin's hand in each of hers and scrambled down the bank. "Should we take our shoes off?" Molly asked, looking at the water with some doubt.

Kerry looked along the bank. Shoes littered the edge of the grass. "I guess so. You don't mind the stones on your bare feet?"

The girls had already sat down and were unlacing their shoes. "Socks, too?" Polly asked.

Kerry nodded and sat down herself to pull off Patrick's big boots. They set the three pairs of shoes in a neat row, then stood and took a first, tentative step into the water. It ran cold and smooth along the tops of their sweaty feet.

Patrick appeared and held a hand out to Polly. "C'mon," he said cheerily. "You can walk from rock to rock and play bullfrog."

Polly looked out at the middle of the river. From the edge the current looked a lot faster than it did from up on the bank. "Not too far out," she said.

"I'll go," Molly answered quickly, and reached to take the hand Patrick was holding out before her sister could do so.

"Careful, now," Kerry cautioned again as the two children started off downriver, stepping from one big rock to another amid giggles.

Charles Kirby, one of Patrick's new friends, offered his hand to Polly, who was looking after her sister and Patrick with some resentment.

Kerry smiled. It was good to see the wagon train's children enjoying themselves. They all worked hard on the journey. At almost every age they had their duties—gathering fuel, preparing food, watching over younger siblings. They deserved some time to play.

Patrick had certainly had little enough of it in the past few difficult years in New York. He'd worked loading fish every day for the past four years. And Kerry had taken care of the small apartment they'd rented above the market. She'd cooked and mended their few clothes and then had gone downstairs to earn extra money cleaning up after the market closed each day. Sean Gallivan had spent the days in the tiny one-room shop just down the street from the fish market, trying to eke out a living with the carpentry skills his father had taught him, all the while dreaming of green acres of land. Rich land of his own.

Patrick deserved all the play he could get, Kerry mused, watching him now far down the river, still holding Molly's hand.

"I guess we all needed this break." Jeb Hunter stood on the bank just above her.

Kerry turned around in surprise. "Oh, Captain Hunter." Her greeting held no warmth.

Jeb regarded her a moment, his eyes drifting down to where white patches of leg showed between the end of her short pants and the water. Kerry backed up a step deeper into the river.

"Are you going to join them?" he asked with a nod toward the children. She wasn't sure, but it seemed as if there was a slight hint of amusement in his eyes.

"I might," she said a little defensively. "There's nothing wrong with a bit of play now and then. I suppose as our captain, you don't do that kind of thing." Standing on the bank, he appeared to tower over her. She took another step backward, away from him, now knee-deep in the water. Her still weak ankle slipped on a mossy rock and she wobbled. In a second, he had stepped down into the river and grabbed her arm to steady her.

"You'll be swimming whether you want to or not if you aren't careful," he cautioned.

He stood so close she could feel the heat of his body all along the length of hers. "I'm...sorry," she stammered. "Now you've gotten your boots wet."

He glanced down carelessly at his feet. "It won't hurt 'em."

His hand still held her arm. "I'm all right. You can...ah...let go of me."

He was looking down at her again, studying her. "I don't know," he said at last. "I don't want to have to fish you out of the river again."

The coldness of the water sent shivers up her legs. Or it might have been something more than the water. She pulled her arm away, but their bodies were still all but touching. "You won't, Captain Hunter," she said through suddenly stiff lips.

There was an odd expression in his light hazel eyes. "The children seem to have the right idea. Hold someone's hand and it keeps you from falling."

If it had been Scott saying such a thing, Kerry would have known what to make of it. The prospector's flirtatious comments were becoming more direct every day. But this was obviously not flirtation by Captain Hunter. He had made it plain the other night that he was not the least bit interested in such things—at least not with her.

"I won't fall, Captain." Carefully, so that she wouldn't make herself into a liar, she stepped along the stones and back up onto the grassy bank. "In fact, I'm done wading." The water had soaked her denim trousers past midthigh. "I've gotten myself all wet."

Jeb's eyes flicked downward again. "Yes, I can see that." He could actually see a sight more than he was comfortable with seeing, he thought ruefully, hoping that his body's signals were not as obvious as they felt. Kerry's long legs, completely outlined by the tight wet trousers were utterly arousing to a man who had not lain with a woman in longer than he cared to remember.

He'd realized the other night on the riverbank that he wanted her. It had surprised him. He'd become so good over the years at suppressing those urges. And he'd made it a strict rule never to allow himself to feel desire for any of the women on his trains. Of course, Kerry wouldn't be on his train much longer. In a few more days she'd be on her way home, out of his reach and his mind. It couldn't happen too soon.

"Why are you still wearing men's pants?" he asked, his voice sharper than he had intended.

She looked surprised and a little hurt at his abrupt change in tone. "They're comfortable."

"For you, maybe," he said grumpily.

"What's that supposed to mean?"

She looked honestly confused, though he didn't think she could be so naive as to not know what effect a body like hers could have on a man. "I mean, it's not exactly modest attire for a young woman."

Kerry looked around her in disbelief, watching as other members of the train romped in the water in various states of undress or in soaked, bedraggled clothes. "We're not exactly in a drawing room, Captain."

Jeb paused. It was unfair to take out the effects of his self-prescribed celibacy on her. "No, we're not," he agreed with a smile. "And it's not really any of my business anyway."

"No, it's not."

"Well, then, consider the comment withdrawn."

She watched him for a moment and her expression

appeared to soften. "All right," she said. Then she
smiled at him. A bright, sunny smile that made Jeb's
heart stand stock-still in the middle of his chest. "I'd
best see what the children are up to," she said, turning to head downriver with a little wave.

He watched her pick her way lightly along the bank
in her short trousers with her short black hair, a nim-
ble, lovely creature as spirited as the fabled lepre-
chauns of her homeland.

Yes, he thought to himself grimly, Fort Kearney
could not come soon enough.

Chapter Seven

The Overland Trail had transformed Fort Kearney from an isolated wilderness outpost into a bustling metropolis. Enterprising entrepreneurs had set up businesses to cater to literally thousands of wagons passing through the fort each season. The companies charged exorbitant prices on goods that the travelers could have purchased for next to nothing back East, if they had only known how badly they would be needed.

Axle grease was selling for two dollars a bucket and salted dried beef for five dollars a box. The travelers from the Hunter train were enthusiastic about this temporary return to at least a semblance of the civilized world of commerce. From wagon to wagon they exchanged information about exactly what each outfit was going to buy and what was the best strategy for getting the lowest price.

Kerry and Patrick listened to their new friends' plans in silence. If Jeb Hunter had his way, Fort Kearney would be the end of the trail for them. In fact, he had suggested that they might want to sell their rig and head back to St. Louis by horseback, carrying the belongings they wanted to keep on packmules. It would get them home much more quickly, he'd explained to a stony-faced Kerry the night before they arrived at the fort.

She hadn't bothered to point out once again that the East would never be "home" to her. She and Patrick didn't have a home—they were on their way to make one for themselves. Since the day when she'd been wading in the river, she'd avoided the captain. The look in his eyes had set off odd flutters inside her stomach, making her distinctly uncomfortable. It hadn't been hard to stay out of his way. In fact, it almost seemed as if he were avoiding her company, too.

But she knew that once they reached the fort she'd have to face him again. She had to somehow convince him to let her stay with the train, and she'd spent hours lying awake at night trying to decide how she would go about it. Dorothy's suggestion of trying to be friendly had definitely not worked. She had the feeling that Jeb Hunter was not a very friendly kind of person.

So she'd taken out the papers her father had signed when he'd joined the train and pored over them, looking for something that would legally force the captain to allow her to continue. But, as the lawyers had told her back in St. Louis, it was quite clear that the wagon train captain had almost total authority to decide who went on his train and what they could and could not do while they were on it.

Captain Hunter had announced that they would take a four-day break at the fort, plenty of time for wagon repairs, restocking, rest from the endless rolling motion of the wagons and the miles of walking through the tall grass.

Time enough for a party, Frank and Eulalie Todd had declared. And it was decided that the members of the train would gather for supper and dancing their second night off the trail. They set up two long tables in front of the sutler's store for the victuals and recruited Charles Kirby's father, Henry, and one of the soldiers at the fort to provide fiddling music for the dancing.

Patrick, who had been off with Charles and two other boys exploring the fort all day, was already dancing with excitement about the occasion. "A real dance, sis!" he exclaimed, jumping down from the back of the wagon where he'd disappeared to change his shirt. "I've never been to a dance before."

Kerry was sitting by the small campfire. She was still wearing her trousers and the same heavy linen shirt she'd worn on the trail. Patrick's grin faded as he looked over at her. "Have you?" he asked.

"Have I what?"

"Been to a dance."

Kerry frowned. Her mind was on the upcoming confrontation with Jeb Hunter. She'd paid little attention to talk of a dance. "No, I guess not."

"Well, come on, then. It's almost time to start."

Polly and Molly came racing up to the wagon, equally excited and even more exuberant than Patrick. Their usually flyaway hair was slicked back and tied with big bows—blue for Polly and red for Molly. Kerry no longer had any trouble telling the two apart.

Polly's eyes held more of a devilish glint, and Molly's face was a bit thinner than her sister's.

"Yeah, c'mon, Kerry. The dancing's about to start," Polly urged.

"You girls look pretty tonight," Patrick said gallantly, causing Molly's face to turn as red as her bow.

"Aren't you going to dress up, Kerry?" Molly asked.

Patrick looked at his sister in sudden surprise. "She's right, sis. You should be dressed up, too. You can't very well dance in my pants."

"I can't dance anyway," Kerry answered dryly.

"We'll teach you, Kerry," Polly offered.

"Or Mama will," Molly chimed in. "She teaches us."

Kerry smiled at the two enthusiastic youngsters. They didn't know how lucky they were to have a loving mother like Dorothy to teach them to dance and tie up their hair in pretty ribbons. Kerry had never had such things, but, then, she hadn't really known what she was missing. And by now it didn't matter anymore. She could do just fine without dancing and hair bows. "You kids go on ahead to the supper. Perhaps I'll be along later."

"Perhaps? You've got to come, Kerry," Patrick said with a worried look on his face.

She gave him a reassuring smile. "I will. You escort these lovely ladies here and go have fun."

The twins giggled and Patrick played his role by making an exaggerated bow and offering an arm to each one. Then they broke the pose and scampered off toward the fort quadrangle. Kerry smiled as she watched them go, then gave a sigh.

"They're right, you know." Dorothy came walking toward her. "You should dress up for the dance."

"I don't know if I'm going."

The petite blonde gave a snort. "Nonsense. Of course you're going. Scott should take you. Where's he gotten himself off to?" She looked over at the prospector's wagon.

Kerry shrugged. "I haven't seen him all afternoon. He said he'd found some men at the fort who'd been out to the gold fields. He wanted to get some advice."

"Well, you'll go to the dance with John and me, then, because you *are* going."

Kerry stood up. "Honestly, Dorothy, I don't know how to dance, and I'm not much in the mood...."

But her friend had turned away to climb up into Kerry's wagon and had begun to open boxes. "You must have some clothes in here somewhere. Come help me find them, Kerry."

Kerry threw her hands up in the air. "I have no idea..."

Before she could finish the sentence, Dorothy turned around in triumph, holding up a green dimity dress, the one item Kerry had taken special care to pack. Her father had once told her that her eyes sparkled as bright as the Emerald Isle itself when she was wearing that dress. She could still see the twinkle in his own identical blue eyes when he'd said it.

"I was saving that dress to wear in California," she said wistfully.

Dorothy's expression became stern. She threw the dress carelessly over her arm and faced Kerry with her hands on her hips. "Which is where you'll never get to if you don't start making some effort to stay on this train.''

Dorothy looked exactly like she did when she was cross with her daughters. Kerry had a sudden urge to laugh, which made her mood lift several notches. ''What do you mean, effort?''

''*Effort,* woman. Come out and talk to people. Make a show. Get some people on your side. Talk to that loutish captain of ours and make him understand that you'll not meekly let him throw you off.''

''I don't think he wants to talk with me. Maybe no one else does either after the problems we caused.''

''Horsefeathers. Everybody's fond of you and Patrick. You'd have lots of support if you just got out and looked for it. And as for Captain Hunter, I think he's more interested in talking to you than you think.''

Kerry walked over to Dorothy and took the green dress from her arm. It *would* feel good to put a dress on again, to feel soft fabric against her skin instead of Patrick's rough trousers. ''What makes you say that?''

''He's a *man,* isn't he? It's like I told you the other day, Kerry. You're a lovely young woman.''

Kerry had a sudden memory of the night by the riverbank. ''I don't think Jeb Hunter is interested in things like that. At least, not with regard to me.''

Dorothy took a step back and studied her friend with disbelief. ''Kerry Gallivan, didn't any boys ever court you back in New York City?''

''I was usually too busy…''

''Well, now you see. There's your problem. It's all a matter of experience. Self-confidence. A little bit of feminine intuition." She took the dress from Kerry again and held it up to her, cocking her head and squinting to picture how it would look on her. Then she handed it back to Kerry with a smile and a wink. "Honey, forget all that, everything I just said. I have a feeling that in this dress, all you'll need to do is show up."

The days were growing longer with the approach of summer. The sun was still hanging brightly in the sky over the western edge of the fort when Kerry arrived at the supper dance with Dorothy and John. When Kerry had finally been persuaded to don the green dress, Dorothy had watched her friend's transformation with amazement. Kerry was about to cause a sensation, Dorothy declared, and insisted on completing the picture by fixing her friend's hair.

"I don't think there's much you can do with this disaster," Kerry had said ruefully, looking in her mother's mirror. But Dorothy had brushed and brushed until the short locks curled glossy and full around her face.

"It's not too bad," Dorothy had said, stepping back to admire her handiwork. "Different, but it suits you somehow. Makes you look kind of like a pixie."

She wished she could disappear like a pixie, Kerry thought ruefully as she walked toward the group that had congregated in front of the supper tables. Most people were still eating. The dancing had not yet begun, and there was a lot of laughing and shouting back and forth as Frank Todd passed around mugs of hard cider and the travelers in general showed the effects of a day's break from the trail.

In front of the barracks, several of the fort's soldiers were watching the festivities with good-natured smiles. They were used to the scene by now, and they knew that the travelers had many tough times ahead of them. It would do them good to let off a little steam with a lively party.

Kerry and Dorothy's arrival caused a number of the soldiers to straighten up on their benches. One poked another in the ribs and gave a nod their way. Another gave a low whistle that was loud enough to reach their ears.

"See, Kerry," Dorothy said with a proud smile. "You're already causing a commotion."

"They're looking at you, Dorothy," she objected.

"Not likely." Dorothy put her arm through John's, who was walking by her side. "I've already got my beau."

Even Kerry had to admit that as they drew closer it seemed that every single one of the soldiers had his eyes on her. It was a heady feeling that she'd never experienced before. "They must not see many ladies out here," she said to the Burnetts, embarrassed and pleased at the same time.

"They don't see many ladies that look like you do, Kerry," Dorothy corrected gently.

The soldiers weren't the only ones impressed. As they made their way toward the food tables, a number of the emigrants commented to Kerry on her transformed appearance. Some of the men who had been resentful after the revelation of her deception were now looking at her, most under the watchful eyes of their wives, with carefully banked admiration.

Even Patrick noted the change, whirling by with

some of his friends and shouting, "Hey, sis, you look grand!"

Kerry looked around for Scott, feeling an unfamiliar anticipation at the thought of seeing his reaction to her cleaned-up and dressed-up appearance. But he didn't seem to be anywhere in sight. Instead, as she scanned the crowd her eyes met Jeb Hunter's. He visibly started when he saw her, then laid his empty plate on the table and started toward her.

Kerry wasn't sure she wanted to talk with him just yet. She wished she could have run into Scott first. She didn't know why, but tonight, feeling feminine and pretty, she would have preferred to face Jeb on Scott's arm.

Jeb tipped back his leather hat as he reached her. "This *is* Miss Gallivan, I presume?" he asked in formal drawing room tones underlaid with a slight touch of amusement.

Damn the man, Kerry thought. He tied her tongue in knots. "I'm not so different that you can't recognize me, Captain Hunter. I've just changed my clothes."

Jeb took one of her hands and held it to one side as if expecting her to do a pirouette to model her dress. She stood stiffly and waited as his eyes roamed over her and warmed. "Yes, I can see that," he said. "Banishing forever the specter of *Kiernan* Gallivan from the minds of the men here tonight."

She looked around for Dorothy and John, but they had drifted off toward the supper tables. She was on her own. Turning back to the captain, she asked, "Does it really make so very much difference—what a person wears?"

Jeb hesitated a moment, dropping her hand. He rubbed a hand across his whiskers, then answered, "I think it depends on what person and what they're wearing."

"Well, I'm the same Kerry Gallivan and I'm wearing a three-year-old dress. Nothing fancy."

"Your hair's different, too."

"No, it's not. It's just...fluffier." She ran her fingers up the side of her head as she spoke.

Jeb laughed and once again Kerry noticed how much he changed when his expression wasn't so serious. It wasn't only *clothes* that made a difference in someone, she decided. "Well, I like it...*fluffy*," he said, giving her a teasing smile that if she'd seen it on one of the Flanagan brothers she would have called downright flirtatious. It made her feel giddy, and she had to tell herself sternly that there was *no way* the serious and stern Captain Jeb Hunter was flirting with her. It was simply the spirit of the evening.

"It's a beautiful night," she said lightly. "And everyone seems to be enjoying themselves."

"Yes." Jeb's smile dimmed a little. "This is good for them. They'll need to remember the good times during the days ahead. We've just barely started, you know."

"Yes." Was now the time to bring up her staying on with the train? she wondered. Now, when Captain Hunter was relaxed and in a good humor, and when he was still regarding her with that...*look* that was making her cheeks as pink as those of little Molly every time she looked at Patrick? "You plan to start out again in three days?" she started carefully.

His expression became guarded. "Yes, three days. Don't worry, by that time I'll have the arrangements completed for you to get back to Westport. You can sell your wagon back to Boone's there and have enough money for transport to New York, if that's where you and your brother want to go."

"You know very well that's *not* where my brother and I want to go, Captain."

Jeb looked down at his boots. "Are we to spoil this beautiful evening with an argument, Miss Gallivan?"

Every time he said her name, it was as if he was reminding himself anew of her deception. "You called me Kiernan before, Captain. I guess you could call me Kerry."

He looked up at her. "Kerry, then. You're right that sometimes it seems foolish to continue to observe the proprieties out here in the middle of the wilderness."

"And, no, I don't want to argue with you," she added.

Jeb's face had resumed its normal, serious expression, but his eyes continued to regard her with a kind of leashed intensity. The setting sun made them look almost golden, tawny, like a watchful lion's. "Good," he said briskly. "Then we won't argue. How about if I get you a plate of supper instead?"

She shook her head. "I'm not hungry."

Jeb made a clicking sound of disapproval. Once again his eyes swept discreetly down the length of her green dress. "You have to eat something, Miss...Kerry. Lord, in that dress you look as flimsy as a milkweed drifting across a meadow."

"Flimsy?"

"Well, slight. Fragile." Jeb looked nonplussed, almost embarrassed, which did not sit well with his usually authoritative demeanor. "Hell, I meant it as a compliment, not an insult. When I think of all the hard work, the lifting and hauling you did when we all thought you were a lad..."

"I've done hard work for as long as I can remember, Captain Hunter. Most women I know do. Harder than men, sometimes. I don't know why that should come as a surprise."

Jeb Hunter grinned. A downright grin. Kerry couldn't believe her eyes.

"I don't think anything you do would surprise me, Kerry Gallivan," he said. "And now, if I'm to call you Kerry, I guess you'll have to be calling me Jeb."

He'd cocked his head and was smiling down into her eyes. It *was* flirting, Kerry decided. She might be a novice about these things, but the signals were unmistakable. The way he was looking at her was making her feel warm inside. And feminine. Maybe it was the dress. She'd feel stronger if she were still facing him in men's trousers. She didn't like this weak-kneed, melting sensation. It was just this kind of female debility that made it possible for men to make laws and regulations such as the one that was keeping her from traveling west with the train.

She drew herself up, which still only brought her as high as Jeb's broad shoulders. "Perhaps I will have some supper after all," she said. "But I can get my own plate."

Then she turned away from him and sent stern messages to her legs to begin walking toward the food tables.

The sun had sunk behind the fort with a spectacular burst of color, as if showing off for the merrymakers. Each member of the wagon train knew that the benign prairie they had crossed was not even a test of the trials that awaited them as they crossed the near desert of the western plains and then the mountains. But for this night, they could forget what lay ahead and celebrate the triumph of completing the first step toward their dreams of a better life.

The evening had started off segregated, with the men hovering around the cider jars, the children scampering about with early-evening energy and the women bustling back and forth with more food. But by now the group had come together for the dancing, old and young alike. Fathers danced with young daughters and old women with the single men.

Kerry had had a constant procession of partners since the dancing began. She was breathless and exhausted. It had been easier than she had thought to follow the simple country steps of the reels and rounds the two fiddlers played, and she was surprised to find that she was enjoying herself immensely. She had not talked further with Captain Hunter. He did not appear to have joined in the dancing.

But she was happy to see Scott when he made a tardy appearance and practically snatched her out of the arms of Ole Estvold, just as the portly Norwegian gentleman had been reaching out a hand to swing her into a Kentucky reel.

"You look wonderful, lass!" Scott said at once. "If a bit breathless."

Kerry laughed. "I am—breathless that is. In fact, would you mind if we sat down for a minute?"

Scott's eyes were lit with admiration. "Let me get you something to drink." He tucked her hand in his arm and pulled her away from the crowd of dancers. At the nearly empty food table, he stopped, poured a cup of cider and offered it to her.

The apple-flavored liquor burned all the way down her throat. "Strong," she gasped.

Scott took the cup from her and sipped. "It's pretty hard," he admitted. "But it seems to be all that's left," he added, looking up and down the tables. He put the cup back in her hands. "Go ahead. It won't hurt you."

It was wet, at least. Kerry scrunched up her face against the taste and drank several swallows. "Where have you been?" she asked Scott.

"Jawing," he said with a grin, "as they say out in these parts."

"With the soldiers?"

"Soldiers, old-timers. There are a couple of real live mountain men who've stopped here after their spring trapping. Foxy and Daniel."

"Foxy?"

Scott chuckled and took her arm again to lead her away from the table and out toward the center of the now dark quadrangle. "Foxy," he confirmed. "That's what they all call him. I suppose it's not his given name. They're colorful characters—both of them."

Kerry reached backward to leave the cup on the table as Scott pulled her along. "Where are we going?"

"Do you want to dance some more?" He nodded back at the circle of emigrants. There were fewer now, for some of the group had started straggling back to their wagons.

"No. I'm still winded. I had more fun than I would have thought."

Scott gave her arm a little squeeze. "I have a feeling there hasn't been an excess of fun in your life, Kerry."

"My father was fun," she said a little defensively. "He'd tell us stories about the little people in Ireland that would have Patrick and me laughing until our stomachs hurt."

They'd continued walking along the row of barracks down to the opposite end of the fort from where the Hunter train was encamped. They were now out of the reach of the lanterns that had been lit back by the dancing, and the only lights were the dim reflections from inside a few of the fort's rough wooden buildings. But the moon shone brightly in the clear sky, and Kerry had no trouble seeing Scott's smile as he shifted his hand from her arm to the back of her waist. "I didn't mean any criticism of your childhood, Kerry. My people came to this country several generations ago. Until I started this journey, I wouldn't have been able to imagine what it would be like to leave your home and travel halfway across the world to seek a new life."

"But now you're doing much the same thing yourself."

"Yes. Which only makes me appreciate more what it must take for all the immigrants like your father to make that move with a family to support."

"With two young children," Kerry emphasized. "Patrick was just six."

"And you were only twelve. Pretty young to have to learn to adapt to a whole new world."

"Papa and Patrick were my world. I didn't care about anything else. Papa told us that things would be better in America."

"And were they better?"

"Well, back home, people were starving. So I guess they were a little better. We always had enough to eat in New York, as long as we were content with fish." She gave a little shudder at the memory, or at a sudden evening chill of air. Scott's arm slipped the rest of the way around her waist.

"I like walking with you this way, Kerry," he said, his voice suddenly grown husky.

The buzz of the insects out on the prairie lent a tranquilizing undercurrent to their conversation. Scott's body felt stable and warm at her side. "I like it, too," she said simply.

And that was evidently enough response for Scott, who stopped walking, gently swung her around to face him and lowered his head to kiss her gently on the lips. He straightened up almost immediately and let out a long breath, at the end of which he said, "I've been thinking about doing that for a long time now, lass."

It was over so quickly that Kerry hadn't had time to even be surprised. But now she could still feel his touch lingering on her lips. The sensation was mildly pleasant. "Have you, now?" she half whispered.

"You're not offended?"

She shook her head. It had been her first kiss—her first *real* kiss. But to her surprise, she wasn't even flustered.

"Good," Scott said, his grin back to normal. "Because I intend to do it again soon."

Kerry put the back of her hand up to her still sensitive lips. "Do you, now?"

"Soon," he said with a firm nod. Then he tucked her hand once again into his arm and turned back toward the bright lights of the circle of dancers.

Chapter Eight

Jeb sat in the darkness on the edge of the sidewalk in front of the fort dispensary. The only sidewalk at the fort, it was bounded by two log pillars that held up a bright green awning. The unusual amenities had been insisted upon by the fort's doctor, Arthur Featherstone. Earlier Jeb had purchased a few supplies from the chatty old major and had sat a spell listening to his various medical stories. Finally Dr. Featherstone had bidden him good-night, and Jeb had gone outside with the intention of rejoining the members of his train. But by then it had grown dark, and something about the circle of warm lantern light and the joyful bouncing of the dancers made him feel particularly lonely. So instead he sat on the sidewalk and looked up at the moon. It was, he decided, more fitting company for him tonight. Any night.

His thoughts drifted to his encounter earlier in the evening with Kerry Gallivan. When he'd first seen her across the crowd of people, smiling and walking along with that natural sway of hers in a new green dress, he'd felt as if a fist had slammed into his middle. He'd already dealt with the fact that she was attractive. But the sudden appearance in a dress had caught him off balance. It was sculpted to the upper part of her body, then cinched at a waist that had never looked so impossibly small when she'd been parading around in men's trousers. A wave of pure desire rolled through his stomach at the memory.

A couple was strolling in his direction in the dark, and somehow he wasn't surprised to discern that it was Kerry herself. Scott Haskell had an arm around her waist and was looking down at her. It was too dark for Jeb to see his expression, but he had an idea what it might be.

They undoubtedly couldn't see him. He was sitting in the shadows of the building behind him. The polite thing would be to make his presence known, he supposed, but instead he stayed motionless, straining his ear in spite of himself to try to hear their conversation. But their voices were low, loverlike, he imagined, in that close position. And, as if to confirm his suspicions, suddenly Haskell leaned down and kissed her.

To his disgust, a surge went through him of something that felt remotely like jealousy. Not jealousy, surely. Envy, perhaps. He was envious of any two people in love who were at liberty to give in to the natural impulses to share each other's body. It was not an impulse he would give in to himself. At least, not with someone he loved. Never again.

The kiss was brief. A damn sight briefer than Jeb would have made it if he'd been in Haskell's shoes, he thought. But he definitely didn't want them discovering him now. He leaned farther back into the shadows and sat almost without breathing until they turned around, arm in arm, and headed back toward the dancing.

The incident had not helped his mood. And it raised some questions. Were Haskell and Kerry in love? If so, they could be married by the fort commander, and she would no longer be a single woman. She'd have the right to continue on with the train. It was an interesting idea. One that would solve everyone's problems.

He stood from the hard wood platform and stretched his back. For several minutes he stood staring into the darkness after the departed couple. It seemed to be the perfect solution—Kerry married to Scott Haskell. Kerry would get what she wanted. He wouldn't have to worry about finding her an escort back East. He'd be able to enjoy Patrick's company for the rest of the trip. Kerry and Haskell—altogether the perfect solution. Which didn't in the least explain why the idea made him want to smash his fist into the log holding up Dr. Featherstone's fancy awning.

When Kerry arrived back at the wagon after her walk with Scott, Patrick was already asleep, curled up on top of some boxes in the back of the wagon, still dressed in his clothes, even his boots. He'd exhausted himself running around all day with his friends, she thought with a smile.

But Kerry wasn't sleepy. She thought about building a fire. Since they'd eaten at the dance, they'd not bothered to build one tonight. Now she found that she missed it—not the warmth exactly. The night was mild. But the comfort of it.

She felt as if she could use a little comfort. She

couldn't exactly state why. She really had had a wonderful time at the dance. Everyone had been nice to her, even the ones who'd been angry after the incident at the river crossing. And she'd enjoyed being fussed over by Dorothy and having her hair fixed, little female attentions that she'd missed growing up.

But nevertheless, now that Scott had said goodnight and headed back to his own wagon, she was feeling melancholy. It probably was due to the confused state of her emotions. His kiss had been nice, perhaps not as magical as she'd imagined her first kiss would be, but certainly...nice. What was bothering her, she decided, was not the kiss, but Scott's goodnight words.

"Sleep well, lass," he'd said tenderly. "You should, you know. Because it's beginning to look as if you won't have to have that showdown with Captain Hunter after all."

When she'd looked puzzled, he'd said with a slight smile, "I told you that single women didn't stay single very long out West." She'd started to say something, but he'd put two fingers on her lips and shook his head. "It's late and your eyelids are drooping, sweetheart. We'll talk about it tomorrow. We'll make some plans."

And then he'd kissed her, on the cheek this time, and had left.

She gave up the thought of a fire and of sleep and decided to sit a spell and watch the nearly full moon. She sank to the ground, heedless of getting dust on her dress, and rested her back against the wagon wheel with a deep sigh. It was no use trying to convince herself that she'd been mistaken about Scott's

meaning. After all, he'd been attentive from that first
day on the trail and tonight he'd told her plainly that
he intended to kiss her again soon. People didn't do
that kind of thing unless they were beginning to get
serious. And it would solve her problems. If she were
married, Jeb Hunter would have no grounds for keeping her off the wagon train. It seemed a bit of an
unusual reason to marry, but she supposed that people
had done it for less cause.

Was Scott in love with her? she wondered. She
wasn't in love with him. At least, she was pretty certain that she wasn't. But she still had vague memories
of her mother and father together, tender and cud-
dling, when she'd been a small child. And she had
more recent memories of her father's face every time
he'd talked about her mother. He'd never forgotten
her, never even looked at another woman until the
day he died. Now *that* was love. And it certainly was
nothing like the mixture of gratitude and friendly af-
fection she felt for Scott Haskell.

"You're still awake." Jeb Hunter appeared suddenly in the moonlight.

She straightened up abruptly, scraping her back
painfully on the wheel hub.

"I'm sorry," he said quickly. "I didn't mean to
startle you."

Kerry reached behind her and tried to rub the sore
spot, but gave up after a moment when she couldn't
reach it. "What can I do for you, Captain?" she asked
without bothering to keep the irritation out of her
voice.

He squatted beside her. "Did you hurt yourself?"
He reached an arm toward her but she scooted away.

"I'm fine." He watched her for a long moment without speaking, so finally she said, "Was there something you wanted this late at night, Captain?"

He let his legs sprawl out beneath him and sat on the ground beside her. "I just wanted to talk to you. But I thought we'd agreed that you would call me Jeb."

"I don't recall agreeing to any such thing."

Jeb gave a reluctant chuckle. "Miss Gallivan, you are one stubborn lady."

"I'm glad you've figured that out, Captain. That way you won't be surprised tomorrow when I come to see you again about staying with the train."

"As a matter of fact, that's what I wanted to speak with you about." Now that he was here, Jeb wasn't exactly sure why he had come. If he admitted the truth, it would be that once the idea had entered his head, he'd not been able to wait until morning to see if his suspicions about Haskell and Kerry were right. But there was no sign of the affable prospector, and Kerry did not seem to be in the humor of a girl who had just received a proposal of marriage.

"Have you changed your mind?" she asked, without sounding too hopeful.

"No. I don't take lone women on my train. I don't know of any wagon master who does."

"So what did you want to talk with me about?"

Jeb shifted to move his back from where it was being poked by the wheel spokes. "Do you want to go sit on the riverbank where the grass is soft?" he asked, still trying to decide how to voice his jumbled thoughts.

Kerry nodded indifferently, but took his hand when

he stood and offered it to her. She winced and her knee buckled slightly as her weight came down on her ankle.

"Are you all right?" he asked, catching hold of her elbow.

"Yes. The foot's almost all better, but I think I danced on it a little too much tonight."

He kept hold of her arm as they walked the few yards to the river. "Perhaps you should wrap it again."

"I'll see. If it's sore, I'll ask Scott about it in the morning."

"There's a doctor here at the fort. You should ask him instead of some blacksmith," he told her, unable to keep the censure out of his voice. "Is this all right?" He gestured to the edge of the bank where the grass was unbroken by patches of dirt.

She nodded agreement and they sat down, her skirts billowing over the lip of the bank. They fluffed up around her as she dropped her hands to her lap. "Why do I get the feeling you don't like Scott very much?" she asked him.

Jeb stuck his feet out straight and looked down at the rushing river. "I have nothing against Haskell in particular. I'm just not too fond of gold seekers."

"Haven't a lot of the people you've guided out West been on their way to the gold fields?"

He nodded. "Yes, I've seen many good men seized by the fever. Usually not much good comes of it."

Kerry followed the direction of his gaze and began staring at the rushing water herself. It was hypnotic. She waited. He said he'd come to talk to her, so let him talk. But when he finally spoke after a long silence, his words jolted her out of her near-trance.

"Have you thought about marrying Scott Haskell?" he asked bluntly.

Kerry's swallow turned into a gulp. Was the man some kind of a wizard? Or had he been standing in the bushes listening to Scott's good-night words to her? The safest way to answer seemed to be "Why are you asking?"

Jeb turned his body toward her. "It looks as if the two of you have become…good friends, shall we say? And I thought it may have occurred to you that if you were married, there would be no reason to keep you off the train."

"Is that true? If I were married, you'd let me stay?" Kerry found herself holding her breath as she awaited his reply, which took several moments.

"I suppose I'd have to. You'd be no different than any of the other women on the train if you had a husband."

The palms of her hands grew moist. "Oh."

"So you *have* thought about it."

"Well…not until tonight."

"Has he asked you to marry him?"

He seemed to have grown tense as he waited for her answer. "I think that would be a matter between Mr. Haskell and myself," she said frostily. "I don't see how it's any of your business."

The smile he gave her was equally chilly. "I think I've explained to you before that everything that happens on this train is my business."

Of course, he was right. It was just that she hadn't sorted out her own head about the idea of marrying

Scott. How could she expect to discuss it with Jeb Hunter? Especially when his presence next to her in the moonlight was starting up those same flutters that she'd felt the night she'd seen him without his clothes. They weren't entirely pleasant flutters, and she wasn't sure exactly what they meant, but she knew that she'd never felt anything remotely like that with Scott. Not even when he'd kissed her on the lips tonight.

She sighed. "Yes, you're right. You have a right to know. And as soon as *I* know, I'll be sure to tell you."

"So you are considering it?"

He yanked a handful of grass by his side and threw it in the direction of the river, then frowned as it failed to reach the water. It almost seemed as if he was angry about the idea of her marrying Scott, Kerry thought with some confusion. Probably because he was looking forward to being rid of her. "To tell you the truth, Captain—"

"Now that would be a novelty from you," he interrupted.

"The truth is that I don't know about marrying Scott. It could be a solution to my problem. But I…I just don't know."

"Are you in love with him?" His face was very close to hers. She could see the slight scar on the right side of his chin and the fleck of dark gold in his moonlit eyes.

"I…" The breath had seemed to stick in her throat and she was finding it hard to breathe.

Jeb's heart had begun to thunder inside his chest. She was so near that he could smell some kind of lavender scent that clung to her dress. Her lips were just inches from him, full and moist. *I don't know,* she had said, sounding lost. The words echoed along with the pulse inside his ears.

Without conscious thought he reached for her, and once his hands folded around her arms, they continued of their own volition until she was hauled totally into his lap, and his mouth found hers, first tasting, then asking for more, then taking it, without asking.

She made a sound at the back of her throat, but it wasn't a protest, and it only served to fuel his blood. Her lips were pliant and rich, her mouth sweet, tasting faintly of apple.

He plundered it, no longer even remotely in control of his raging senses. Her breasts grew hard against his chest and he pressed her closer, trying at once to clear the whirling in his head and to purge his body of the hunger that had been clawing at him since the moment he had seen her in Scott Haskell's arms.

It couldn't have lasted for more than a couple of minutes, but it was enough to steady the throb inside him. It was enough for Kerry to come to her senses and begin to push on his arms.

Her sensuous moan now turned itself into a protest. Alarms rang inside Jeb's head and he relaxed his hold on her with something akin to horror. What in the name of sweet Jesus had possessed him?

Without speaking, Kerry pulled herself out of his arms and back to her seat on the bank. He let her go immediately, his insides churning. The palms of his hands felt as if they'd been scalded. Totally unsettled, he flopped backward to lie on the bank and put an arm across his eyes. He didn't want to see the accusing look in her eyes. Never in his life had he made advances to a woman who was unwilling. But then, he asked himself as his breathing began to slow toward normal, had she been so completely unwilling? Was it just inexperience that had made her lips mold to his as if their mouths had been designed to fit together?

"I'm sorry," he said finally, a little less sorry than he had been when she'd ended the embrace.

"I...you..." She was sputtering, sounding more lost than ever. And young.

He sat up. Even if she hadn't been totally unwilling, he'd had no business kissing her. "It's the moonlight," he said lightly. "And your green dress. I was carried away by your...charms."

"You had no right..." she began with a scowl.

"Of course not. I took shameless advantage of a helpless female alone in the wilderness." He suddenly saw how he could use the incident itself to assure that there would be no repetition of it. "Which is precisely the reason that rules get made about single women on the trail. You have no protection against bounders like me."

Kerry hunched over her knees and hugged them. "So this was all a show, Captain?" she asked, her voice low with anger. "You were trying to prove to me how helpless I am?"

Jeb was torn. Part of him wanted to deny her accusation. If Kerry had had any experience at all with men, she would have known that his body's response to her was anything but show. But perhaps it was better for them both if she believed him an unfeeling scoundrel. "Did I succeed?" he asked with a forced grin.

Kerry released her tight hold on her legs and jumped to her feet. "You only succeeded in showing me that I have to choose my company more carefully."

He stood more slowly. "You'll encounter worse company than me if you persist in heading West."

"I doubt that, Captain," she snapped. Then she spun around on one heel and marched away toward her wagon.

"What would you say if I decided to marry Scott?" Kerry asked Patrick as they rebuilt their fire for breakfast the next morning. The log Patrick was holding slid from his hand and landed on the dead fire with a flurry of ashes.

"Marry? Get *married* to him?"

"Well, I'm not sure if that's exactly what he had in mind. But if I were married to him, then they'd have to let us stay with the train."

Kerry had spent a good portion of her nearly sleepless night trying to convince herself of the logic of the move. And trying to assure herself that her consideration of the idea had nothing to do with the kisses she had shared with Jeb Hunter the previous evening. But in the end she was too honest to deny even to herself that she'd been frightened by what had happened by the river. Frightened not of Jeb, but of herself.

"But..." Patrick had unloaded the rest of his logs and stood watching her with a confused look. "I mean, you can't just *marry* someone you've barely

met. And, besides," he finished with a sudden look
of relief, "Scott isn't even going to Sonoma. He's
heading to the gold fields. He can't marry you."

"Well, maybe he could marry me for a while, and
then go off to the gold fields."

Patrick looked more confused than ever. "Do people do that? Marry for just a while?"

Kerry gave an exasperated shrug. "I don't know.
The whole idea's probably crazy."

They worked in silence for several more moments,
Patrick lighting the fire and Kerry scooping coffee
into the pot. Finally he said, "It wouldn't be so bad.
I like Scott."

"I like him, too," Kerry said wistfully. She *did* like
him. He'd been kind to her and helpful. He went to
great efforts to do nice things for her and for Patrick.
He was a good man. And his kiss had felt sweet on
her lips.

Sweet. She gave herself a little shake as once again
the wave rolled through her middle at another flash
of the memory. But the memory was not of Scott's
sweet kiss. The kiss that had her insides melting into
a liquid pool every time she turned around was that
other one. Jeb Hunter's kiss.

After years of avoiding the entire idea, she'd been
kissed by two men in one night. And the two kisses
had been more profoundly different than the devil and
a holy choir.

It wasn't until midmorning that Scott came back to
find her at her wagon. Kerry'd been expecting his
appearance all morning, and had changed her mind at
least two dozen times about what she hoped he'd say.

Patrick had been sober over breakfast. They'd discussed the possibility she'd raised a bit more, and he'd posed the same questions that she herself had been pondering. Did she love him? Would she be happy? Was it the right thing to do? What would Papa have said about it?

That last one was a sticky issue. When Kerry's mother had died, Sean Gallivan had let most of his faith in the Mother Church bleed away from him. He'd never taken his children to Mass. But Kerry knew that he hadn't entirely abandoned the church's teachings. And more than once she'd heard him say, "Marriage is for life, children. You be darn sure it's what you want before you take the vows."

Was Scott Haskell what she wanted? For life? When he finally showed up, whistling and holding a sheaf of wildflowers, which he presented to her with a gallant bow, she still hadn't made up her mind.

"I guess you knew what I was talking about last night, Kerry," he said, detecting her serious mood. "It would make sense, you know—you and me."

Make sense? Is that what love was all about? She put her nose down into the bunch of flowers to inhale their delicate fragrance and consider her reply. "Scott, you've been a godsend to us from the beginning. But now you're sacrificing your own plans to try to make mine work out."

He sat next to her on the log that they'd pulled up to their campfire to act as a little bench. "Sacrifice! What a way to talk, lass. I'd wager there's not a man within five hundred miles who'd not feel the luckiest man on earth to claim you as his wife."

Kerry had donned her trousers again today. They

made her feel stronger, less vulnerable. "Well, there aren't so very many men within five hundred miles," she said with a slight smile. "So that's not much of a test."

Scott reached for her hand. "I'd feel privileged to marry you, Kerry Gallivan, if you'll have me." He looked around at the dusty campsite. "Shall I kneel?" he asked with a touch of humor.

"Please, don't." She shook her head. He made her laugh, and he said pretty things. He hadn't said that he loved her, but she wasn't so sure that love was the most important thing when it came to a marriage.

"So what do you say? Shall I go talk to the fort commander? We could be married today and then march right up to Jeb Hunter and tell him that Kerry *Haskell* and her new husband will most definitely be continuing on with the train when it leaves in two days."

She didn't know if it was the odd sound of her name coupled with Scott's or the mention of Jeb, but suddenly Kerry saw the situation with total clarity. She slowly pulled her hand away from Scott's and let it fall heavily into her lap. "I'm sorry, Scott. I can't marry you."

He pulled his head back a little in surprise. "Why not?" he asked abruptly, his smile gone.

"I think it would be hard to put into words, but I have a certain idea about marriage...." She gave herself a little shake. "I don't think I want to be married."

Scott gave a little huff. "I thought every girl wanted to get married."

"Well, not this one. I just want to go to California and build my father's ranch...."

"And how are you going to do that if they won't let you get there without a husband?" Scott's hurt feelings made his voice sound a little angry.

"I'm not just sure yet, but I only know that it wouldn't be fair to you for me to marry you just so I can get to California."

"I guess I should be the one to say what's fair for me," he protested.

"Fair for either of us, then. I appreciate your offer more than I can say." She turned and rested her hand on his knee. "But I'm turning it down. If Jeb Hunter won't take me to California as an unmarried woman, then I'll just have to find a way to get there on my own."

Chapter Nine

Scott had continued trying to persuade her for some time before he'd finally given up and gone into the fort to find his new mountain men friends. After his initial hurt reaction to her refusal of his proposal, he'd regained his typical, cocky good spirits. "I've got two days to wear you down, lass," he'd told her with a wink before he left.

But she knew that she wasn't going to let herself be worn down. With the decision made she felt as if a great weight had been lifted from her. No matter what happened with the wagon train, she'd not continue on as Scott Haskell's wife. But her brief satisfaction over the resolution of that question soon faded. She was still in the same coil she'd been in before the idea of her marrying Scott had occurred to anyone. There was only one person who could be of help to her now, and, in spite of the fact that after last night she didn't care if she never laid eyes on him again, she would have to seek him out.

It would do no good to put off the meeting. As Scott had pointed out, she had only two days to make a change in her prospects. She stood, slapped her hands against her trousered thighs and took several long steps toward the fort. Then she stopped. Perhaps she should take Patrick with her for support. Jeb liked Patrick.

No. It would be bad enough facing him with the memory of their hot kisses last night flaming her cheeks without having her little brother along. She turned and started out once again, only to slow her pace more and more until she finally came to a stop. Maybe she should put on her green dress. It had seemed to make him…susceptible to her in some way.

There it was—the warm flush up her face as the memory came of exactly how susceptible Jeb had been to her last night. And she to him. She stuck out her lower jaw and blew air up to cool her cheeks. She'd see him dressed as she was, she decided finally. In trousers. Man to man.

Jeb finished off his last mouthful of stew and looked across the table at Foxy Whitcomb and Daniel Blue. He enjoyed listening to the old-timers' yarns about the early days of exploration across the Rockies. Foxy had first crossed back in '26, in the days of Jim Bridger and Jedediah Smith. Thirty years of wilderness had put lines on his face and left his hair snow-white, but his body was honed and fit, a match for any man at the fort.

"This is gonna be a dry one, Jeb," Foxy had warned him.

"No rain all spring," Daniel agreed.

"The tribes'll be hurting, especially the Sioux. And

they're not taking kindly to white folk after Blue Water.''

Two years before the U.S. Army had killed an entire encampment of Lakota Sioux at a place called Blue Water. Many had been women and children. Jeb's stomach gave one of its familiar twists every time he thought about it.

Jeb nodded and listened carefully to their advice. He'd made the crossing himself many times now, but he wasn't so much a fool as to make the mistake of not paying attention to men who'd done it that many times over.

Wagon guides generally held their breath all through Indian country, even in a good season. Leaving Fort Kearney, they'd cross through Pawnee territory. The prairie tribe's buffalo herds had been decimated by the encroachment of the white man. They, too, had a right to be resentful, Jeb reckoned. But neither the Pawnee nor the Sioux had the right to retaliate by taking the lives of innocent settlers. Especially not on one of his trains.

He wasn't surprised coming out of the sutler's store to see Kerry striding resolutely toward him across the quadrangle. He knew he'd have to see her today, but had been putting it off. He didn't walk to meet her, waiting for her to come to him, but did her the courtesy of sweeping off his hat as she approached.

''I want to talk with you, Captain.''

Her eyes were hard, bearing little resemblance to the passion-softened ones he'd looked into last night as he held her a breath away. That was last night, and today was obviously another day as far as Kerry Gallivan was concerned. He knew at once that she would not bring up the subject of their encounter on the riverbank. Which was fine with him.

"Of course, Miss Gallivan." He kept his voice carefully pleasant. "You want to know the details of how you're going to get back to Westport."

"No. I want to persuade you to take me to California. I'm ready to stand here in the sun all day long arguing with you until you'll agree to it."

She stood in her trousers, legs slightly apart, hands on her hips. If she'd been wearing a sidearm, she would have looked as if she were preparing for a gunfight. She *definitely* did not resemble the woman he'd held in his arms last night. "I've already given you my answer on that score. Standing in the sun is not going to change my mind."

"I don't understand how you can be so darn stubborn," she fumed.

Jeb smiled. "In a battle of stubbornness with you, Miss Gallivan, I'm not sure I'd come out a winner. But you still can't come."

"Because I'm unmarried."

"Because you don't have anyone to protect you—"

"Any male," she interrupted.

"Yes, any male." He should just tell her, he thought angrily. He should just sit her down and tell her exactly what horrible things could happen to an unprotected woman in the West. A woman like Melly, who'd been sweet and helpless and never meant to be alone. Who had married him trusting that he'd be there to take care of her, instead of off roaming the gold fields following a crazy dream of instant wealth. He wondered how Kerry Gallivan's beautiful, stubborn face would change if he told her what had happened to Melly.

"Your only requirement is that I need a male to protect me. Which means that if I married Scott Haskell, you would let me stay."

There it was. He'd been waiting for it. Perhaps it would be easier to forget the fever she'd created in his blood when he knew she belonged to someone else. He hoped so. Otherwise this could turn out to be the longest summer of his life. "If you were married, I'd have to let you stay."

He could almost see the steam rising from her as she pondered what she obviously considered to be the gross injustice of this ruling. Well, Jeb had always viewed his overland emigrants as something like his children. And sometimes you had to make decisions for children that did not set entirely well with them. "So are you going to marry Haskell?" he asked.

She let out a long breath and looked off into the distance. Finally she said in a tired voice, "No, I'm not."

Jeb was surprised at her answer and doubly surprised at the relief that washed through him when he heard it. "Why not?" he blurted.

"Because I'm not in love with him, Captain Hunter, if that's any of your business."

"Everything on this train…"

She held up her hand in interruption. "I know, everything on this train is your business. Well, Captain, as you have informed me numerous times, I'm no longer with this train. So that means that nothing about my life need concern you any further."

"I said I'd help you make plans for returning."

She turned her back in the middle of his sentence and began to walk away. Over her shoulder she told him, "Don't bother. My brother and I will just wait here at the fort until a train comes through that will agree to take us."

"You might have a long wait."

She was already a third of the way across the quadrangle. "But that's no longer any of your business, Captain, remember?"

By the time he thought of a reply she was well out of earshot.

"Scott's by himself...and Rudy Popovich," Dorothy held up the fingers of her right hand and started to count.

"Mr. Ingebretson," Patrick contributed.

"There are lots of single *men* on the train," Kerry agreed. "It's just single *women* who aren't allowed."

"And you're not even single—you have me," Patrick put in, his adolescent voice squeaking with indignation.

"And you have lots of friends who would help out," Eulalie Todd added.

"We all would. Charles will be heartbroken if Patrick has to leave." Charles Kirby's mother, Frances, had joined the group of women who had gathered at the Gallivan wagon to discuss their wagon captain's banishment of Kerry and her brother. Most of them had been secretly admiring of Kerry's daring in disguising herself as a man to be allowed on the train in the first place. And resentment about her current plight was building.

"You know, we're all going out West because we

want things to be different—for ourselves and our daughters,'' Dorothy told the group.

"I've heard there's even talk that women out West are going to be given the vote,'' Frances agreed.

As the oldest, Eulalie had been given a spot in the center of the circle. "It's like a fresh breeze out here,'' she said. "Change in the wind.''

"Well, things might be changing out West, but they're just the same as they were back home as far as this wagon train is concerned,'' Kerry said. "It's a man's world.''

For a moment no one spoke. Patrick shifted on the ground, a little uncomfortable to be the sole representative of this obviously negligent gender.

"I'll be darned if I can see why,'' Dorothy said finally. "The wagon train is us—all of us. Men and women alike. And if we want you along with us, I don't see how one *man* can keep you off. Even if he is the wagon master.''

"The papers say…'' Kerry began.

But Dorothy had already stood and was dusting off her hands with a determined expression on her face. "People can shout a sight louder than papers, Kerry. Especially when we shout together.'' She looked around the group with a smile. "C'mon, ladies. We have some work to do.''

Jeb Hunter looked around at the group of women in disbelief. He'd retired early to the bunk he was borrowing in one of the fort's half-empty barracks. He'd thought staying there would give the Todds a break from his company and would give him a chance to talk with some of the soldiers. But tonight he hadn't felt much in the mood for socializing with his emigrants or exchanging tall tales with the motley assortment of soldiers, trappers and adventurers who could always be found at the fort no matter what season of the year.

He'd been happy to find the barracks empty. Perhaps he'd be able to get to sleep before the beginning of the typical night's symphony of snoring and heavy breathing. But he'd no sooner stretched out on his bunk than he'd been jolted upright again by the sudden grand entry of what looked to be about half the women on the train. Led by Frank's wife, Eulalie. And, of course, Kerry Gallivan.

He suppressed a groan. He had a feeling that he could predict what the women had on their minds. And he could predict that he wasn't going to like it.

"Captain Hunter," Eulalie began. This was a bad sign to start because the motherly, white-haired woman had been calling him Jeb since the second day of the trip. "We've come to discuss a certain matter with you."

Slowly Jeb brought his stockinged feet to the floor. He wished he had his boots on. A man single-handedly facing down a pack of determined women ought to at least be allowed boots. He stood, ran his hand back through his tousled hair and plastered a smile on his face. "Evening, Miz Todd...ladies," he said.

"It's about the Gallivans. Kerry, here."

"Yes," Jeb acknowledged dryly. "I imagine it is."

Dorothy Burnett took a step forward and put an arm around Kerry's waist. Kerry gave a half smile and put her arm around Dorothy's in return. In spite of the fact that Kerry was still wearing men's trousers, the gesture seemed to imply some sort of special female communication that totally excluded Jeb or any other man. "We understand you've told her that she can't continue with the train," Dorothy said in a pleasant but firm voice.

Jeb felt uncharacteristically on the defensive. "It says so right there in the association papers," he began, then chided himself for feeling the need to use legalities to back up his actions.

"We know that," Dorothy continued. "But we—" she paused and looked around at the women by her side "—we women have decided that that particular provision is unfair."

"And since the association is us," Eulalie continued, "*all* of us, we don't see why we just can't change the rules."

Jeb resisted the urge to rub the back of his neck. Kerry, he noted, had wisely not said a word so far. She didn't have to with half the women on the train speaking for her. Half the women usually meant half the men as well. Nights could be long and cold on the trail when a man was out of favor with the woman of the household. "I've never allowed any of my trains to change the rules in the middle of the trip," he said, but his argument held no energy, even to his own ears. Somehow he'd known from the minute he'd seen the women streaming in the door that this was a battle he wouldn't win.

"Well, that's another rule that could be changed, I would think," Eulalie said pleasantly.

Jeb looked down at the floor. How hard was he willing to push this thing? he asked himself. Not just the nights, but the days as well would be pretty long and cold for him if the women of the train turned against him. It would make for a miserable crossing. And perhaps even a dangerous one. Dissension among the group was one of the surest ways to get into trouble. It was a sticky decision. He had to balance the benefits of capitulation at this point with the possible undermining of his authority from appearing to cave in on a major issue. He couldn't allow that either.

He took his eyes off the worn spot in the toe of one of his socks and looked up again, meeting Kerry's level gaze. "I'd be willing to have it put to a vote," he said finally. "To let the members of the train decide."

"A vote that would, of course, include all the *women* members of the train as well," Dorothy specified.

Jeb's gaze went to the pretty blonde, then to the wrinkled face of Eulalie, who was watching him with an expression as stern as was possible for her naturally soft features. Finally he looked back at Kerry. "A vote that would include women," he agreed.

There was a sudden leap of light in Kerry's eyes. Jeb felt as if it had reached out and scorched him. This was a mistake, he thought with frustration. She wasn't going to marry Haskell, and she was going to stay with the train where he'd see her daily, hourly for the next several weeks. Her constant presence would not allow him to forget how her lips had melted under his, how it had been to feel her breasts pressed against his chest. He was remembering it now, in spite of the risk of the telltale signs of his body embarrassing him in front of all these women.

He sat back down on his bunk, heavily. "If that concludes our business, ladies, I'll say good-evening," he said curtly. "I was about to retire."

"So tomorrow we put it to a vote?" Eulalie asked.

Jeb nodded, keeping his eyes on the older woman and off Kerry. "I'll talk to Frank about it in the morning."

"Thank you, Captain," Kerry said softly, speaking for the first time. Her gaze held his for a few endless seconds before she turned and followed the procession of quietly triumphant women as they filed out of the room. Jeb waited until the door shut softly behind them, then he flopped back down on his bunk with a groan.

Kerry's newly united women friends were jubilant when the vote went their way and the Gallivan wagon was allowed to continue on when the train pulled out of Fort Kearney two days later. But Kerry herself was wondering about the cost of her victory. She was delighted to be forming friendships with other women, something she'd never had the chance to do before, but at the same time, the two men who had become important to her seemed to have withdrawn from her life.

Scott had taken her refusal harder than she would have thought. She hadn't really considered that his proposal was anything more than another of his kind offers to help her out of a problem. But evidently his feelings had been more deeply involved than he'd shown with his happy-go-lucky manner.

And Jeb was totally avoiding their wagon. He hadn't even come by to give Patrick his morning rides, which had her brother watching the wagon master's progress up and down the train with puzzled, hurt eyes.

Well, Kerry thought, she'd said she could make it in the West on her own, without the help of a man, and it looked as if she was going to have the chance to prove it.

She and Patrick had taken to making campfire with the Burnetts each night now that neither Scott nor Jeb seemed to want their company. Molly was finally feeling less self-conscious about her crush on Patrick, and the three children got along well, accomplishing their tasks with little fuss, then running off to join their friends along the train for a few games before the late summer sunset.

At first Kerry had tried to take her leave when the children did, thinking that Dorothy and John might want time to themselves. But at the continued urging of both, she'd begun staying later, sitting by the fire and sipping coffee. She appreciated the company. There was little joy for her sitting alone at her wagon, cramped as it was.

They'd reached the dry portion of the western Nebraska prairie—the desert, it was called. It was still covered with grass and dotted with wildflowers, but there was also more and more sagebrush and the occasional cactus. The dust from the trail was thicker, sometimes almost seeming to hang in the air as they passed through. Even with their handkerchiefs, the emigrants coughed.

Today had been the worst yet. The Burnetts and

the Gallivans had coughed intermittently all through supper, sometimes just from thinking about the dust.

"It's going to be hard to start up again tomorrow morning," Kerry said with a little sigh.

"It certainly is," John agreed. "It's a wonder there's any prairie left out there—I feel as if I've got it all inside my lungs."

"We should wet down the kerchiefs tomorrow," Dorothy suggested.

John shook his head. "They'd dry in a minute in this heat. And, anyway, we can't afford the water. You know what the captain said about this dry piece."

"Not even for the girls?" Dorothy persisted. "They walked most of the way today, and they're closer down to the dust."

"I don't know. Maybe we should ask Captain Hunter about it," John said.

"What are you and Patrick doing for the dust, Kerry?" Dorothy asked.

"Same as you. Kerchiefs that within minutes turn so dusty themselves that they hardly seem to have an effect."

"We could go look for the captain now," Dorothy suggested. "At least he could tell us how long we're going to be in the desert."

Kerry felt a bit of a chill run down the back of her neck. She'd scarcely seen him in a week, but the memory of what had happened between her and Jeb back at the fort was as vivid as if it had occurred only minutes ago. "I should probably get some sleep," she said quickly. Too quickly for the sharp-eyed Dorothy.

"What's the problem between you and the captain?

Before Fort Kearney he was coming around your wagon almost every night. Now we never see him."

Kerry shook her head vaguely. "He's busy, I suppose."

Dorothy frowned. The line between her eyebrows had gotten more pronounced after all the days in the sun. She watched Kerry a moment, then turned to her husband and said, "Why don't you go find Captain Hunter, dear, and discuss the matter with him? Ask him what we can do to keep our girls from coughing."

John nodded agreement, then untangled his long legs and stood. "I'll be back after a spell," he said, and started down the line of wagons at an easy lope.

Dorothy's eyes followed him with a fond gaze.

"You're a lucky woman," Kerry said. "John's a good man for you."

"A good husband and a good father," she agreed with a smile. "But I sent him away so that we could talk about you. Tell me about Captain Hunter."

Kerry was closer to Dorothy than she'd ever been to any woman in her life, but there was absolutely no way she could get herself to talk about that night on the riverbank with another living soul. "What about him? You know he was against my continuing on the train. He would never have agreed to take me if it hadn't been for all of you."

Dorothy leaned to throw a couple fat sticks on the fire. They landed on the pile with a flare. "And...?" she asked patiently.

"And what?"

"And what else about you and Jeb Hunter?"

Kerry shifted away from the sudden intense heat of the fire. "And nothing. He's angry with me, I think."

"Hmm." Dorothy's blue eyes had a devilish gleam. "My grandma once told me that men only get angry with women they're sweet on."

Kerry flushed. "Don't be silly, Dorothy. Jeb Hunter is definitely not sweet on me. As a matter of fact, he strikes me as the kind of man who wouldn't be sweet on anyone."

"Well, I imagine he was sweet on his wife."

"Wife?" Kerry didn't know why the news surprised her. The captain must be close to thirty years old. Few men reached that age without marrying.

"You never heard his story? He had a beautiful young bride. They'd only been married a few months when she was killed while she was staying alone in their cabin, murdered, they say."

Kerry gasped.

"I guess he's never completely recovered from the shock. I try to think of that when he gets a bit, you know, *overbearing*. I suppose going through something like that would turn any man kind of hard."

"I suppose," Kerry agreed softly with a little shudder. "How very awful for him."

"But it's been several years now. He's been guiding wagons ever since. I suppose he figures it would be hard for him to settle back down in California."

Kerry's mind was whirring with the news she'd just heard. The tragedy of Jeb's young bride might have something to do with his adamant stand against single women on his train. Suddenly it made more sense, and made her feel more charitably toward the handsome captain for the first time since they'd left Fort

Kearney. It made him seem a little less like some stubborn male who simply wouldn't acknowledge a woman's capabilities.

"So what do you say?" Dorothy asked.

"Hmm?" Kerry had entirely lost the thread of the conversation.

"Haven't you been listening to me, Kerry? Maybe you're too sleepy to tackle this tonight."

"Tackle what?" Kerry asked contritely, now turning her full attention back on her friend.

"Talking to Jeb Hunter. I was suggesting that we go find John and join in the discussion about the desert, then John and I could just sort of leave and you'd have a chance to be alone with him."

The very idea made Kerry's stomach flutter. She didn't want to be alone with Jeb. Especially not this minute. Not until she'd had some time to digest this new information Dorothy had given her so casually. "I don't think that's a good idea," she answered.

Dorothy stood up and shook out her skirts. "Nonsense. You two have been pussyfooting around each other for days. Poor Patrick can't get his rides anymore because the captain's afraid to come within ten yards of your wagon. And you're moping by yourself every night because you've turned down one eligible male and have talked yourself into being scared of another."

As usual, Dorothy's plain speaking made Kerry feel as if she were taking everything a little too seriously. Her friend was right. It was silly for her and Jeb to avoid talking to each other. The same with Scott. She should just march up to them both, stick out her hand and say, "Truce. Let's be friends."

Slowly she got to her feet. "I'll go with you," she said, "but just to find out about the desert crossing and to be...friendly. I'm not interested in having you leave me alone with him."

"Coward," Dorothy said with a smile.

Kerry chuckled reluctantly. "You're right about Patrick. He misses his morning rides. It's only natural for a boy who's just lost his father to look up to someone in authority like that. But as far as my relationship with Jeb, it's strictly business. My father paid a fee for his services as a guide, and I'm now availing myself of those services. That's as far as it goes."

"*Jeb?*" Dorothy asked as she put her arm fondly around Kerry's waist and started walking with her up the line to the Todds' wagon. The smile in her voice deepened her Virginian accent. "Kerry, girl, you can talk until the creek starts flowing upstream, but find someone else to try your 'strictly business' tale on, because my mother's daughter was not born a fool."

Chapter Ten

Kerry might have expected that Dorothy would pay no attention to her request not to be left alone with Jeb Hunter. They'd arrived to find John and Jeb sitting around the Todds' campfire with Eulalie, Frank and the two mountain men, Foxy and Daniel, who had joined up with the train at Fort Kearney. The grizzled veterans had decided to walk with them for a spell just to have some company until they headed back up into the mountains for another round of trapping before the snows came.

Kerry had been happy to see the size of the group. It meant that there would be no question about her having to carry on a conversation by herself with their wagon master. But they hadn't even had time to finish the cup of coffee that Eulalie had pressed on them when Foxy and Daniel stood up and said they were going to seek out their bedrolls. Frank and Eulalie agreed and retired to their wagon. And in short order Dorothy, just as she had promised, stood, hauled John to his feet and said, "We have to go track down the girls. It's past their bedtime. But I believe Kerry has some more questions for you about this next stretch of trail coming up. We'll just let you two talk it over and she can pass on any useful information to us tomorrow.''

John stumbled, a little off balance at being suddenly yanked from his comfortable seat by the fire, but he took one look at his wife's raised eyebrows and followed along without protest.

Suddenly everyone was gone. Kerry hadn't even had time to think up her own excuses for saying goodnight.

''You had some questions about the trail?'' Jeb asked, pleasantly enough, but his voice was nowhere near as cordial as it had been during the earlier part of their trip.

The evening was warm and still. The dust that had hung around them all day had finally settled, and the black prairie sky was clear overhead. It was too beautiful a night to feel resentful. In fact, Kerry gave a half smile at Dorothy's impudence. She couldn't very well complain about her friend's determined behavior. After all, Dorothy's toughness and Eulalie's gentle insistence were a big part of the reason that Kerry was still with the train.

But unlike Dorothy, who'd been raised by Southern belles, Kerry had never learned how to play those dissembling male-female games. ''I think my friend was trying to leave us alone together,'' she said bluntly.

The careful veneer of politeness on Jeb's face slipped a little. He licked his lips and then said, ''And just why would she want to do that, Miss Gallivan?''

She gave another half smile. Good. It appeared that

he was ready to be equally blunt. Perhaps they would get something accomplished after all. "She thought I should ask you why you've been avoiding our wagon. I can understand that you might still be angry with me, but surely you have no particular bone to pick with Patrick."

Jeb reached for the coffeepot to pour himself another cup. He gestured to the cup she still held in her hands, but she shook her head. She had the feeling that he was stalling for time while he considered how to answer her.

"Are you still angry with me, Captain?" she asked softly.

He put the pot back near the fire and looked up at her. "No," he said.

"Then, why…"

"I think you know the answer to that question, Kerry."

Now there was a look in his eyes that took her back instantly to the moment just before he had reached for her on the riverbank. It was a look more palpable than a touch. A swift stab of feeling plunged through her middle and she drew in a breath. "Because of…" She tried to make her breathing even out so the question wouldn't sound stammered. "Because of what happened back at the fort?"

Jeb looked angry, but this time she didn't think the anger was directed toward her. "Because of what happened back at the fort," he said brusquely. "And because of the possible consequences if that should ever happen again."

"It…it won't happen again," Kerry said in a small

voice. "And...I'm not upset about it anymore, so you don't have to worry."

He was several feet away from her, but she could feel a certain heat between them, much the way it had been that night, when it had built so suddenly into something she still found herself remembering every night as she closed her eyes to sleep.

He felt it again, too. She could see it in the quick flare of his nostrils, the predatory look in his eyes. She had to get out of here...quickly. She rose to her feet and held out the cup. "I have to go," she said nervously. "I...ah...should go find Patrick."

He was on his feet the second she stood. He reached for the cup, but then held both it and her hand in his without letting go. His fingers were warm and strong, hers slender and cool, even holding the luke-warm coffee.

"You're not upset about it anymore?" he asked in a low voice. "Which means that you were upset at the time."

"Well, yes, but then I realized that it really had been just a little kiss and hadn't meant anything...."

Her voice trailed off as his eyes denied her assertion.

She tried again. "It's just that I'm not very experienced in these things, so it took me by surprise."

She tugged on her hand a little but he held it firm. "That much, at least is obvious," he said dryly, and when she began to protest his rudeness, he shook his head and continued, "because if you were at all experienced, you'd know that what we shared that night was not 'just a little kiss.'"

She pulled on her hand again, feeling silly over the

minor battle of it, but this time he let her go, keeping the cup. In spite of the return of her nervous flutters, his vehement words made her smile. "All right," she agreed. "It was more than a little kiss. I guess I'm experienced enough to know that much."

"Good," Jeb said curtly. "Then you should also know enough to understand why I'm avoiding a repetition of that event."

"You...didn't like it," she ventured.

Jeb rolled his eyes in exasperation. "Your naiveté, child, would try the patience of a saint. And I'm no saint, Kerry Gallivan."

"And I'm no child," she snapped, glaring at him.

He threw his head back and laughed. "Lord, no. You're no child. And when you get that hell-for-leather look in your eyes, I'd match you up against any woman west of the Mississippi, regardless of age. But that's precisely the problem."

"What is?"

Jeb took a step back from her and set down her cup on a rock. He didn't look in her eyes as he confessed, "I'm attracted to you, Kerry. I...*remember* that kiss. All too well. In fact, just looking at you makes me want to do it all over again. So it's easier not to look at you."

Kerry hesitated a moment, then asked, "So you intend to travel all the way from here to California without looking at me?"

Realizing the absurdity of that notion, Jeb grinned at her. "I could wear blinders like the mules."

She was forced to smile back at the ridiculous suggestion, and she couldn't resist saying, "There are people who might say you share some characteristics with those animals, Captain.''

His grin stayed in place, as he shook his head at her and said, "I thought it was going to be Jeb now.''

"Not if you refuse to look at me for the next ten weeks.''

The touch of humor had dissolved the tension between them, and for the first time in days they stood in comfortable companionship. It felt good to Kerry, and she suspected it was feeling good to Jeb, too.

"Well, I guess I'll just have to make the sacrifice every now and then and look at you. Does it have to be every day?''

Kerry giggled. He was actually playing with her now, which was a side of Jeb Hunter she'd never seen before. "Well, let's say once a day. I'll try to keep it from being such an onerous task," she teased. "At least I don't have to rub dirt on my cheeks anymore.''

Jeb's smile dimmed a little. "I'm afraid none of us will have to rub extra dirt on our cheeks over these next few days. We'll all have plenty naturally.''

"So it *is* going to get drier?" she asked.

He nodded. "Foxy and Daniel say there's been hardly any rain in the territory since clear last fall.''

"But there's enough water along the trail.''

"As long as we stick by the rivers.''

She could hear some hesitation in his answer. "Then we'll stick by the rivers, right? It's the only thing that makes sense.''

He looked up at the sky and around the camp before his eyes finally swiveled back to her. "Yes, it's what makes sense.''

Certain that he was avoiding telling her something, she persisted, "Except for what?"

He sighed, but this time did not look away. "Except that with a season this dry, it's the only thing that makes sense for the Indians, too."

The slight warmth that had taken over his voice and his expression when they'd been bantering earlier disappeared. Once again his face was stern. Kerry would have liked to ask further details about the Indians, but his cold demeanor seemed to shut off their discussion.

"Do you expect problems?" she ventured.

"My only problem will be falling asleep in the saddle tomorrow if I don't get some sleep," he said, throwing the remainder of his coffee on the dying fire.

The comment was again just at the edge of rudeness. Kerry took a step backward with a little trip. "I'll say good-night, then," she mumbled. And he answered her only with a nod as she turned to make her way back up the line of wagons.

Kerry had not told anyone about Jeb's comment regarding the possibility of an encounter with the unfriendly natives, but somehow word had spread through the train that such a meeting was a possibility, especially when water in the region had grown so scarce, which meant that everyone would be seeking the same limited resources.

The children had replaced their river games with make-believe plays about settlers and Indians. The adults watched with bemusement and said inner prayers that the childish fantasies would not have any real-life counterparts.

In spite of the new worry, Kerry was feeling happier than she had since before her father's death. The morning after her discussion with Jeb at the Todd wagon, he had appeared to collect Patrick for their morning ride as if there had never been any break in the routine.

Patrick had tried to appear nonchalant about the resumption of his friendship with Jeb, but Kerry knew that secretly he was delighted about it. And Kerry had to admit to herself that the wagon master's resumed visits to their wagon were also brightening her days. She began to look forward to seeing his tall form riding toward them, straight and proud on Storm's back. She found herself taking a little more care with her appearance in the morning, tugging with frustration each day on her cropped hair and wishing that the glossy black strands that had been cut off back in St. Louis could somehow magically appear again.

She'd started wearing her own clothes again. She told herself it was so that she wouldn't alienate the women on the train who had helped her. It had nothing to do with the way Jeb looked at her in her more shapely attire.

Scott was still staying away. She'd tried to talk with him one night, and the conversation had embarrassed them both, so she'd decided to give him time to let the hurt of her rejection of his suit heal.

Which left a clear field for Jeb, and each day he seemed to take a little more advantage of that fact. He'd started coming for Patrick both morning and afternoon. Then a couple of afternoons he casually stayed on to help them build their evening fire, at which point she'd felt obliged to invite him to stay to supper. And so the custom had been born. Now it was understood up and down the train that at the supper hour, Captain Hunter could be found at the Gallivan wagon. Secret bets were placed on how long it would take the serious captain to admit that he had fallen for the spirited young Irishwoman.

Kerry and Jeb were oblivious to the talk, but had developed their own version of gambling as each night brought them closer and closer to a repetition of their first shattering kiss.

Kerry, in fact, was ready to let it happen. Jeb had made it clear that he was not interested in settling down or taking a wife. So exchanging a few kisses with him in the moonlight would pose no risk to her plans. It would simply be another lesson to add to the many she would have to learn out West, she told herself.

Jeb was the one who resisted. After that first discussion when he had admitted that he was attracted to her, his conversation had been totally circumspect. He talked with her in tones no different from those he used for Patrick. Occasionally she thought she could see that *look* in his eyes, but it was always carefully shuttered by the time she tried to be sure.

The train was making painfully slow progress along the broad, dry plain of the Platte River. There had been no sign of Indians, though Jeb carefully checked for tracks or evidence of recent campsites. But when the women asked for a break, he'd shake his head. He wanted to get through this territory as quickly as possible.

"We keep pushing until we reach Independence Rock," he'd told them at a camp meeting. "Gateway to the Rockies. If we make it there by the Fourth of July, we've done it. We'll be over the mountains to California before the early fall snows.''

Kerry felt the closeness developing between them almost as powerfully as the physical attraction. She would have liked to know more about his wife, but had been hesitant to bring up the subject. She sensed that it was the one topic that could bring back the aloof Captain Hunter, that would drive Jeb away from their nightly campfires.

"Jeb's not coming until later," Patrick informed her one evening. "He's riding ahead to scout around the bend of the river and be sure there aren't any Injuns lurking there ready to scalp us."

"Patrick!" Kerry scolded. "I'm sure if there are Indians around, they're not lurking. The Indians are a very proud people. And I don't think they'd do any scalping, either, unless we bothered them first."

"Jeb says the white folk have bothered them plenty. That they have a right to hate us."

"And why are you calling him Jeb? It's not respectful."

Patrick grinned at her. "You call him Jeb. And, besides, he told me I could."

"Well, I think it would be more polite if you called him Captain Hunter, at least if there are other children around."

Patrick didn't seem daunted by her scolding. "All right. But I'll call him Jeb on our rides. We have such swell rides, Kerry. You ought to try it some day."

"As you have frequently pointed out, little brother, we don't have a horse."

"But you could ride with Jeb, like I do. Storm can take two people easy."

"I'm not sure Captain Hunter would be interested in..."

She stopped speaking as Jeb rode up and Patrick ran over to his horse. "You could take Kerry on a ride sometime, couldn't you, Jeb?"

"On a ride?" Jeb asked, swinging his long leg over the saddle and jumping lightly to the ground.

"Up behind you on Storm. Like you do with me. I told her how much fun we have."

Jeb looked amused. "I don't think your sister would want to ride bouncing along behind me the way you do, partner. It's kind of a man thing to do, you know."

Kerry gave a little sniff. "Is that right? What makes it a 'man thing'?"

Jeb flicked a glance over her serviceable blue cotton dress. "Well, for one thing...the clothes. Though it's done out here in the West, most women from back East are too embarrassed to ride astride in skirts."

"Ah, but that's an easily solved problem. All the woman has to do is put on a pair of pants."

Jeb's eyes glinted at the tone of challenge in her voice. "Most women wouldn't want to do that, either."

"Well, I'm not most women, then," Kerry said breezily.

"You'd go for a ride with me?" Jeb asked skeptically.

It was not what she had intended. But now it seemed that the issue had become a matter of pride. "Certainly. If Patrick can do it, so can I."

Jeb chuckled. "All right, if you say so. There'll still be plenty of light after supper. We'll go then."

Jeb had known the moment he agreed to this evening ride that it was not a wise plan. For days now he'd tried carefully to keep his head clear concerning Kerry. He'd told himself that he regarded both her and Patrick as younger siblings, people he was fond of, nothing more. He'd quickly turn his gaze away whenever he'd discover that his eyes had fixed themselves on the wispy black hair at the back of her neck or the way her slender wrists turned as she prepared the evening meal. He'd been *so* careful.

And now, like a blamed fool, he'd let her put on those clinging male trousers and climb up behind him so close that inevitably her firm, small breasts pressed against him every time Storm's front hooves hit the ground. As if that wasn't bad enough, he'd agreed to take her to see a panoramic view of the river valley up on one of the little hills that had lined their route all day. They'd left the wagon train behind, and with it the safety provided by the constant presence of onlookers.

Her arms were around his waist, holding tightly, though more relaxed now than the first few minutes. "Are you doing all right?" he asked her over his shoulder.

"As long as I can hold on to you. It's not a bother?"

Her hands squeezed into his midsection, just above his belt, just above the area of his groin that had started to ache from the constant contact with her. "No, it's not a bother," he lied. And then he distracted himself by starting to count the clumps of sagebrush.

"Would it be easier if I sat in front of you?" she asked.

"No," he said simply.

They rode in silence for several minutes, then Kerry said, "Patrick loves to be with you. And it's good for him. I think it makes him miss Papa a little less."

"He's a fine boy. Tough to lose your father so young in life."

Here, perhaps, was the opening for her to find out a little more about Jeb Hunter's own life. "What about your parents, Jeb?" she asked.

"I lost mine, too, though I was a bit older than Patrick."

"I'm sorry."

Jeb shrugged. "At the time I was already on the verge of going out into the world to make a life for myself. I missed them, but for a long while it seemed as if I'd been the one who'd left them instead of the other way around. By the time it really sank into me that they were dead, I..." he hesitated. "I was ready to start my own family."

Kerry's heart sped up a little. Would he tell her about his wife? she wondered. Did she dare ask him?

"Your own family?" she asked casually.

"Mmm." He spurred the horse up the last piece of hill and pulled back on the reins. "This looks like a good place to stop and see the view, if you've a mind."

"Certainly," she answered, though she regretted the interruption in their conversation.

He dismounted with a jump and then reached his hands up to her. Storm was a big horse and Kerry was happy to have Jeb's arms to slide into before she hit the ground. The contact was brief, but she felt a wave of warmth at the pressure of his hands on her waist. He let her go almost instantly.

"Thank you," she murmured. "That was enjoyable."

"Are your legs holding up all right?" he asked with a smile.

She took a couple of steps. "I can still walk."

His smile grew broader. "We have all the way back yet to go, you know."

"Don't worry about me, Captain. I'll ride as far as you want to take me." She turned around to look behind her at the view of the valley below and gave a little exclamation of pleasure.

Jeb was following the direction of her gaze. "Beautiful, isn't it?"

The yellowish green grass was crisscrossed with late afternoon shadows where cottonwood trees grew singly or in groups of two or three. At the far end of the valley the wagons formed an uneven circle, looking small and lonely in the vast expanse of land, like a neglected set of children's toys. Across the meadow, another long ridge of hills, much like the one they were standing on, cut a wavy silhouette across the nearly golden sky. Kerry was enchanted. "It's almost sunset," she breathed.

"Yes, we should have headed back by now. It'll be dark when we return."

"Oh, please. Let's just watch a little longer." Without waiting for his answer, she flopped down on the grass, her trousered legs sticking straight out in front of her, and took in a deep breath of air. "It's a little like what I remember of back home in Ireland. Green hills and lots of land."

"Not enough land to feed everyone from the accounts of the immigrants," Jeb disagreed mildly. He let Storm's reins trail on the ground and sat beside her.

Kerry gave a twisted smile. "I know. I imagine my memories of Ireland are all mixed up with my father's fantasies. Once we got to New York City, it seemed as if that was all he could talk about. 'Breathing room,' he called it. Land enough for a body to have breathing room."

"And that's what he wanted to find in California."

Kerry nodded. Tears stung her eyes, but she realized that they were the first she'd felt in days. Perhaps time would finally start to work its healing on her as it already had on Patrick.

They were quiet for several moments, watching the orange orb of the sun sink beyond the far western end of the ridge of hills. The few wispy clouds had turned a pink that was growing darker before their eyes. "This would be a nice moment to freeze," Kerry said wistfully.

"To freeze?"

She chuckled. "It was a kind of game of my father's. When he'd tuck us to sleep at night, he'd ask us what had been our favorite moment of the whole day. We'd tell him about it, then he'd make us close our eyes and say, 'All right, now, freeze it behind those sleepy eyelids.' And it would mean that we'd dream about that happy moment all night long."

Jeb smiled. "What moments did you freeze?"

Kerry was now thoroughly in the grip of nostalgia, but the memories were more benevolent than any she'd had since her father's death. They felt warm and pleasant. She lay back on the grass and closed her eyes. "I suppose they weren't anything so very important. Eating a sweetmeat or maybe having Mrs. McElroy agree to help me with the stalls so I could leave early. Sometimes I froze a scene from a book when I could get my hands on one."

Jeb could hardly keep his mind on her words. He was battling his own memories—more recent ones. Memories of the last time he'd sat next to Kerry on a hillside, of how easy it had been to scoop her up into his arms. Of how quickly her lips had softened under his. Of the liquid heat of their kisses.

She opened her eyes. "I wanted to learn more about you, and here we are talking about me again."

"There's not much to learn about me, I'm afraid. From listening to you and Patrick talk about him, I'd say your relationship with your father was closer than anything I remember from my childhood."

From where she lay on the ground, Jeb was silhouetted against the darkening orangish-purple sky. The light gave his brown hair a rusty tinge. It was gently ruffled by the sudden picking up of a late-evening breeze. The strong features of his face were shadowed. A moment to remember, Kerry thought to herself. A moment to freeze. "You must have some special memories," she said.

His deep breath was ragged. "The only one that

seems to come to mind at the moment doesn't have anything to do with my childhood.''

She gazed up at him with a questioning look.

''What I'm remembering is the taste of those red lips of yours.''

Chapter Eleven

He might as well have been touching her. The mere sound of the words had the same effect. She drew in a quick breath and waited, her lips already feeling swollen. And his actions swiftly followed the words. He bent over her, blotting out the sky, and then the world turned to darkness as her eyes closed and his mouth pressed against hers.

She twisted her head slightly toward him, seeking the warmth, and he acknowledged her acquiescence with a low groan. Barely withdrawing his lips from her, he murmured, "Lord, sweetheart, you make me want you."

This time his words burned, down her middle and straight to the place where an incredible, yearning feeling was building. She opened her eyes to find that his were gazing at her with a hooded intensity that made the burn hotter.

He hadn't touched her with anything but his lips, but these were thorough and skillful, taking their time in slow, patient, long kisses that focused first on the center of her mouth, then slipped to the corner, then finally along the line of her jaw and up to her eyelids, which had once again drifted closed as she lay on the grass in delicious lethargy.

It was endless minutes before she felt his weight shift over her, his chest pressed gently on hers. One of his legs moved between hers, hard and warm against the insides of her thighs, which were already sensitive from bouncing along on top of Storm.

She squirmed a little, not in protest, but just reflexively, trying to find an outlet for the waves of sensation. He pulled his head back and smoothed the hollows of her cheeks with his thumbs. "Look at me, Kerry," he said in a husky voice.

When she once again opened her eyes, his expression had changed. The predatory intensity was gone, replaced by a gentle smile. "These lips were meant to be kissed, sweetheart," he said, lightly doing so.

Kerry was trying desperately to regain control of her racing senses. They scared her. She didn't want to think that another person could do this to her, scramble her head this way. She'd already turned down one offer of marriage this trip because she didn't want to give anyone else power over her life. But somehow it seemed as if Jeb had a power over her that she'd neither given nor anticipated. Her brain told her to roll out from beneath him, but her body would not cooperate. Instead her head rose just enough to make contact once again with his mouth.

This time he was exquisitely slow. He kissed her, starting from gentle pressure, then his tongue made a smooth tour of her lips, seeking entrance, and then entering her with a careful, persistent rhythm that made her hips rise from the grass to meet the hard barrier of his thigh.

He groaned again, then pulled his mouth away from hers and shifted downward to let his head fall heavily on her chest. "This is totally against my rules," he said in a voice tight with frustration.

Kerry felt as if he'd splashed cold water on her face. There were *rules* about things like this? "Am I supposed to apologize?" she asked when she could get her breath to speak.

He gave her shoulders a squeeze, then sat up. "No," he said briskly. "I am. I've taken six trains across country and have never once let this happen to me."

The unfulfilled feelings in her center still raged, making her voice sound angry. "I'm the lucky one."

He pushed back his tousled hair and gave a harsh laugh. "The unlucky one, you might better say."

The self-condemnation was so evident in his tone that her anger began to dissipate. She sat up slowly. "It wasn't *that* bad," she said softly with a touch of humor.

His laugh was more genuine this time. "Well, thank you for that, anyway. It's still not something I intended to allow to happen."

"Perhaps I was the one allowing it."

He shook his head. "It doesn't matter. I have no business kissing you or any other woman under my protection."

Kerry's body was finally returning to normal. She stretched her legs and smoothed out her shirt. "You're just our wagon master, Jeb, not our father."

"A wagon master is a father, husband and policeman all in one."

"What about friend?" It was beginning to get quite dark, but Kerry could still see the hard lines of tension that had taken over his face as he remembered his duty.

"No," he answered after a minute. "Not friend. And certainly not lover. It doesn't pay to get your feelings involved with people you have to control."

Kerry gave an exasperated click of her tongue. "Haven't you ever considered that developing some of these feelings you're talking about just might help you get the cooperation you're looking for on a train?"

He gave a firm shake of his head. "No, ma'am. You can't be a leader one moment and one of the bunch the next. It doesn't work."

"And you can't be a wagon train leader and also enjoy a few kisses on a hillside."

"That's right." He stood and held his hand out to her. "C'mon. We're going to have to make our way back in the darkness. I don't like doing that over this rough prairie. We could hit a prairie dog hole that would break Storm's leg."

His tone was all back to business, effectively shutting off all further conversation about anything more personal. But she wasn't about to let Jeb Hunter turn back into his comfortable role of authoritarian wagon master. Not after what they'd just shared.

She took his hand and let him pull her up. Then she dusted off the seat of her pants. "Well, Captain, I bet this is the first time you've kissed someone wearing trousers. At least *that* kind of kiss."

He was already throwing the reins over Storm's head and getting ready to boost himself up on his back, but her words made him turn back to her. He hesitated a minute, then his face relaxed into a smile. "Not *that* kind of kiss," he agreed.

"It was...a nice kind of kiss," she said, remembering with a flush of heat exactly how nice it had been.

Jeb looked as if he was struggling not to let her words soften his resolve. He gave a quick puff of air, then swung himself into the saddle. "Yes," he said curtly. "It was nice. But it'll be better for us both if it doesn't happen again."

His voice was so distant that Kerry gave up trying to make it go soft again as it had been just moments before when he had called her sweetheart. The trip back was mostly silent.

The breeze had picked up, causing Jeb to comment, "Maybe this wind will bring some rain. We could sure use it."

And since the weather was not the topic that was occupying Kerry's mind, she made no reply.

They rode more slowly than they had on the way there, letting Storm pick a careful trail through the dark grass. The gentle rocking motion of the horse was soothing, and by the time Jeb pulled Storm up next to her wagon, she was almost drifting off to sleep.

"What took you so long?" Patrick came running up to them from the direction of the Burnetts' wagon.

"Nothing in particular, sprout," Jeb answered breezily, then took a closer look at the boy's face. "Is something the matter?"

Patrick's eyes were worried. "Dorothy's been looking for you. Little Molly's awful sick."

"Sick?" Kerry asked in alarm, jumping from Storm's back without bothering to take the hand Jeb held out to her.

"Polly says she was holding her stomach and moaning all afternoon, but now she's just lying there. She looks so tiny."

There was a bit of a crack to Patrick's voice at the end of his statement. Kerry put an arm around his shoulder. "Children get sick fast, Patrick," she said reassuringly. "They usually get well fast, too."

But when she and Jeb climbed up into the Burnetts' wagon and saw Molly lying on the bed they'd cleared for her, Kerry felt her throat constrict. Molly did look suddenly tiny. Her skin was stark white and her breathing heavy. "Good Lord," Kerry said under her breath, then mentally berated herself for her words as she saw Dorothy's stricken face.

"She's had…you know…the 'relax' for a couple days now, Captain," Dorothy explained. "She was too embarrassed to tell anyone, but now it's as if all the life has just drained out of her."

Jeb's face was set in a hard mask that Kerry could hardly recognize. Though everyone's fears were always of the Indians, dysentery was by far the deadliest of killers on the vast plains. "She needs to drink something." He sat down beside Molly's slight form and lifted her limp wrist, feeling the weak pulse.

"I can't get her to take anything anymore," Dorothy said.

"She has to. Even if we have to dribble it down her throat little by little." Jeb turned to John, who sat in one corner of the wagon looking hollow-eyed and frightened. "How much cider do you have—not the hard stuff?" When the girl's father shook his head, Jeb continued, "Find some. Go up and down the wagons."

"I've been trying to give her water—" Dorothy began.

"Not water," Jeb interrupted. "This is what I was afraid of with the water so low. The river's gotten brackish, infested. We'll have to ride up into the hills and find some smaller streams where the water will still be fresh."

He leaned toward the opening of the wagon to speak with Patrick. "I want you to go to every wagon and tell them not to drink the water they've taken from the river. They'll have to drink cider or milk or whatever else they can find tonight. We'll find a fresh supply tomorrow."

Patrick looked relieved to have something to occupy him, to have an excuse to move away from the tense faces of the adults at the Burnett wagon. "I'll go talk to all of them, Jeb."

He turned to leave, but then stopped as Jeb called one further instruction. "Ask at every wagon if anyone else has taken sick."

Patrick looked around once more at his sister and the two older Burnetts. Then his gaze went to Polly, huddled on top of a flour bag, her eyes swollen from tears. "I reckon I'll need help," he said to her. "Will you come with me?"

The usually lively child gave a solemn nod and slid from her perch. Kerry sent Patrick a grateful smile. Then the two children headed off into the darkness.

* * *

Kerry had always thought that the night she had spent with her anguished father as her mother lay dying would be forever after remembered as the longest night of her life. But the hours she watched Molly Burnett fight for her life eclipsed that childhood memory. The seconds echoed as Dorothy's pretty face stretched tight with anxiety and John's bright eyes dulled. They seemed to be aging overnight.

It was Jeb's presence that held them all together. He never left his post by the child's side. Without wasting time on commiserations, he ministered to the fragile body, forcing swallows of liquid between the inert lips and wiping down the fever that flared in the early hours of the morning.

He told the Burnetts in calm, strong tones that it was not uncommon for children to be hit this suddenly and this hard by dysentery. His guess was that it was from the brackish water they'd been drinking, and not something that would be transmitted from Molly to the rest of the family or the rest of the train. There was no particular reason to think that Polly would be similarly afflicted.

He did not say, though Kerry heard an implication behind his words, that at least they would still have one daughter left if the worst should happen.

And for long hours of the night, it appeared as if that was exactly what might happen. It was hard to believe that a human could change so quickly. In just a few hours Molly's skin had become lifeless, grayish almost. She'd been passing blood, they'd told Jeb. And it looked as if she'd passed so much that there was no longer any left inside her to provide the warmth to keep her alive.

The Todds came by and the Wilkses, and many of the other wagon train members, sober and frightened. It appeared no one was sleeping that night. Patrick and Polly were assiduously visiting every single wagon, making frequent trips back to the Burnett wagon to see if there had been any change in Molly's condition. So far they had brought no reports of other people being stricken.

Kerry could hardly believe that an evening that had started out with a golden sunset and the exhilarating discovery of a passion she hadn't even known she possessed could end in such agony. Once she caught Jeb's eye and had the fleeting impression that he, too, was remembering their kiss up on the hill. He gave her a smile that was half reassurance and half something with a deeper sort of warmth.

By dawn they all had the feeling that the illness had reached a crisis stage. The soul that was fighting inside that tiny, ravaged body was either going to give up the battle or start to win it.

Jeb was dribbling liquid down her throat again, this time some clear soup that Eulalie had brought. Kerry sat next to Dorothy on the food sacks, an arm around her back. John was crammed up against the other side of the wagon, leaning back against the cover, his eyes closed. But everyone knew that he was not asleep.

"She moved her lips," Jeb said, a low excitement in his voice.

Dorothy and John both sat up straight.

Jeb turned to Dorothy with a cautious smile. "She just swallowed that mouthful of soup. On her own."

There was a soft moan from the bed. Jeb turned back and spooned in more soup. This time all of them could see that, though her eyes were still closed, she was definitely responding to the food in her mouth.

"Thank the Lord," Dorothy whispered, tears streaming down her face.

Kerry swallowed the lump in her own throat and nodded agreement with her friend's prayer.

When Frank and Eulalie appeared for the third time shortly after dawn, they informed Eulalie that her soup seemed to be performing miracles.

With a broad smile of relief, the older woman said briskly, "I could have told you that. Everyone's always said that my turnip soup could raise the dead."

By midmorning, Molly was intermittently opening her eyes and seemed to be enough aware to be shy about the fact that the wagon master was sitting by her bed. She even responded with a little smile when Patrick climbed up into the wagon and said to her, "You gave us all a scare, Molly. You'd better get all better quick."

The hours without sleep and the tension had Kerry feeling numb, which at least left her with no more energy to think about Jeb's kisses. She wouldn't think about them until after she'd had some sleep, she decided, but found the resolution wavering when Scott came around to check on Molly's progress. The mere sight of the kind young man who had offered to save her dream by marrying her, made her feel a little sick to her stomach.

Jeb stayed in the Burnett wagon until noon. He told John and Dorothy to come and find him if there was any change for the worse, then climbed down, stretching the muscles of his back. There was no question about moving the train that day, but if Molly was out of danger, he had other tasks he could see to. He was just starting to enumerate them in his mind, trying to decide if he should try to get a couple of hours of sleep first, when the prospect of a productive afternoon was abruptly shattered. Frank Todd had come back to the Burnett wagon to find him.

"We've got two more cases," he told the wagon leader with a grim face. "And one of them is Hester Hamilton."

Hester was the oldest settler on the train. She was too much a lady to tell her age, but she and her husband Samuel made no secret about the fact that she was older than he was by several years. And Samuel had several years over Frank Todd. Jeb had been a little skeptical about their ability to undertake such an arduous journey, but he'd been convinced by their evident good health and, more than anything, by the strong bond the two had with each other.

"She snatched me out of the cradle," Samuel had said with a twinkle in his eyes, "and we've been rocking along together ever since."

It was a special sight to see a couple so in love after all these years. The Todds seemed to have had similar fortune. It shouldn't be that much to ask of life, Jeb had thought with a twinge of bitterness, yet it seemed to be as rare as a blossom in the snow.

Jeb was cursing himself now as he strode grimly toward the Hamilton wagon. Perhaps he should have flatly refused to let them join the train, he told himself. He'd known the dangers, the strain. He hadn't figured on dysentery, that grim reaper of the young and the elderly, but then, something unexpected always arose—every trip. It was his job to be ready for all contingencies and to ensure that his people were up to handling them.

Mrs. Hamilton's illness had come on as swiftly as Molly's. By the time Jeb got to their wagon, she could no longer sit up, could not even lift her head. Samuel was seated next to her, holding her hand and talking to her semiconscious form in low, soothing tones. Remarkably, though his face was pale and grave, he conveyed no sense of despair. The anguish that had been almost palpable in the Burnett wagon was missing.

When Jeb climbed into the wagon, Samuel looked up at him and gave a sad smile. "We've said goodbye," he said softly. "Just in case."

"We need to get liquids into her. We'll try some of Mrs. Todd's soup that seemed to work well for Molly." The desperation in Jeb's voice sounded out of place in the face of Samuel's serenity.

"I'll do it," Samuel said. "If you would just be so kind as to fetch it for me." Obviously he was not going to relinquish his place by his wife's side to anyone.

Jeb spent the afternoon and evening traveling from the Hamilton wagon to the wagon of the other victim, the Crandalls' sixteen-year-old son, Homer, whose case fortunately turned out to be mild, and finally back again to the Burnetts to check on the progress of Molly. The little girl was now drinking on her own and smiling a little at her sister's sallies. Kerry was still there with Dorothy and John, so the child had plenty of nurses.

In between visits to the sick, Jeb consulted with Frank, Scott, Henry Kirby and several of the other men about the water supply. All barrels that had been filled from the river were to be dumped and rinsed with vinegar. To fill the train's immediate needs, a group of five men was dispatched with a team of mules to head into the hills and bring down water from the cleanest spring they could find.

Hester Hamilton died just before midnight. The goodbye Samuel had mentioned to Jeb had, indeed, been their last. Jeb asked him if he wanted some of the women to come tend to her. But Samuel had said simply, once again, "Thank you, Captain, but I'll do it." Jeb had left him still holding her hand.

He hadn't slept in two days, and as he walked away from the Hamilton wagon he swayed a little on his feet. He should make one more check on Molly and the Crandall boy, but he was afraid that he'd keel over if he didn't sleep for a spell. That is, if he could *get* himself to sleep. The death of Mrs. Hamilton sat like a stone in the middle of his chest. It didn't help that she'd been old, that perhaps it had been her time. It didn't even help that her husband seemed to be accepting the loss without casting blame. Jeb would cast enough blame to satisfy anyone. And the blame would be squarely on his own shoulders.

Most of the wagons were dark. No one had slept much the previous night, and the fires had been put out early. But down across the circle from the Todds' wagon he could see Kerry sitting up by her campfire. He crossed over to her. "Why aren't you sleeping?"

"I just left the Burnetts. I need to settle my thoughts a moment before I try to lie down. How's Mr. Hamilton doing?"

"Far better that I would be in his place. How's Molly?"

Kerry gave him a tired smile. "She's become shy about having Patrick see her in her nightgown, which I think means that she's close to recovery."

"Is Patrick still there?" He looked around the camp.

"He's sound asleep inside the wagon. He's had a rough day, like we all have. I think he's fonder of Molly than he'd like to admit."

"Young love. It's so simple, isn't it?" Jeb moved closer to her. She'd washed up and changed clothes sometime during the day and was wearing the green dress he liked.

Kerry shook her head. "No, I don't think love's particularly simple at any age."

"Since you're such an expert," Jeb couldn't resist saying.

Kerry didn't try to refute his sarcasm. "It's not simple, but I don't think you have to be an expert, either. You do what feels natural."

They were both silent, remembering what had felt natural to them up on the hillside. Had it only been one night ago?

She looked up at him. His face in the firelight looked drawn and tired, and she had a sudden desire to hold him. What had he said? It would be better for them both if it didn't happen again. She looked away and stared into the flames.

Jeb felt the exhaustion drain out of him, replaced by a more stimulating sensation. Kerry was utterly appealing in the dancing light of the fire. Her big eyes stared up at him from underneath her cropped hair.

He'd best spin right around on his heels and march away, he warned himself. Because right now it was just too damned tempting to kneel beside her and draw solace from those magic lips of hers.

There was no light from any of the nearby wagons. They might as well have been alone together in the middle of the prairie, caressed by the warm night air and serenaded by the rhythmic drone of insects from out in the fields.

"Patrick's asleep, you say," he said, moving not away, but closer.

She turned her head away from the fire and held his gaze with her wide eyes. "Yes," she whispered.

And then he knelt beside her and drew her into his arms, finding her mouth in a blinding instant.

Kerry sensed from the moment he took hold of her that this time a kiss would not be enough. Instead of gentle and exploring, his mouth felt needy, almost desperate, as if he was seeking comfort from her, seeking to forget the tension and guilt of the past few hours. Well, she'd wanted to comfort him. But as soon as his lips touched her she knew that comforting was only part of what she wanted.

She didn't know how it had happened. She'd fought the notion from the first time she'd looked up and seen him on his big horse. She'd fought it across miles of prairie. But she couldn't fight it anymore. She was in love with Jeb Hunter.

She'd told herself it was lunacy. He obviously was not interested in love. He'd flat out told her that kissing her had been a mistake. Yet here he was again, seeking her out at her campfire in the middle of the night. He'd vowed that their kisses would not happen again. Yet here he was.

She put her head back and let him explore her neck with his mouth and tongue. If it was a mistake, Kerry thought hazily as she slipped into that deliciously aroused state that she was just beginning to learn, she and Jeb were about to make it together.

Chapter Twelve

Jeb knew exactly what he was doing. Afterward he wouldn't be able to tell himself that it had happened because he'd gone two days with no sleep. Or from drinking hard cider on an empty stomach. He wouldn't even be able to put the blame on the need for some sort of reaffirmation of life and love after his most recent losing struggle with death.

None of it mattered. The only thing that was important was Kerry, her bright eyes and lush body, the valiant spirit that had made her deceive him, badger him, refuse to give in when he wanted to send her home. Kerry, who had not yet finished shedding her own tears of grief for her father, but who seemed to be willing to open her heart and her body to offer him comfort.

She gave and he took, filling his hands with her curves, finally reaching the firm globes of her breasts, which had hardened against the tight bodice of the green dress. Without conscious thought, he loosened tiny buttons that ran from her neck to her waist, seeking flesh and warmth.

She leaned back against his arm and let him peel back her clothes until her breasts were bare to his gaze and his touch. His lips fastened gently on a peaking nipple. In age-old rhythm he tugged at it as his own body grew swollen and urgent.

Kerry's eyes were closed. She lay docile in his embrace. But when he stopped sucking she murmured a protest and said, "It feels so..."

She stopped and he lifted his head a moment to encourage her words. "What, sweetheart? Do you like that?"

Her eyes flickered open, and her smile was sensual. "Mmm, yes," she said. "Please, do it some more."

Jeb would have been amused at her characteristic plain speaking if he hadn't been too busy being aroused by it. Ignoring a surge of lust from the lower portion of his body, he took the other breast in his mouth and lavished on it the same attention as he had the first.

She rolled her head against his arm, thoroughly caught up in her first experience with erotic pleasure. Jeb continued his slow lovemaking. When her nipples were swollen and wet, he moved back to her lips, then turned her a little in his arms to kiss the sensitive back of her upper arm and then make his way up the side of her neck.

He didn't know when he decided that he was going to take their lovemaking to its preordained conclusion. It was too late now for anything else. Her face had the telltale flush, her moans had become urgent and entreating. Her fingers dug into his shoulders, then loosened, in rhythm with his tongue's invasion of her mouth.

Her acceptance was so complete that it banished any doubts about propriety. In spite of her seeming innocence, surely she must be experienced in these matters. She was, after all, a city girl, not any city, but New York. Perhaps she'd even lain with Haskell. The very idea made him renew his onslaught. With his last vestige of good sense he lifted his head and looked around, checking for signs that anyone had awakened in nearby wagons. It was not an ideal setting—he could not leisurely be the way he preferred to ensure that the lady's pleasure equaled his own. But from the urgency of her hands on him, he figured that quickness would do them just as well.

Unfastening his trousers, he pushed up her dress and sought the warm moist core of her through her underclothes. She lifted her hips and moved sinuously against him, firing his blood, and without further preliminaries he entered her.

She gave a great gasp and her fingers at his neck gouged so hard that he could feel her nails through his shirt. He pulled back in horror, realizing that he'd just plunged heedlessly through a thin barrier of skin. Kerry Gallivan was a virgin. *Had been* a virgin, he corrected himself with a sick feeling rising in his throat.

He stopped all movement, holding himself above her, his eyes closed. He didn't want to look at her face.

"You haven't done this before," he stated dully, finally opening his eyes.

"No," she said in a voice he could hardly hear.

"Do you want me to stop?"

He was still inside her, and little by little Kerry

was becoming accustomed to the odd sensation. In fact, it was turning pleasant, and even stimulating. She'd been on the verge of such ecstasy before the unexpected, sudden pain. Now the ecstasy was creeping back, little by little. "No," she said again.

He kissed her and mumbled, "I'm sorry," then he was gone from inside her, leaving her feeling empty. But before she could even protest, he whispered, "Shhh," and the hardness of him was replaced by his fingers, gently playing, caressing and finding a place on her that soon had her shifting her hips once again in search of some relief.

She'd grown moist, she could tell, and this time when he slipped into her there was no pain, only a pleasurable sensation of fulfillment that escalated as he slowly moved in and out. The pleasure became hunger and finally almost pain again as their movements became more frantic. Then she cried out as the waves hit her, endless, incredible waves of feeling radiating up from her loins. She was dimly aware that he'd pulled quickly out of her again, shifting positions to turn himself a little away from her. And she heard his own deep breath of release.

Then they both were still, exhausted. Kerry closed her eyes and felt as if she was floating on a blissful sea. She wasn't even entirely sure what had happened to her. She'd never had a mother to explain these male-female things to her, and she certainly would never have dreamt of asking her father. She'd had to gleam little bits and pieces of information from eavesdropping on the conversations of the women who came into the market. But she had the notion that Jeb's sudden withdrawal had had to do with having babies. Or rather not having babies. Which was a sobering thought that had not even entered her head when he'd taken her in his arms tonight.

She wasn't too concerned about the virginity issue. Since she'd never been all that interested in finding a husband, she hadn't worried about needing to save her body to give as a gift to one particular man, the whole notion of which had always struck her as rather silly.

But babies were another matter entirely. It would be mighty hard to build a ranch if she were with child. Now that the glow of the experience was literally fading from her body, she began to chide herself for her impulsiveness.

Jeb sensed the change in her immediately. She was already regretting the encounter, which was only natural. She'd been a *virgin*, for God's sake, and he'd taken her on the ground next to her wagon, a few feet away from her sleeping brother. She, who was one of his pilgrims, totally under his care. He'd never in his life done anything so despicable. Well, that was not true, he amended bitterly. Deflowering a virgin under his charge was really just one more sin to add to his toll. He'd already paved his road to hell when he'd left Melanie alone in the wilderness.

"Are you all right?" he asked stiffly.

She sat up a little and smoothed down the skirt of her dress. Was this the way it was supposed to end? she wondered. His voice had become distant. He'd just done the most intimate things that she'd ever had done to her body, and now he was sounding like a stranger. She wanted him to lie back down and draw her into his arms again. She wanted him to whisper warm and low into her ear. Instead he pulled entirely away from her, discreetly closing up his trousers and repeated his question.

"Are you all right? You're not hurt?"

She shook her head, dazed. She had never discussed the matter with another woman, but some inner sense told her that this was *not* the way people ended their lovemaking. Perhaps he hadn't liked it very much, though that was a cruel thought when she considered the incredible feeling it had produced in her own body.

She pulled herself upright and began to fasten up her dress. Mustering all her dignity, she said, "You didn't hurt me, Captain."

Her voice was as cold as a January dawn. Jeb resisted the urge to shiver. He deserved it. He deserved her contempt and more. If her father had still been alive, he'd be within his rights to take a shotgun to Jeb right now. And Jeb thought he would almost have welcomed it. In the months after they'd butchered Melanie, he'd had that thought often.

"I'll leave you alone," he said. "I... It won't even do any good to apologize. It happened and there's nothing we can do about that."

It happened? Was this the sum total of discussion that she was going to have with her first-ever lover? Kerry felt her Irish temper begin to rise. It wasn't a quick temper as they painted it in the stories, but once it was aroused, it could be fierce and unforgiving.

She jumped to her feet. "Captain Hunter, you and I are going to continue to travel together for a long time, months yet. I think you'd better leave now before I say something to you that will make those months highly uncomfortable for us both.''

Jeb got more slowly to his feet. ''I want you to know that...''

She waited while he hesitated, then looked down at the ground and shook his head. He looked immensely tired.

''Never mind,'' he finished. ''It's late. I'll come by in the morning and we'll see if we can make some sense out of this thing.''

She watched in disbelief as he picked up his hat from where it had fallen to the ground and walked away.

He didn't come by in the morning. There was an early morning meeting with the men who had gone into the hills for water. The fresh water supply was already almost gone. No one else had been taken ill, and some of the settlers had begun using the convenient water from the river, in spite of Jeb's warnings. He wanted to get on the trail as soon as possible to move farther upstream.

But first there was Hester Hamilton's funeral to arrange. Samuel had made no fuss about burying her in a shallow grave between two cottonwood trees.

''It's not my Hester there,'' he'd said with misty eyes that belied his calm voice. ''She's in here,'' he ended, pointing to his heart.

Everyone had stood around the small hole as they'd lowered Hester's body into it, wrapped in a sheet. Frank Todd had read the verses and at the end, while Scott, Jeb and several of the other men filled in the grave, someone started up a hymn. Their discordant voices sounded weak and lost in the middle of the prairie, almost drowned out by the whistling of the wind through the grass.

So they'd started up again, wagons rolling and people walking, mostly in silence, thinking now and then of the still mound of dirt between the cottonwoods. And Jeb had not come to the Gallivan wagon.

They kept moving until almost twilight, trying to make up for the day and a half they had lost. Everyone up and down the train was subdued and tired. Even the children refrained from their usual antics. Patrick had ridden beside Kerry all day, not caring to seek out the company of his friends. He'd looked for Jeb to come by and offer a ride, but when the wagon master did not make an appearance, he made no comment.

By the time they stopped, everyone was too tired to form their circle. They camped right where they were in line, most of the wagons not even bothering to build a fire. Mothers up and down the line offered cold dinners of meat cakes and the last of the apples, which were now shriveling with the heat.

Kerry was exhausted. She'd slept little the previous night after her encounter with Jeb and none at all the night before. When Scott appeared at their wagon shortly after they'd stopped to camp with a plate full of biscuits and cold meat, she greeted him as if he'd been sent from heaven.

"Some of us went hunting for sage hens while we were laying over yesterday," he explained. "Cooked them last night."

Kerry didn't know which made her happier, the thought of fresh food or the fact that Scott seemed to be back to his normal happy-go-lucky self. Both were welcome developments, she decided as she, Patrick and Scott sat down on the ground and began to eat.

Scott's gentle teasing was exactly what she needed tonight as an antidote to her bitter experience with Jeb. She couldn't believe that he'd not come around all day. It was as if he was angry with her for an event that had certainly been at least half his fault, that had seemed at the time like something that both of them wanted equally.

"Are you going to be friends with us again, Scott?" Patrick asked between mouthfuls of sage hen.

"Patrick!" Kerry remonstrated, but Scott waved her reproach aside with a good-natured grin.

"Of course I'll be your friend, Pat, my boy. If you and your sister want me around."

"Why, sure we want you around. Don't we, sis?"

Kerry nodded and met Scott's eyes with a look of apology that communicated far more than could be said in words.

Scott gave her a reassuring wink. "Then I reckon you've got me. At least until we hit the gold fields."

Patrick threw the completely clean leg bone down on the plate. "And then you'll be off to make your fortune, right?" he asked with enthusiasm.

"That I will, lad."

"I wish I could do that," Patrick said wistfully.

"We'll be building our own kind of fortune, Patrick, as you well know," Kerry said. "We'll be building the future that our papa planned for his family."

Patrick fell silent, but his expression said that somehow farming didn't seem anywhere near as romantic to a boy of thirteen as finding a fortune in gold.

"Never mind," Scott said, reaching to put one of his own pieces of meat on Patrick's plate. "I'm sure you'll have plenty of adventures in California. And you have many years to have them in."

Patrick nodded and picked up Scott's offering of meat. "I can't wait," he said with a full mouth.

Kerry smiled at them both, happy for the first time all day. She would just put Jeb Hunter out of her mind, she decided. She intended to have her own rich, full life with Patrick in California, and she didn't need the company of an erratic wagon master to do it.

There was a sudden sound in the shadows and all three looked up to see Jeb Hunter standing next to their wagon. He cleared his throat, then asked, "I'm sorry. Am I interrupting?"

"As a matter of fact, we're about to turn in for the evening," Kerry said quickly. Both Scott and Patrick turned their heads to look at her. Her chin went up.

Jeb looked uncomfortable. "I'll say good-night then. I'm just checking on everyone. Nothing important."

Scott looked from Kerry's tense face over to Jeb. Then he said in a hearty voice. "Join us if you like, Hunter. I'd offer you some bird, but it appears that this growing boy and I have finished up the last morsel."

Jeb shook his head. "No, thanks. I'll be moving along. We all could use a good night's sleep."

Kerry's hands clutched at each other in her lap. Had Jeb had trouble sleeping last night, too? She fervently hoped so.

"Can we go riding again tomorrow, Jeb?" Patrick asked.

Jeb's eyes were on Kerry. "Hmm," he answered noncommittally.

Patrick smiled, evidently taking his answer as an affirmative. "Say, I never got to ask you, Kerry, about your ride the other night. With all the fuss over Molly it just went out of my head."

Kerry tore her eyes from Jeb and turned toward her brother. Scott was watching her, his expression guarded. "The ride was fine," she answered.

"Did you gallop? And did you hold fast to Jeb's waist? It's kind of hard sometimes, isn't it?" he commented with the pride of experience.

Kerry hoped her flush did not show in the dim light. "I said it was fine, Patrick. But you heard the captain say that it's time for everyone to get some sleep."

"I just wanted to know if you galloped," he said, sounding disappointed that he could not spend more time on a topic about which his experience far outweighed his sister's. "I can gallop with him just fine. Can't I, Jeb?"

"Sure thing, partner," Jeb agreed, but his voice was distracted.

Scott stood up. "So are we going to turn in or are we going to sit here talking all night?" he asked.

Kerry gratefully stood next to him. "I'm going to turn in," she said. "I don't care what the rest of you do."

"We'll be heading out at the usual time tomorrow," Jeb told them.

"Fine," Scott answered. "We should be a happier

group. Today's been rough on everyone. How's Mr. Hamilton doing?''

Jeb shook his head in amazement. "He seems to be so much at peace that I can hardly believe it.''

"He says his Hester will be with him always," Patrick added with a nod. "He does understand that she's dead, doesn't he?''

"He understands it,'' Jeb answered. "He just seems to have an acceptance of it and a faith…'' His voice trailed off as he pondered the mystery of Samuel's peace. "I've checked in with him off and on today, and, instead of pitying him, I keep wanting to say 'what a lucky man.' It doesn't make sense.''

"It makes sense to me," Kerry said. "My father is with me inside, just like Samuel's Hester. I'll never completely lose him.''

Jeb was quiet a moment, his eyes on her. Then he said, "I guess that makes you lucky, too.''

"I guess it does." She gave him a brittle smile, then nodded to Scott and Patrick and turned away to get herself ready for the night.

In spite of his promise, Jeb did not come to collect Patrick for a ride the next morning. The boy waited all day, finally giving up hope by late afternoon. He made no comment on his disappointment, but Kerry knew that it wasn't only the ride that he had looked forward to. He'd come to appreciate what he considered the man-to-man exchanges he'd had with Jeb. He'd been able to talk with the wagon master in a way that he never could with his own father. He'd learned from Jeb. Their daily discussions had covered such diverse topics as the terrain of the West, horses, hunting—things that a young boy could listen to for hours without tiring. If Jeb cut off their friendship at this point, Kerry thought, it would be a blow for Patrick.

She told herself that it was fine if he wanted nothing further to do with *her*. It was obvious that he was a cad and worse for introducing her to such sensual delights and then turning harsh and distant. She'd be far better off without him. She would concentrate on getting to California and realizing her goals. And she would not waste time regretting her encounter with Jeb Hunter. In fact, she did *not* regret it. Her brief experience with lovemaking had opened up feelings and sensations in her that she had never known existed. And in addition, it had taught her a valuable lesson—that loners like Jeb Hunter were better left to their loneliness. They were incapable of anything else.

She greeted Scott with more enthusiasm than ever before when he made his way once again back to their camp at supper time. Maybe Jeb was going to crush Patrick's hopes, but Scott would not. From the very first, he'd been attentive and friendly to the boy. At noon that day he'd brought over an armload of clothes for him. Her brother seemed to be growing into a man before her eyes. His voice had lowered and rarely squeaked these days. And he could hardly fit in his clothes. The previous evening Kerry had commented that if they didn't find a solution, Patrick would end up having to make the trip to California stark naked.

Her only reservation about the friendship was that Patrick was always a little too interested in Scott's gold mining stories. But she supposed that when they got to California, they'd go their separate ways and Patrick would forget about it.

Scott looked pleased at the warmth of her welcome, but made no move to take advantage of her change in attitude. He no longer tried to take her arm or make a personal remark with that charming smile of his. It was almost as if he'd decided to assume the role of a helpful and protective older brother, and Kerry found herself overwhelmed with a feeling a gratitude toward him.

They had a merry supper, relieved to be a full day's trail now away from the specter of sickness and death. After the meal, the Burnetts joined them, John carrying Molly in his arms. She was a little weak, but almost back to normal. It was impossible to believe that she'd been so close to slipping away only three nights ago.

After an agreeable hour of conversation, John took the twins back to put them to bed and Scott said goodnight as well. Patrick climbed up into their wagon, leaving Kerry to sit with Dorothy. The close call with her beloved child had left the usually spunky Southerner shaken. Kerry provided a sympathetic audience as she listened to her friend's hopes and dreams for her two daughters. For the first time, Kerry felt as if she could understand what it might be like to have a family, children of her own to love and plan for. Of course, that was not for her. She had a ranch to build. She had Patrick to care for.

And, besides, in order to have a family, she'd have to have a husband. She'd have to be in love. Jeb's face as it had looked when he'd been holding her flashed through her head. He hadn't come to their wagon—even for Patrick. She shivered. She still didn't know exactly what had happened between them. But it hadn't been love. That was for *darn* sure.

By the time another full day had gone by without so much as a sign of Jeb Hunter, Kerry was starting to get angry. Even disregarding the fact that a gentleman would have at least checked on her welfare after what they had done together, disregarding the fact that he'd promised Patrick to take him riding, he was their hired guide, and it was his business to check in with them on a regular basis.

"Where is he?" she demanded angrily the next night at supper.

Scott shrugged, but John Burnett, who'd come over to use their fire to heat a kettle of soup, answered, "I think he's been busy dealing with the water issue. He's insisting we have to bring our supply down from the hills, even for the animals. A lot of folks aren't too happy about it."

"Even after what happened to Molly and Hester Hamilton?" Kerry asked.

John shook his head. "People have short memories, evidently."

"Well, anyway, he should have been back here to keep us informed about what's going on."

"Frank Todd came around," Scott supplied. "He said Hunter has flat out prohibited drawing from the river until further notice."

Patrick was away paying a visit to the twins, so Kerry said, "He'd promised to take my brother riding with him. Patrick's been terribly disappointed that he hasn't come around."

"Well, why don't we take a couple of my mules and go for a ride ourselves?" Scott asked. "They're not as elegant as Hunter's stallion, but good enough for an evening outing."

Kerry's face brightened. "That would cheer him up."

John was disapproving. "Hey, you know the rules. We're not supposed to wander away from the train by ourselves."

"We wouldn't go far," Scott said. "Just enough to give Pat the feeling that he's had his daily ride."

"Let's do it," Kerry agreed. She turned to John. "If Captain Hunter should finally decide to show his face around here, please tell him that we've gone riding."

John looked grave. "I still don't think it's a good idea," he said, but by then Kerry was already running toward his wagon to fetch her brother.

"They've gone *where?*" Jeb asked.

"They took a couple of Haskell's mules. I don't think they're planning to be gone long." Frank's tone was placating.

Jeb sat on Storm and looked down at the earnest young settler in total disbelief. "The damn fools," he said finally.

"They said they'd be back before sunset."

"If the Pawnee don't find them first."

"The Pawnee?"

"We're smack in the middle of their hunting grounds."

John's broad forehead furrowed. "What should we do?"

"The same thing we've been doing for the expeditions to bring down water—get together a group of armed men. *Men*," he emphasized. "Not women and children."

"They've got Haskell with them."

"Great. And just how many guns did they take along?"

John shook his head.

Jeb looked out at the hills in the direction John had said the trio had traveled. "Damn fools," he said again under his breath.

Chapter Thirteen

Riding on the bristly back of Scott's mule was not as exhilarating as the run on Storm had been, but it was pleasant to get away from the train for a while. The dust didn't seem as thick, and the wind teased their nostrils with the gentle scent of the tall grasses around them.

When they'd ridden away, Kerry had kept watch over her shoulder, expecting to see an irate Jeb chasing them at any minute, but it appeared that no one had taken any notice of their leaving. The wagons receded slowly in the distance, and by the time they'd reached the first of the hills, she relaxed and forgot all about them.

She and Patrick were riding one mule and Scott another. Patrick had been ready to try an animal by himself, but Kerry had not been so sure, so he'd agreed to ride with her, as long as he could be in the front.

Scott had entertained them along the way with stories about mules from his blacksmithing days. The time passed quickly, and before they knew it they were at the top of the hill, looking out over the broad expanse of prairie. The river flowed out as far as they could see to the east and west, looking silver and majestic, not at all brackish and dangerous from this viewpoint.

"Too bad we can't just hop on a river and float all the way to California," Kerry said dreamily.

"Jumpin' Jehoshaphat, that would be wonderful," Patrick agreed.

His American speech was becoming more colorful from his association with the other boys on the train. But Kerry did not chide him. They were in the wild West now. She supposed Patrick could talk a little more wild if he chose.

"You'd have a tough time floating over the Rockies," Scott protested with a laugh.

Patrick refused to let his enthusiasm be dimmed. "It would be great, just the same."

"Look. Some riders are heading out from the train." Scott's voice grew sober.

Kerry squinted far across the prairie in the direction of the train. Riders? She had expected to see Jeb. In fact, if she examined her motives for accepting Scott's offer, she might even have had to admit that her agreeing to the ride had something to do with her pique over Jeb's inattention. But she hadn't expected an entire posse to fetch them back like some kind of horse thieves. It made their expedition suddenly seem like a greater transgression than she had imagined.

"We'd better ride down to meet them," she said.

Scott nodded. "I hope we haven't caused a problem. John was right. We probably should have at least told Hunter before we came out tonight."

Patrick caught the tone of his elders. "Will Jeb be angry with us?" he asked.

Kerry didn't answer, but Scott turned to the boy and winked at him. "He won't be angry with you, lad. If he has a problem, I reckon it'll be with me."

They rode down the hill without further comment. The men across the valley had evidently seen them, because they stopped. By now they could make out that the lead horse was Storm with Jeb riding him. They continued closing the distance between the two parties as they watched Jeb turn to the other men and send them back to camp. He came on alone, riding hard.

It was another ten minutes before they met. By then Kerry was thoroughly regretting their impulsive excursion.

Jeb's expression was harder than the granite from the hill they'd just left. He turned the brunt of his wrath on Scott.

"What in hell did you think you were doing, Haskell?" he shouted while their mounts were still several yards apart.

"We didn't go far," Scott said defensively. He, too, was obviously feeling remorse for their actions. "What are you getting so fired up about?"

Jeb reined in his horse and jumped to the ground, stalking toward them. He waved his hand toward Kerry and Patrick. "What am I fired up about? You ride off alone and unarmed into Pawnee territory. Would you like me to give you a graphic description of exactly what they might do to a young woman and a boy?"

When Scott remained silent, Kerry came to his defense. "It was partly your fault," she said.

"Partly *my* fault?"

She wouldn't let his badgering tone intimidate her. "Yes. We wanted to take Patrick for a ride after he's been waiting for you to come for him the past two days."

Jeb looked nonplussed for a moment, and when he spoke again, his tone had become a little less angry. "That's no excuse for taking a risk like you all just did."

"Obviously we didn't realize that it would be any risk," Scott said stiffly.

"Which is why *I* make the rules on this train and not you," Jeb shot back.

"Well, there was no real harm done." Kerry tried to soothe their feelings. "I'm sorry you felt you had to come look for us. We won't do this again."

"You're damn right you won't," Jeb agreed. He turned his angry eyes on her now instead of Scott, but after a couple of moments, they seemed to soften. "I suppose I should apologize for not stopping by your wagon. I've been up to my ears in problems."

The words sounded hollow even to Jeb. He *had* been dealing with a lot of problems, chief among them the water supply. But he could have made time to ride back to the Gallivan wagon for a few minutes. He could have taken Patrick with him for part of the day. He'd been avoiding it. He'd been avoiding *her*. He'd been an abject coward.

He looked at Patrick. "We'll ride tomorrow, partner. I promise. And now I want to ask you to do me a favor."

"What?" Patrick asked in a small voice, as though aware that he had been the cause of a lot of trouble.

"Can you ride that animal by yourself? Take it on back to camp?"

"Sure," the boy answered, sounding confused. "But what about Kerry?"

"I'll take your sister up on Storm with me. I want to talk with her in private for a few minutes."

Patrick twisted around on the mule's back and looked at Kerry. She gave him a nod of reassurance, then said, "Hold her still," while she slid off the mule's back.

"You don't have to go with him, Kerry," Scott said.

"It's all right. You and Patrick go on back to the wagons and we'll just bring up the rear."

She waited, standing on the ground while both Scott and Patrick gave her a last doubtful look, then kicked their mules to start them walking sedately back to camp. Kerry walked over to Jeb and reached a hand up, but instead of helping her to swing up behind him, he dismounted himself. "We'll just let Storm walk a spell," he said, then belatedly added, "that is, if you don't mind."

Kerry's insides felt shivery. It appeared that the conversation that she'd been both wanting and dreading to have with Jeb was finally going to take place. "What about the Indians?" she asked.

"We're close enough to camp here. I'm not worried."

Leading Storm behind him, he started in the direction of the camp and she fell into step beside him, waiting for him to speak first. It took him so long, the thought occurred to her that they might walk all the way back to camp before he decided to open his mouth. But finally he said, "This has been poorly done."

It wasn't exactly what she had expected to hear. "What has?" she asked, understanding his meaning more or less but wanting to make him state his case more clearly.

"All of this." He made a vague spiraling motion with his hand. "You and me. Patrick. Haskell…"

Now she was legitimately confused. "What's Scott got to do with anything?"

He gave her a sidelong look. "What do you think?"

Her embarrassment about the trouble they'd caused was fading and she was beginning to get irritated with him again. "I have no idea, Captain."

"I suppose you want me to believe that running off with Haskell tonight had nothing to do with the fact that I haven't come around to talk with you since…since we made love."

Kerry stopped in her tracks, forcing Jeb to do the same and making Storm halt so abruptly that he almost ran right into them. "I did *not* run off with Scott. What an absurd thing to say."

"Well, you *went* off with him."

"And with my *brother*. Does that sound like some kind of clandestine activity to you?"

Jeb took a closer hold on Storm's reins. When the big animal began snorting restlessly, he reached back automatically and rubbed its nose. "Why did you do it, then?"

Kerry shook her head in exasperation. "So that my

brother could go out riding—just like I said before. It had nothing to do with you, Jeb Hunter. I'm sorry if it's difficult for you to understand that the world doesn't revolve around you. Or around your precious rules for that matter.''

Jeb looked a little discomfited. "I should have stopped by to talk with Patrick and explain how busy I was today.''

"And yesterday.''

"And yesterday,'' Jeb agreed.

Her breathing calmed. "Well, we agree on that much, at least.''

"And I should have come by to talk with you. I tried the other night but you were eating with Haskell. I couldn't very well discuss things with him there.''

"Discuss what things?'' she asked, though she knew very well. Against her better judgment, she was already beginning to forgive him—for not coming to their wagon, for disappointing Patrick, for yelling at them tonight. He'd wanted to talk with her, he said. He'd tried. And now, tonight, he'd been *jealous.* Of *Scott.* It was unmistakable. And it made her heart soften dangerously.

He looked at her with an expression that was almost shy. "Would you like to, uh…'' He gestured to a small cluster of trees about fifty yards to the south of them. "Shall we go tie Storm up for a while and sit down?''

Across the prairie the wagons were lighting up like puffy white lanterns as the settlers lit oil lamps inside to prepare for bed. "Don't we need to get back?'' she asked, alarmed to notice that her throat had suddenly gone dry.

He shook his head. "They'll know we're here. They can probably see Storm from the camp." He took her hand then and led her toward the trees. "You're cold," he said as his big fingers closed around hers.

"No, I'm not," she said with a little shiver.

He stopped and walked back a step to pull a rolled-up blanket from the back of his saddle. "Here, put this around your shoulders."

They walked in silence to the group of trees. "I'm not really cold," she said more emphatically. "But we can sit on this if you like."

He nodded approval and she spread the blanket over the tall grass. It made a cushiony bed beneath her as she sank to her knees. Jeb tied Storm to a low hanging branch, then lowered himself beside her.

"So, here we are," he said, clearing his throat.

The domineering wagon master was nowhere in evidence. It made her feel more self-confident. "Yes," she said pleasantly.

"As I was saying…"

"You weren't saying much of anything, Captain," Kerry said with a touch of humor.

He rubbed a hand against his chin. "No, I reckon I wasn't." Then he turned to face her and said, "Would you mind calling me Jeb?"

His face was only inches from hers. "I wouldn't mind," she said, her voice growing softer.

"Good. Now I reckon what we have to get past here is the fact that we let ourselves get carried away the other night…."

"Is that what you call it?"

"Well, you know what I mean. We were both tired and overwrought from Molly's illness…"

Kerry's amusement faded. "Captain—Jeb, I most assuredly did not let you make love to me because I was tired and overwrought."

"Damn it," he said, striking his leg with his palm. "I'm trying to apologize, woman, and you keep interrupting me."

"Apologize? Is that what this is all about?"

He let out a deep breath. "That night, I didn't know you were…" He seemed to be struggling for the words. "I didn't know that you'd never done that kind of thing before."

"I guess you could have asked if you'd wanted to know."

He nodded. "I should have asked. Or rather, I had no business putting us both in such a position, no matter how much experience you might have had."

The features of his face were drawn taut with strain. All day long she'd been angry with him for his seeming indifference to what had passed between them. Now it appeared that he was anything but indifferent. In fact, he appeared to be suffering from a soul-searching far more painful than her own. She put a tentative hand on the sleeve of his buckskin shirt. "It wasn't that bad, Jeb," she said gently.

He groaned. "Your first time with a man and you have to say 'it wasn't that bad.' Lord, Kerry, it's not supposed to be bad at all. It's supposed to be wonderful—magical. It's the most intimate experience that a man and woman can share."

She gave a half smile. "Well, actually, it was rather nice—most of it anyway. I'm not angry about it."

"You should be. I'd feel better if you'd just slap me across the face and call me a bounder."

She didn't know whether to laugh or to offer him comfort. This remorseful side of him was harder to deal with than his arrogance. It set off tender feelings inside her that she didn't want to have—not for Jeb or any man. "I'll call you whatever you like, but I refuse to slap you. I'm sorry, but I don't believe in violence."

Her words brought a reluctant smile. "You're a forgiving woman, Kerry Gallivan," he said.

"And am I forgiven for our mule excursion?"

His eyes held hers. "Yes."

"And you won't make any more wild accusations about me running off with Scott?"

"Is he in love with you?"

"I hope not. I think he felt protective toward both me and Patrick, and that made him think he should make his offer of marriage. But what he really wants is to get to those gold fields."

"The lure of the mythical Golden Fleece."

Jeb's voice again had that tinge of bitterness. "You don't like prospectors very much, do you?"

Jeb hesitated a moment, then pushed back with his long legs to rest against the tree trunk behind them. "No," he said.

It was as if a shutter had closed across his face. Kerry had seen it happen before, but this time she wasn't going to let the matter go. "Why not?" she asked, turning around on her knees to face him.

He rolled his head against the bark of the tree, stretching his neck. The headache that had been pounding at him since John Burnett had told him that

Kerry had left camp was blessedly beginning to recede. In answer to her question, he said, "Because I know what blamed fools they are."

Kerry pursed her lips. "Well, there is gold, right? Why do you say they're fools?"

"From firsthand experience."

"You were a gold prospector?"

Jeb nodded. "I had the fever as bad as any of those young idiots."

"But you didn't strike it rich?"

He gave a contemptuous sniff. "Hardly. I couldn't even pan out enough to eat most days."

"Maybe you didn't keep trying long enough."

Jeb closed his eyes, his expression once again tightening. Kerry felt the breath stick in her chest as she realized that he was about to tell her something that would not come easy in the telling. She waited, and finally he opened his eyes and looked at her with an expression that sent a chill down the back of her neck. "I kept trying long enough to give a band of marauders time to rape and murder my wife."

The blood pounded in waves at Kerry's cheeks and she had the feeling that she might faint. She shifted from her knees to a more stable sitting position. "Lord have mercy," she breathed.

Jeb stared past her out at the dark night. "Yeah. Well, He didn't. No one had any mercy on my sweet Melanie. Starting with me."

Kerry searched for something comforting to say, but the enormity of his tragedy was so total that no words came. Finally she reached out and took his hands in hers. He hardly seemed to notice. Once he had established the worst, he seemed to have the need to tell the rest of the story. Reciting the tale with a voice that had grown curiously dead, he told her how he had left her as a young bride, in spite of her protests, in order to find his strike while the pickings were rich. Forty-niners were streaming into the territory daily, and the men who were there knew that they had to get their claims made before the gold was all gone. Gold fever had seized the minds of the young men of the territory like a disease. And Jeb Hunter had been another willing victim.

It had taken him a mere three months to realize that only a small, lucky percentage were ever going to realize the overblown dreams of wealth. Like thousands of others, he was hardly scraping enough to get by. But in the meantime, some of those others had formed themselves into bands of lawless thieves and plunderers. They'd decided if they couldn't mine the riches of California one way, they'd take what they wanted by thievery and violence. He'd left his wife alone in their small cabin in the foothills at the mercy of such men.

By the end of his story, tears were streaming down Kerry's cheeks. The terrible tale made it easier to understand the hardness that sometimes settled over his expression, the bleak look in his eyes. Jeb Hunter was living with two tragedies. The murder of his wife was only the first one. The second was his own, relentless, tormenting guilt.

Somewhere during the course of his recital, she'd moved closer to him, still holding his hands. He was clenching her fingers so tightly that they had gone numb, but she was sure that he wasn't even aware that he held them.

"You couldn't have known," she said after a long moment of silence. "How could anyone imagine something like that?"

"I took her as my bride and said the vows to protect and cherish her. Till death do us part," he added with a hollow, horrible sound that was half laugh and half sob.

She moved against him and drew his head against her shoulder. It wasn't sexual, only the normal human instinct of reaching out to another soul in pain. Not much different from the way she had comforted Dorothy the other night at Molly's bedside. But after a few minutes, in spite of herself, she realized that her breasts had hardened against his warm body. He realized it, too.

He straightened back up against the tree and pulled her across his lap, seeking her mouth with his. She couldn't heal the gaping wound of grief that still bled inside his heart, but she could make him forget the pain, at least for a while. She could make him lose himself in the sensations he had taught her the other night. She wanted to do that for him...and for herself.

Jeb's reason was slowly returning just as his body began spinning out of control. He was once again aware of surroundings. He knew it was Kerry he held in his arms, not Melanie. He'd never hold Melanie again. It was sweet, lush Kerry with tears on her cheeks that she'd shed for him. Precious drops that seemed to be falling on a dusty, dry spot inside him that had lain fallow for years.

He kissed her with gratitude and longing that turned almost immediately to intense desire. He knew somewhere in the sensible, reasonable part of his brain that he should not let this happen again. But his heart and his senses were not willing to listen. He overruled himself with the simple argument that he owed it to her to make up for the other night when he'd taken her virginity so abruptly.

He forced himself to breathe deeply. He would stay under control, he vowed. He would show her what it was like to be thoroughly and properly loved. He would make her body sing.

He laid her down on the grass and started by covering her face with soft, gentle kisses. And when her eyes drifted closed, he opened her shirt and started to lavish the same attention on her breasts. "Look at me, sweetheart," he said then, lifting his head. She opened her eyes to look straight into his so that he could watch them change and grow wider as his fingers gently tugged her nipples and then drifted down beneath the waistband of her brother's trousers to find the dewy area below. He could tell from her still open eyes when he touched the right spot.

His slow, erotic exploration was sending waves of sensation radiating up her body. She wriggled a little beneath his hand and pushed against him, all of her being seemed to be focused in that one region and in the tawny depths of his eyes. Desperately, she tugged at her trousers and pushed them down her hips to give him freer access. He pulled back long enough to help her slide them off.

"Relax, sweetheart. Just lie back and feel." And then she was totally naked on the rough wool blanket and he was kissing her from her toes to her neck and back down. His fingers were inside her again, stretching just slightly, and suddenly his mouth was there above the fingers, finding her, rolling that particularly sensitive place with his warm tongue. And she grabbed the blanket with her fists and gave a keening cry as her body exploded.

He held her, rocked her with an amused, "Shush, sweetheart. They'll hear you all the way back to Fort Kearney." Then after he had kissed the new tears on her cheek, tears of passion this time, he rid himself of his own clothing and lay back down beside her.

"That's how it should be, how it should have been the first time—you, sweet and melting in my arms," he told her.

His voice was thick and sensual in her ear. Kerry was already feeling the need building inside her again, even as the meadow breeze cooled the first flush from her body. Unlike their hurried experience of the other night, he was entirely naked against her, his body hard, his skin rougher than her own. With curiosity and daring, she reached out a hand to explore him. It only seemed fair. He'd already visited every part of her. Parts she hadn't even been aware of herself, she thought with a smile.

"What are you purring about, kitten?" he asked her with an answering smile of his own.

"Happy kittens purr, I believe," she said.

"Did I make you happy, sweetheart?" he asked more seriously.

"Mmm. That's a small word for such a big feeling."

He kissed the tip of her nose. "I'm glad. That's what I wanted to do."

Her hand arrived at his stomach, which was flat and covered with silky hair. He gave a moan of pleasure and encouragement. "Are you purring, too, Jeb?" she asked archly.

He put his hand on top of hers where it had halted its progress and moved it gently downward to his erection. "Men don't purr," he protested, but as her slender fingers closed around him he gave another half groan.

"Sounds like purring to me." She moved her hand on him in a motion she'd never been taught but that seemed to come to her naturally. As he swelled to her touch, she felt the answering response inside her own body. "But it's fierce purring," she continued, whispering in his ear, "like a tiger."

He gave a growl much like the feline she'd described and rolled over with her, flattening her on the ground and spreading her legs with his own. Hurriedly his hands checked to see that she was still moist and receptive, then he entered her with a deep breath of satisfaction.

There wasn't the least pain this time, only an exquisite sense of fullness, then a more urgent one of building passion that soon had her meeting his rhythm with a rocking motion of her hips. He kissed each breast until the nipples were wet, then picked up the pace of his motion and once again brought his face just above hers. "Open your eyes, sweetheart. Watch mine while I take you over the edge."

She opened her eyes and then seemed to see herself spiraling into his as he stopped deep within her and the feeling began to rack her. At the very height he pulled away from her and she clutched at him, mur-

muring a protest. But he was gone, leaving her with a feeling of emptiness. "I'm sorry, sweetheart," he said, his voice tight and breathless as he ended his own release.

Chapter Fourteen

She lay limp beneath him, thoroughly sated. Her body felt lavish and miraculous. What a feeling. No wonder people fought wars for love, she thought hazily. No wonder men and women did all kinds of foolish things in the name of romance.

Only the end had been a little disappointing when he had left her so suddenly. Was the pleasure still as great for him? she wondered. Was he able to experience the same kind of completion she did?

He seemed to be as satisfied and exhausted as she. He pulled her into his arms and rolled the blanket up around them.

"Let's hope no one else got the idea to take an evening ride," he said with a tired smile.

She chuckled. "I just hope that Scott and Patrick didn't decide to turn back and look for us."

Jeb's smile faded. "I can't believe I've let this happen again. I should be horsewhipped."

Kerry pulled her head away to look into his face. "You said something like that about the first time we were together. Hasn't it occurred to you that perhaps I'm the one who's allowing it to happen, not you?''

"It's the man's responsibility..."

"Hogwash. Not everything important in life is the man's responsibility, Jeb. Some things are shared propositions. And I would think that what we did together would most definitely be one of those things."

She laid her head back down against his arm. "I thought it was beautiful."

Jeb gave her a squeeze and said gently, "I thought it was beautiful, too."

"So that settles that." They lay quietly for some moments, each lost in thought. Kerry was trying to figure out what this whole new side of herself meant for her future, for the future she planned with Patrick. She wasn't about to give up on her father's dream, but for the first time she began to consider that she might be willing to share that dream with someone else—with Jeb. He'd evidently planned to settle down to his own place with his wife before her horrible death, perhaps after all these years of wandering he'd be ready to give the idea a try again.

If she was already carrying his child, he'd have no choice. The notion gave her mixed emotions. It didn't horrify her as it had when she had first thought about the possibility. It would be hard to build a ranch if she were pregnant, but it could be done, especially if she had a husband helping her. Of course, she'd prefer that she and Jeb didn't have to start out their lives together under those circumstances. Again she wondered about the actual mechanics of the matter. It was one of the many times when she missed not having had the counsel of a mother. Well, there was only one way to find out what she needed to know.

"Jeb," she began tentatively.

"What is it, sweetheart?" He sounded almost asleep.

"There at the end...you were, you know, *gone* all of a sudden. Was that..." She took a deep breath and made herself say the words. "Does that mean we didn't make a baby?"

Jeb boosted himself up on an elbow and looked down at her. "Didn't you know what I was doing?"

She shook her head, embarrassed.

He let a long breath stream through his nose. "If I stay inside you when I...finish, then, yes, there's a possibility we could make a baby. That's why I pulled away."

"Thank you," she said with a soft smile. "I don't think we should make a baby just yet either."

Jeb's hand, on his way to smooth back her ruffled hair, froze. Just yet? What was she thinking? He thought back over their encounters trying to decide if there had been a time when he'd led her to believe that he could be committed to her for any kind of future. He'd made love to her. He supposed that in itself was a statement of commitment to a girl like Kerry. But he'd never said it in words, of that he was certain. Those were words he never intended to say again in his life. He'd said them once and failed so miserably that he deserved to live with the sound of them ringing hollowly in his ears for the rest of his life.

"I was deliberately careful, Kerry," he said slowly. "It was wrong of me to make love to you, but it would have been despicable for me to leave you with a child growing inside you.''

The wind had picked up and flapped the ends of the blanket around them. Kerry shivered and felt a sudden cold that went deeper than her exposed skin. "Leave me with a child?" she asked. "Isn't it customary when people...make babies, to raise them together?"

Jeb moved his arm from beneath her back and lifted her to a sitting position against the tree. Then he started to pull on his clothes. "That's why I was careful that we didn't make a baby, Kerry.'' His voice sent the chill even deeper, all the way to her core. "That kind of a life is not for me.''

"You must have wanted that life once.''

He shook his head. "Yes. If I'd only been content to stay with my wife and build that life, I'd be a different person now. But I wasn't, and now I've lost the right to even think about such an existence.''

Kerry pulled the blanket tightly around her shoulders. "I don't believe that, Jeb. No man should forever lose his chance for happiness because of one mistake.''

He'd finished dressing and the expression he turned on her was almost angry. "It wasn't just a 'mistake,' Kerry. I was responsible for the brutal murder of a helpless young woman who trusted me to protect her and provide for her....''

Something clicked inside Kerry's head. "Helpless?" she said. "Maybe she was helpless against the band of scum who killed her, but surely she wasn't helpless. A pioneer woman?"

"A *woman*,'' Jeb corrected. "Just like any woman

who should have the protection of a man in order to survive in this country. Just like you, Kerry, though you think yourself so invincible. The same thing could happen to you as happened to Melly. And who would protect you? A thirteen-year-old boy?''

"I'd protect myself. Just the way I intend to build my ranch *myself*. Just as I've come this far by myself."

"By making moves such as the stunt you pulled tonight, which might have ended up getting you and your brother both killed."

They were both on their knees now, facing each other, all tenderness gone from their voices and their expressions. "I've already apologized for that, Captain," she said frostily. "And if you would be so kind as to hand me my clothes, I'll let you get back to the train where you can be the masterly protector of all the poor women and children, assuaging your guilt as much as you like."

"What's that supposed to mean?" he asked angrily, tossing her clothes into her lap.

Her own anger died as quickly as it had arisen, and she spoke sadly. "There's nothing noble about spending a life wallowing in the past, Jeb, no matter why you think you're doing it. I'm sure that your Melanie was a staunch woman if she was willing to start a home in the wilderness. And I'm equally sure she would not want the circumstances of her death to mean that you should forfeit the rest of your life as a penance."

Jeb was silent as Kerry quickly put on her clothes. When she was finished, he said simply, "We'd better get back."

She nodded and waited for him to mount Storm and pull her up behind him. She put her arms gingerly around his waist but tried to keep her own body as far as she could from his as they trotted back to the camp without another word.

Patrick and Scott were both waiting, looking out into the night for them as they rode up. Scott started to ask why they had taken so long to return, but evidently thought better of the question after one look at their tense faces.

Jeb pulled his horse up beside the wagon. He turned around to her and held out a hand to lift her to the ground. Out of earshot of Patrick and Scott he murmured, "I'm sorry."

She looked him in the eyes, then glanced at his extended hand. Ignoring it, she grasped the back of the saddle and boosted herself to the ground. "I'm sorry, too," she said tersely, then walked around the back of the wagon and out of sight.

As he had promised, Jeb showed up early the next morning to take Patrick up on the horse with him. He was still having problems with a group of settlers who didn't want to follow his water-rationing plan. It did not help matters that Foxy Whitcomb and Daniel Blue were scoffing at the wagon master's fears about drinking from the river.

"I've drunk every kind of water from here to the coast," Foxy boasted. "Including those Satan's holes John Colter discovered northwest of here. Never been sick a day in my life."

But it wouldn't make much difference to his problems to have the boy ride along. He'd already disappointed one member of the Gallivan family. He could at least make things up to her brother.

It lifted his spirits to see Patrick's smile of welcome, and it felt good to have his company. Jeb tried to put thoughts of Kerry out of his mind as he concentrated on the daily duties of keeping the train moving west. In spite of the sickness and the water problems, they were still making good time. They would reach Independence Rock in another couple weeks. Each crossing he felt that if he could get his group there with good spirits, the hardest part of the job had been done. The mountain passes still lay ahead. But no matter how arduous the physical labor of those climbs, it did not take the same kind of mental toll on the group as the prairie and desert.

Kerry's "good morning" had been barely civil when he picked up her brother. He'd looked up into her eyes, those same blue eyes he'd watched glow with passion the previous night. And there'd been a knife twist at his gut such as he hadn't felt since shortly after Melly's death.

"I'll bring him back when we stop for the nooning," he'd told her. She'd nodded without speaking.

As it turned out, the nooning that day was the most turbulent they'd had since the train left Westport. He and Patrick had ridden up to the Crandall wagon to find a group of settlers crowding around Foxy and Daniel. The two old-timers were mixing cornmeal into a kettle of dirty river water. When the meal settled to the bottom, so would the mud and so, Foxy announced loudly to the group, would the evil spirits.

"The Injuns do it this way," Foxy told the group of mostly male settlers. "They never get sick."

In fact, the resultant water at the top of the kettle looked remarkably clear, nothing at all like the greenish sludge that was flowing along the river. Several of the men brought cups to scoop some out and take a sample.

"Fresh as spring water," Thomas Crandall said approvingly.

His son, Homer, who was only now recovering from the effects of the dysentery that had struck him, stood by his father's side and viewed the water doubtfully. "The captain said we shouldn't be drinking it yet. Not till we get farther up toward the mountains."

"Well, the captain doesn't have a whole family to haul a supply to every day," Crandall replied. "I don't see why we should be getting up before dawn to ride out to some creek when we've got a perfectly good river right alongside our wagons."

Several of the other men murmured agreement.

"That boy next to you is the reason, Crandall," Jeb said sternly as he rode up to the group. "You almost lost him, and now you're risking losing someone else in the family or killing yourself." He swung down from his horse and walked over to knock the cup out of Crandall's hand. "Don't be a blasted fool," he ended angrily.

Crandall looked almost as if he was going to take a swing at the wagon master, but he held back. His face had gone white with anger. "I reckon Whitcomb and Blue, here, have taken this route a sight more times than you have, Hunter. If they say it's all right to clean up the water this way, then it's all right by me."

"Well, then, it's lucky that you're not the one running things around here, because you could kill us all. I say that no one drinks from the river until further notice, and if I see anyone disobeying my orders, they'll be off this train the minute we reach Fort Laramie."

He took the kettle from Foxy and emptied the contents on the ground, then remounted Storm. "There are plenty of streams in the hills we're passing through. There's no point in taking needless risks. I'm not going to lose another one of my charges."

He rode off, leaving the milling crowd looking after him, several with looks of dissatisfaction on their faces.

"These young whippersnappers always were too quick to see a problem," Foxy said.

"I think Hunter just likes the feeling of ordering people around," Crandall added. "Maybe it's time he got reminded that *we're* the ones who hired *him.*"

The trouble continued that evening when Jeb called a camp meeting to organize teams of lookouts for the night and advance and rear guards for the next few days' travel.

"We're at the heart of Sioux country now," he told the gathering. "And they haven't been friendly these past couple of years."

From the back of the group Foxy drawled, "Ain't a Sioux within a week-long goose flight of here."

Jeb had kept himself awake much of the previous evening with tortured thoughts of Kerry, at turns remorseful and erotic. He'd ridden hard all day and had had several disagreeable encounters about the water problem. He was not in a humor for any more of Foxy's folk wisdom.

"Have you been up flying like a goose, Whitcomb, to be able to make a statement like that?" he asked sharply.

Foxy got to his feet and came slowly toward the front of the crowd. The majority of eyes were on him and he preened a little at the attention. "How many buffalo have you seen in these parts? None, right? The Sioux have followed the buffalo up north."

"The numbers are thinning," Jeb acknowledged. "That's precisely the problem. The Indians can't survive without them, and they're none too happy about the streams of white folk coming into their territory and decimating their herds."

"They're well north of here," Foxy insisted.

Jeb shook his head in exasperation. He waved a hand around the crowd. "You may be willing to risk the lives of all these folks on that assumption, but I'm not. We'll post lookouts and we'll ride guards. That's the way it's going to be."

As he looked around the group he was distressed to see the number of skeptical expressions. When they'd started out on this journey, they'd taken anything he had to say as gospel. But he knew that this stretch was in many ways the most demoralizing part of the journey. They'd been on the move now for nearly two and a half months, through endless, boring, dry, hot prairie. It was the time when every overlander started to feel as if the journey would never end. The fresh food was long gone. They were sick of insects, sick of dust seeping into every seam of their clothing and every possession. Many had developed chronic coughs, yet still had to get back on the trail each day to breathe in several more hours of it.

Once they reached the Rockies, attitudes changed. Remarkably, everyone felt new energy to tackle the obstacles ahead. The goal was finally in sight. On the other side of those mountains was the promised land. It was not to say that the arduous passage over them would be easy. But morale at that point usually soared, at least for a while. And if things went right, it stayed that way until they reached the coast.

Jeb knew all this, and usually he worked hard to keep his own temper even and pleasant during these last tedious days of prairie. But he'd never had a crossing quite like this one. He'd never before found himself so distracted by one of his emigrants that at times he'd totally forget his responsibilities, by one who'd so fired his blood that he tossed at night with restless dreams.

"Frank has some paper," he said wearily. "I'd like every man over eighteen to check in with him and sign up for a watch."

Out of the corner of his eye he saw Kerry looking up at him with something like sympathy in her gaze. He had a fleeting memory of when she'd comforted him by drawing his head into her arms last night. He hadn't deserved the comfort, but it had felt good. Too good. For the sake of the train and for the sake of his own soul, he'd have to be damn sure that he never gave himself the opportunity to take advantage of it again.

Jeb looked exhausted, and when Kerry listened to him outlining the details of the extra safety measures he wanted to put in place, she got a sense for the first time of exactly how much did weigh on those broad shoulders of his. It wasn't only the burden of his wife's death that Jeb was carrying, she realized. He carried the burden of every single settler he took across the country each season. What a fitting atonement for his supposed crime—the crime of having the same foolish aspirations that thousands of other young men were having at the height of the gold fever.

It made her sad to think about. Sad for Jeb and for herself. When she closed her eyes she could still feel the ecstasy he had brought to her body. When she opened them, she could look into his face and feel a special warmth that was nothing like she'd ever felt. She'd loved her father and she loved Patrick. But Jeb seemed to have worked his way inside a little place in her heart that she hadn't known existed.

It didn't matter. For them to have a life together, he'd have to be free of his demons. And he didn't want to be free of them. They were the link that kept the memory of Melanie alive in his heart. It didn't matter that it was a destructive, painful link. It kept her there. And Kerry didn't think that he would ever be willing to break it and let her go.

After the meeting she and Patrick wandered slowly back to their wagon with Scott. Scott was so open and uncomplicated. It would have made much more sense if he had been the one who had unlocked that special door in her heart. But, as she had said to herself many times since her father had died just on the verge of realizing his greatest dream, life didn't make sense. It simply didn't.

"There's talk of a mutiny," Scott said when they were out of earshot of the other settlers.

"What on earth do you mean?" Kerry asked.

"Against Hunter. People are getting sick of his high-handed ways."

"That's the most ridiculous thing I've ever heard of."

"You yourself said he was high-handed, if I recall," Scott pointed out.

"He's the wagon master, isn't he? I guess he wouldn't be worth his salt if he didn't know how to use some authority now and then."

"He's not high-handed with me," Patrick contributed. "I like him."

Scott didn't look pleased with his comment.

"Well, I certainly hope that people will come to their senses and stop talking nonsense. That's not what we need when we're about to enter a dangerous portion of the trail."

"If it *is* dangerous," Scott added.

"Well, Jeb says it is. I believe him."

"Jeb, is it?" Scott gave her a sideways look.

Kerry flushed. "We hired him to lead us and I think we ought to let him do his job."

"I don't know. Some folks are saying that Foxy and Daniel would be better scouts for us." They'd reached Scott's wagon and he stopped, evidently not intending to accompany them back to their own.

"I can't believe anyone would be foolish enough to think that. Why, those two have more tall tales than a shipload of sailors."

Scott squinted to see her face in the moonlight. "What is it with you and Hunter?" he asked.

"You've changed your mind about him since the beginning of this trip."

"I've just seen that he's efficient and knows what he's talking about. And it's obvious that he cares about everyone on the train."

"Some more than others, I'd wager."

Kerry did not try to refute Scott's implication. The way Jeb was ignoring her, there was no way anyone could accuse him of harboring special feelings for her. "He's been right about everything so far. He was right about the weight of our wagon and evidently about the bad water. No one else has gotten sick since we stopped drinking it."

"That could be coincidence. Are you saying he was right when he tried to keep you off the train, too?"

Kerry sighed. Patrick had continued on to their wagon so she and Scott were alone. "I'm not saying that you have to like him, Scott. But it's going to hurt the whole train if people begin to divide into factions. You know what Jeb has stressed from the beginning—we all need to work together."

"We may just decide that what we need to do is work together without our current wagon master," Scott argued.

"I hope not. Because I want to get to California. I think you do, too. And I'm convinced that the person who's going to get us there is Jeb Hunter."

By the next day, almost everyone on the train knew of the whispers against the captain. After Jeb came by for Patrick, greeting her only with a nod, Kerry spent the rest of the morning wondering if he was aware of the degree of dissatisfaction among his charges. She should talk with him, she thought, but she was afraid that any kind of private conversation would be impossible after the way their last encounter had ended. She was sure that Jeb Hunter would be happier if he never had to set eyes on her again. And whereas she didn't try to convince herself that she'd stopped caring for the difficult captain, she knew that the best thing for her would be for this trip to be over with quickly so that she would never have to see him again. She could put her heart and her energies into building her father's ranch.

The hot sun overhead meant that soon they would be stopping for lunch. Dorothy walked up beside the Gallivan wagon to ask Kerry if she was aware of the mutinous talk. At Kerry's nod, she exploded. "It's the men again—that Thomas Crandall and that old fool mountain man, Foxy." A paroxysm of coughing stopped her tirade.

"Walk farther out from the wagon, away from the dust, Dorothy," Kerry suggested. "I can still hear you." When her friend moved away, she continued, "What do you think we should do?"

"Why don't you talk to Captain Hunter?" Dorothy suggested. "You know him better than anyone."

Kerry shifted her eyes to the oxen in front of her. "I don't think he'd want to listen to me."

Dorothy put a hand up to shield her eyes from the sun as she looked up at Kerry. "Are you two having a lover's squabble?" she asked.

Kerry bit her lip. She hoped Dorothy's words were a figure of speech. She'd hate to think that her friend or anyone else on the train knew that she and Jeb had become lovers. It was humiliating enough that *she* knew how thoroughly he had rejected her. "We're just not getting along that well at the moment."

"A lover's squabble," Dorothy confirmed with a nod of her head. "Don't worry. You'll work it out. That is if these hotheads don't have their way and replace him."

"It wouldn't really come to that, would it?"

The wagons were slowing to a halt as the lead wagon stopped for the noon break at Jeb's instructions. "I don't know," Dorothy said, sounding worried. "If you don't want to talk with him about it, maybe we should both go now and see what Eulalie has to say."

Kerry felt a surge of relief. Soft-spoken, strong, kind Eulalie would know what to do.

"I think you should talk to him, Kerry," Eulalie suggested. "I believe he's developed a fondness for you."

"Aha! What did I tell you?" Dorothy clapped her hands together in delight to hear her suspicions shared by the older woman.

Kerry felt the sweat beading on her upper lip, and realized that it wasn't only from the intense heat of the noon sun. It appeared that there was no help for it. She'd have to confront Jeb. They would both have to move beyond their own personal discomfort with each other and think about the good of the train. "What should I say to him?"

"Just warn him. Let him know how people are talking." Eulalie urged.

"Wouldn't it be better from Frank? After all, he's supposed to be the people's representative."

"Frank's so angry with everyone that he can't even see the thing straight. He says he won't dignify all this blamed fool talk by bothering the captain about it."

"So it's up to me?" Kerry felt the beginnings of that now familiar weakness in her stomach.

"Go to him, Kerry," Dorothy said gently. "Ask him what he'd like us to do to stop this nonsense."

"I'll give it a try." She looked at the hopeful faces of her two friends. "But I have to tell you that there's a possibility that Jeb Hunter won't want to hear a word that I have to say."

Chapter Fifteen

She would have preferred to get the meeting over with, but Jeb had kept the nooning short, as was his custom lately while they were traveling through what he called the heart of the Indian country. He'd been pushing to cover a few extra miles for several days now, which merely added to the grumbling among the emigrants. The short noon breaks, the long days, the extra patrols—all of it seemed unnecessary when they continued to go mile after mile without any evidence of the presence of even friendly Indians, much less hostile ones.

Kerry had had to climb back up on her wagon as the line began to roll again, and Patrick had joined her with the news that he wouldn't be riding with Jeb that afternoon as the wagon master would be doing some scouting out ahead of the train.

So she'd had a full afternoon to contemplate their encounter, and by the time evening came, she'd decided that she was overreacting to what was really a very simple task. She and Jeb had made love. There was nothing that could be done to change that. But they were two adults, and they could certainly move beyond their personal difficulties to deal dispassionately with the situation at hand. She wouldn't even bring up their last private meeting. She wouldn't even think about it, she resolved, as she put away the supper dishes and prepared to walk to the Todds' wagon to find him.

"Eulalie said you wanted to speak with me."

His voice made her drop the tin plate she was holding. It fell to the ground with a clatter and rolled toward Jeb. He leaned over to pick it up and asked with a twisted smile, "Throwing dishes at me already?"

Her hand fluttered at her throat. This was not the calm and collected way she had wanted to greet him. "You startled me," she explained unnecessarily.

His half smile stayed in place. "I'm sorry. But then, you must be getting tired of my apologies by now. I should probably stop making them."

She took the plate from his hand and put it back in the provision box, slamming the cover. "There's no need for apologies. You've done nothing to offend me."

"Except take your virginity while you were under the false impression that I was doing so with the idea of marrying you."

Kerry looked around, checking to be sure that Patrick was not within earshot. Jeb was being careless bringing up the subject here where anyone might come along to hear them. She sensed an anger simmering beneath the surface of his bland expression that made him uncharacteristically blunt and heedless.

"Is something wrong?" she asked.

"What could be wrong? I'm leading a group of wagons through the most dangerous part of the Overland Trail. It's possible we're being watched by a Sioux war party this very minute. We have no water to drink. And now I find that my settlers have decided that it's no longer important for them to follow my orders. To top it off, I've thrown away every principle I ever had to commit a total breach of trust and perhaps ruin the life of one of the women on my train."

"That would be me?" Kerry asked.

"That would be you," he confirmed. The anger now showed clearly on his face, and once again Kerry realized that it was directed almost entirely toward himself.

She decided to leave the personal issue alone for the moment and stick with the problem of the dissatisfied members of the train. "So you know about the grumbling among the settlers?"

Jeb nodded. "Frank's filled me in. Plus most of the disgruntled members have not been too particular about keeping their feelings a secret."

"Well, I want you to know not everyone feels like that."

Jeb's expression lightened for a moment. "Thank you," he said. "You have more reason to dislike me than anyone."

"I don't think anyone dislikes you, Jeb, though sometimes you do seem a little...hard. You could make more of an effort to be friendly, to joke with people."

"I'm not exactly a funny guy, Kerry."

"I don't mean that. We need a leader, not an entertainer."

"They should just let me lead then, and stop complaining."

"Yes, you're right. I don't know what's the matter with some of these people."

Jeb turned and went over to crouch down next to their dwindling campfire. Absently, he began building it up again with the wood that was stacked next to it. Kerry had been going to let it die for the night now that supper was finished, but she sensed that he needed something to do, so she didn't comment. After a few moments, he said in a dispirited voice, "I know what's the matter with them. It happens every trip about this time. The prairie madness, we call it. Everyone goes a little crazy. But crazy people can be dangerous, and it's my job to protect them from their own foolishness."

"What are you going to do?" She walked over and went down on her knees next to him by the fire.

"Well, for one thing, I'm going to tell Whitcomb and Blue to take their beaver traps and skedaddle. I don't need them undermining every word I say."

"They seemed like such agreeable old gents."

"Oh, I think they are. It's just that they're mountain men. They have their own way of looking at life. Climb one taller mountain, kill one bigger bear and, most important, always have one better story than the next guy."

Kerry sat back, crossing her legs to keep them out of the way of the fire. She was pleased that Jeb was talking with her in this way, opening up a little. He seemed to carry so much bottled up inside him. "Do you think they're the ones causing the problems, then?" she asked.

Jeb moved to a sitting position beside her. "No, not particularly. I'm sure they have no idea of the damage they could be doing to these people. They're loners. They go where they please, when they please—camp when they're tired, knowing that they can always live off the land if their supplies run out. They've never had the responsibility for getting fifty wagons full of women and children across half a continent."

"Like you do."

"Yes, like I do." He rubbed the bridge of his nose and then his forehead.

"Does your head hurt?"

He nodded. "It's something I live with. My headaches seem to take pleasure in coming on just when everything else is going haywire."

"Don't you have powders or something?"

"No. I just live with it."

Men, Kerry thought with exasperation. Her father had been the same way, never wanting to admit that anything could be wrong with him. She'd thought more than once that it was probable that he'd felt pain in his heart before the attack that killed him and had just never said anything to them about it. But as she watched Jeb continue to rub his forehead with two tanned fingers, she realized that Jeb's reaction to his headache went beyond typical male ego. It was almost as if he welcomed the pain. Another piece of his penance.

She jumped to her feet and went back to the wagon to rummage in a pack that included medicinal supplies from the Boone store. She found one of the headache powders and mixed it in a cup with some of the fresh water that the men of the water brigade had brought to each wagon.

"Drink this," she said, returning to the fire and handing it to him.

He looked at the cup as if it were poison.

"It's spring water," she assured him. "I'm not disobeying your orders about the river."

"You seem to be the exception, then," he said, gulping the drink down in three big swallows. "This tastes awful," he added, making a rasping sound with his throat.

Kerry laughed. "Don't be a baby. Just finish your medicine like a good boy."

"I finished it." He handed the cup back to her, then added grudgingly, "Thank you."

The whole exchange made Kerry feel tender and a little sad. Jeb Hunter was so set on protecting and taking care of his flock. But who took care of him? He didn't seem to think that he deserved to be cared for.

"Would you like a cold cloth?" She asked. Without thinking, she leaned toward him and pressed her cool fingers against his forehead. He gave a murmur of approval as he tipped back his head and closed his eyes.

"That feels better than a cold cloth," he said softly.

Her fingers soon took on the heat of his skin so she exchanged them for the fingers of her left hand, and let her right move to his temple to make gentle circles. "A cloth would be cooler," she said.

"You smell good. Lavender or something."

Kerry knelt beside him, continuing her gentle massage. "My soap. It only takes up a little space," she added quickly.

Jeb opened his eyes. The anger was entirely gone from them and much of the pain. He regarded her with gentle amusement. "I'm not going to tell you to leave your soap behind, Kerry. I'm not that much of an ogre. Especially not when it makes you smell like an English garden."

She blushed. "An Irish garden, you'd better say. Papa said the same thing when he gave it to me. He said my mother always used it."

Slowly he reached his hands up and pulled hers away from his head. "I think that had better be enough."

"Are you feeling better?"

He gave a rueful chuckle. "My *head* is."

Kerry sat back on her haunches. His meaning was obvious. "Should I be the one to apologize now?" she asked.

He studied her in the firelight. "Apologize for making my blood race every time I get near you? I hardly think it's anything you can help, sweetheart. It's just something I'm going to have to learn to live with over these next few weeks."

"Until you can be rid of me."

"Well, yes, to be blunt. Until I can see you safely to your destination, which is what you and all these people hired me to do. And which is what I'm going to do, whether they want me to or not."

His voice became stronger as they moved back to a topic that was safer than the more personal ones. Kerry let her hands drop back into her lap. At the moment, Jeb was right, the welfare of the train was more important than any feelings between the two of them. Whether they would be able to keep that resolve through the weeks they still had of traveling closely together was another question.

"The Todds, the Burnetts, Samuel Hamilton and several of the others are on your side. We are, too, of course," she told him.

"What about your friend Haskell?"

Kerry hesitated. "I think Scott has enough sense to do the right thing in the end. He doesn't like you much, though," she admitted.

"I wonder why," Jeb said dryly.

Kerry shrugged. If he didn't want to deal with his own feelings for her, she wasn't about to discuss Scott's. "Is there something you want us to do—to persuade the others?"

Jeb leaned back on his hands. "If they would just hang on for a few more days, we'll be starting to go up in elevation and we'll hit the Sweetwater River, where we'll have as much fresh water as we need without leaving camp."

"You have to tell them that, Jeb."

"They don't even want to listen to me anymore. They're too busy listening to Foxy's boasting."

"We'll just have to make them listen, then," Kerry said firmly.

Jeb sat watching her with a look of admiration. "You don't give up, woman, do you?"

"That shouldn't surprise you. There are a lot of women on this train who don't give up. You found that out for yourself back in Fort Kearney."

Jeb rubbed his chin. "Yes, I did."

"You might want to remember that every now and

then. Men might have the brawn to go out and wrestle with this West of yours, but women can have something even more important—the will.''

His eyes darkened in memory. ''Having a strong will doesn't always save you from disaster.''

''Brawn doesn't either.''

Jeb fell silent. The rare times that he wanted to give himself a little break from his guilt, he'd admitted deep down that if he'd been at his cabin with Melly when the renegades came, there would probably have been little he could do against them. Most likely he would have died alongside her. Kerry was right. Sometimes neither physical nor mental strength could prevent evil things from happening.

''You're quite a woman, Kerry Gallivan,'' he said finally. Then on a sudden impulse that overruled his best resolutions, he leaned over and kissed her. It was meant to be a kiss of gratitude for her support, but the moment their lips touched, it blazed into something more. Once again, the heat between them was instantaneous and devastating, blotting every sane thought from his mind.

He reached for her, his hands finding her slender arms and then cupping themselves around her neck to hold her steady as his lips and tongue plundered her mouth.

''I'm sorry to have to interrupt.'' Scott's voice was harsher than Kerry had ever heard it before. And beneath the harshness was something else that had her sitting up straight in alarm.

Jeb rolled to his feet. ''What's on your mind, Haskell?'' His tone was not friendly.

''One of my mules is missing...''

"Did you tether them securely...?" Jeb interrupted, but Scott continued angrily.

"One of my mules is missing and so are Patrick and the twins."

Kerry's face went white. "Patrick was just here for supper a few minutes ago."

Scott looked from her to Jeb, his face stony. "More than a few minutes, I'd say. It appears that you may have lost track of time."

Kerry ignored his accusing tone. "Why do you say they're missing?"

"Dorothy and John say Patrick took the girls right after supper, over an hour ago. They've searched up and down the train and can't find a trace of them."

"Patrick wouldn't go off by himself. He knew how upset Jeb was the other night when the three of us went out."

"Did either of the two of you ever take the time to explain to him why he shouldn't ride away from the train?" Scott asked them.

Kerry felt sick to her stomach. "Well, he knows about the Indians. Everyone's been talking about it."

"Yes, everyone's been talking about it, and Foxy and Daniel have been busy reassuring everyone that there's nothing to worry about," Jeb pointed out. He walked briskly toward Scott. "I'm sure the children have heard that, too. Where are your animals, Haskell? I want to take a look."

Kerry followed the two men to the other side of the wagon where five of Scott's six-mule team grazed quietly in the darkness. Please let it be a mistake, she prayed silently. She looked along the line of wagons, *willing* Patrick to come running up with a twin on each hand. What had Jeb just said? A strong will doesn't always prevent tragedy.

"Bring a lantern over here," Jeb said curtly to Scott.

Kerry stood to one side as Scott brought the light and held it aloft while Jeb studied the ground. "I don't see any signs of other riders," Jeb said finally.

"Other riders?" Scott asked.

"Indians. It doesn't appear that they were taken away by anyone."

"If Indians had been here, we would have seen them. There's no way they could just ride in and snatch them right from under everyone's nose," Scott said, sounding as if he thought the wagon master was crazy.

Jeb straightened up and gave Scott a withering glance. "They could snatch your hat right off your head without you ever seeing them, if they'd a mind to. But it looks as if these youngsters have just taken off by themselves."

"I can't believe Patrick would go off in the dark," Kerry said again, her voice cracking.

Jeb made a movement toward her, but stopped as Scott stepped back and put an arm around her. "We'll find them, lass," he said, pulling her against him.

Jeb watched for a minute in silence as she buried her head in the prospector's comforting shoulder. Scott's strong, blacksmith fingers sifted through her short hair. Then Jeb turned to go raise men for a search party.

Within a half hour, at least thirty men had gathered at the Burnett wagon. Jeb kept them back from Scott's animals so that they wouldn't trample any trace of a trail, though he admitted that it would be almost impossible to follow a trail through grass on a dark night. He'd asked the searchers to carry lanterns. Every horse that was accompanying the train was being used and a number of mules. Even Foxy and Daniel had put aside their storytelling for the moment to join the group.

Kerry had dressed in her trousers and one of Patrick's sweaters and was untying one of Scott's mules when Jeb came up to her. "What do you think you're doing?" he asked with none of the gentleness that had been in his voice earlier when they'd been sitting by the fire.

"Getting my mount," she said. "Scott says this one's the most docile."

Jeb looked at her in amazement. "Tie it back up. You're not going anywhere."

Kerry paid no attention. "Excuse me," she said, brushing past him, leading the animal. "Scott's borrowed a saddle for me from the Kirbys."

Jeb put a hand on her arm. "I said you're not going."

"Yes, I am." Her voice was calm.

"Kerry, remember what we were just talking about? I'm the wagon master. I make the rules. We're not taking women."

She looked at him, then, with a sad shake of her head. "I know that you're the wagon master. And I'm willing to follow you every step of the way, but it's my brother out there. He's all I have left in the world. And I'm not going to stay home just because my wagon master is so busy blaming himself for losing one woman that he can't see that another one might be capable of helping out. Of helping *him* out.''

The speech hadn't come out quite the way she had intended, but perhaps it had said, after all, what she had been wanting to say to him for some time now.

Jeb opened his mouth and looked as if he was about to renew his protest, but no words came out. Finally he dropped his hand from her arm and let her walk by him leading the mule toward her own wagon where Scott was waiting with the borrowed saddle.

Dorothy looked as if she was considering following Kerry's lead in insisting on accompanying the party, but finally she merely clung to her husband for a few seconds before he mounted a borrowed horse, then watched as the group rode out into the night.

They stayed in a tight bunch, holding the lanterns high as Jeb pointed out that Scott's mule seemed to be following along a small trail through the grass. If they continued on the path, perhaps there would be a chance to catch up to them. The three children made a light load, which meant the tracks were not deep. Periodically, Jeb held up his hand for the others to stop. Then he climbed down to study the ground and be sure they were still going in the right direction.

There was very little speaking. Once when Foxy Whitcomb started in on a story about Indian captives, Jeb turned around and rudely told him to shut up. The old mountain man was silent after that.

Scott's mules had been tethered near a small grove of trees, which was evidently what had prevented anyone from seeing the departure of the children. The tiny trail appeared to lead directly north, vertical to the river, and headed straight for the scrawny patch of woods covering the base of a line of hills some distance away.

When they had covered about a third of the distance to the trees, Jeb dismounted and spent a longer time than usual looking at the dark ground. When he straightened up, his eyes in the lantern light were troubled. "There are three more tracks now," he told them. "Horses."

Scott jumped from his horse and Kerry struggled down from the broad back of the mule she'd been riding. It was the first time she'd ever ridden by herself and under any other circumstances she would have taken the time to be proud of her accomplishment, but at the moment all she could think about was Patrick and the girls.

"They're not shod," Scott said as he looked down at the hoofprints Jeb was pointing to in the dusty ground.

"No," Jeb agreed quietly. "They're Indian mounts."

A murmur went around the group of riders. For days, weeks now, they'd heard the stories of the Indians. They'd ridden patrols, posted guards. Now, just when many of them were becoming convinced that Jeb Hunter had been crazy to be so worried about a bunch of mythical savages, here they were. Only three of them from what Jeb could see, but where there were three, there could be three hundred. And Patrick, Polly and Molly were with them.

Kerry lost track of how long they'd been searching. It probably had not yet been two hours, but it seemed as if the search had been longer than their whole westward journey thus far. The two mountain men had confirmed Jeb's conclusion that there were now four animals traveling together, still following the tiny overgrown trail through the grass. The trail was more evidence that this territory they were crossing was not exactly wilderness, after all. People had lived here for years, centuries, perhaps. Jeb had been right when he had said that the white folks were the intruders. At the moment the important thing was that the old trail was enabling them to follow the children's progress. If they'd been riding through the tall grass, there would have been no way to determine in which direction they had gone.

Scott let his mule drop back to fall into place beside hers. "How are you holding up, lass?" he asked.

"I'm fine. Patrick's the one we have to worry about—and the twins. Molly's not even fully recovered from her illness."

"She looks healthy enough to me. You just have to have faith that they're all going to be fine."

"Do you think the Indians are taking them to their camp?" she asked, gulping down a wave of fear. They'd all heard the tales of white women and children taken off to live with the Indians and never heard from again.

Scott reached out a hand and patted her knee where it rested on the mule's broad back. "We'll find them, Kerry. We won't go back until we do."

Scott's cheerful, reassuring voice buoyed her spirits as it had done so many times on this trip. He didn't deserve to have come in second in her affections, she thought, fighting back tears. "I'm sorry, Scott," she said.

He looked startled. "Sorry for what?"

She looked down at her hands clutching the horn of the unfamiliar saddle. "About what you saw back there at camp. Jeb and me."

He didn't answer for a moment. Then he said, his voice determinedly light, "Hunter's a lucky man."

"I don't think he would agree with you."

"Why not?"

"Because..." She pressed her lips together as she searched for the words. "Because he doesn't want me. I mean, he doesn't...want to marry me or anything like that."

Scott's expression was unreadable. "He's told you this in so many words?"

"Yes."

The two mules lumbered along another few steps. Finally Scott said, "Then maybe the men on the train are right. Hunter *is* a fool."

Kerry didn't respond. She couldn't think about Jeb right now, about either his problems with the men on the train or his problems with her. She couldn't think about anything but Patrick. She'd already lost her father. She couldn't lose her brother.

Ahead of them the lanterns started to close together in a bunch again as the lead animals drew to a halt. "What's happening?" Kerry asked.

Scott boosted himself up in his stirrups. "There's someone up ahead," he said, then continued with excitement. "Kerry, I think they've found them."

Chapter Sixteen

A half moon had risen over the far hills, providing some light in the dark night. As Kerry struggled to make her recalcitrant animal move faster, she could make out the silhouettes of Patrick and two girls sitting on the back of another mule up ahead. Tears filled her eyes and her limbs tingled with relief. "Patrick," she hollered, and the relief became sheer joy when her brother gave her a weak wave in return.

He was all right, that much was obvious, and with that knowledge she turned her attention to the three horses that surrounded her brother's mule. She could not see very well, but their riders definitely were Indians. Two of them appeared to be half-naked. The rest of the men moved their animals aside to allow her mule to pass through. By the time she'd reached the front, Jeb had dismounted and had lifted both the twins down from the mule. All three children seemed to be in good condition, if a bit subdued. Patrick was sliding off the mule's back. The three Indians remained mounted. When she drew near, Kerry was surprised to see that they were boys, not much older than Patrick.

"It appears we've interrupted an impromptu cultural exchange," Jeb told her as she held tightly to her saddle horn and swung off the mule. Scott came up behind her and dismounted as well.

Kerry ran to fling her arms around Patrick, who hung back and did not look at all pleased at the attention. "That's enough, sis," he grumbled, shooting a look over at the three mounted Sioux, who sat watching the emigrants from the backs of their horses without moving.

"What happened to you, Patrick?" Kerry asked, ending the unwelcomed embrace and stepping back from him. Now that the fear was receding, the anger at her brother's foolishness began to build. "How could you have done such a thing?"

Polly answered for him. "We just came out to meet these boys, Kerry. They were waving to us to come."

"We weren't planning to ride this far," Molly said, her voice full of tears.

Jeb stepped up and put a hand on Patrick's shoulders. "Is that what happened, partner?" he asked gently. "You saw these three Lakota and wanted to come out to meet them?"

"They were signaling to us," Patrick explained, allowing Jeb's touch, which was evidently not as embarrassing as his sister's. "And we didn't want to wave at them to come in to us, because what if one of the lookouts had shot at them or something?"

"Well, you may have been right about that," Jeb acknowledged.

"So we thought we'd just ride out and see if we could talk to them."

"And how did you end up way out here?" Jeb's tone was patient. He seemed to sense that the three children were shaken by their adventure and that yelling at them at this point would not serve any purpose. Kerry knew that inside he must be furious with Patrick for risking his own life and the lives of the Burnett girls in such a way. His restraint was admirable.

"By the time we got Scott's mule, they'd moved out farther, but by then we really wanted to know what they'd be like, so we kept going."

"Then they were going to kidnap us," Polly added with a note of importance.

"They were not," Patrick said quickly.

"They *maybe* were," Polly argued.

Molly was left to explain the real events. "When we got out to them we realized that they didn't understand us, and we couldn't understand them. So one of them grabbed the mule's bridle and they started leading us off to the other side of the meadow."

"We tried to tell them we couldn't go with them," Patrick explained, "but they just laughed and kept going."

"I was so scared," Molly added.

"I wasn't," Polly said. "It was exciting."

Jeb looked up at the three Indians who hadn't moved a muscle while the discussion had been going on. He smiled at them and held up his hand, palm outward.

One of the young Indians made a similar gesture in return, but none of them smiled.

Jeb said a few halting words that they seemed to

understand. The one who had held up his hand answered in rapid speech that had Jeb shaking his head.
"I'm not good enough at their language to understand
all of it," he said. He continued to listen intently as
the boy finished his speech, then he gave a grave nod.
"I think he's trying to say that they were taking the
children to someone in their tribe who speaks English.
They just wanted to talk with them."

Kerry studied the somber faces of the three Indians.
Close up, they looked much like her brother, the same
earnest look in their eyes, the same slim bodies, not
yet filling out into manhood. Her fear of them disappeared. They might have been three young Irish
boys coming to collect Patrick after a day at the fish
market. "Shall we invite them back to the train?" she
asked, noting that Patrick's expression brightened at
the suggestion.

Jeb shook his head. "Not with the current mood of
the folks back there. I don't need more problems."

"It doesn't look as if these boys would be any
problem," she objected.

"No, but what about when their people come looking for them, the way we had to come looking for
Patrick and the girls?"

"Oh." Kerry saw the look of disappointment on
Patrick's face. "You think there are more around,
then."

"I know there are more around," Jeb answered,
casting a look back to where Foxy and Daniel were
waiting quietly on their horses. Perhaps this would
shut up the two old geezers, Jeb thought with a little
sigh. He turned to Patrick. "Say goodbye to your new
friends, Patrick. It's dark and late, and we have no

idea when these boys' elders are going to decide to come along, so we're getting back to the train."

"I think they're friendly," Patrick said wistfully.

"I do, too, partner, but I'd rather not risk a meeting. Especially not in the middle of the night with your sister and the girls out here."

Patrick gave a reluctant nod and turned to the three young braves. He held up his hand the way he'd seen Jeb do, and this time all three Indians held up theirs. Then they wheeled their horses and rode away in a cloud of dust.

Everyone on the train who hadn't been on the actual search party was waiting near the Burnetts' wagon when they arrived back with the children. Dorothy hugged her two girls so hard that their feet left the ground. Patrick seemed a little ill at ease when Charles Kirby and his other friends crowded around. It was as if he couldn't quite decide if he'd been the hero of a great adventure or a naughty child who should be ashamed of himself.

It was quite a while before folks started drifting off to their own wagons for bed. Before they left Jeb asked for volunteers for extra guard duty.

"The three Indians were just children, Captain," Thomas Crandall protested. "Not as old as my boy Homer. I don't see any reason to put on more guards."

Jeb had had about enough of Thomas Crandall. At least this time Foxy and Daniel were keeping their mouths shut. They had sense enough to know that the three young lads they had seen wouldn't be traveling alone. It was true that they had seemed friendly, but it would be downright stupid not to take precautions. "Don't volunteer then, Crandall," he said curtly. "I'm sure there are plenty of other men here who are willing to lose sleep in order to be sure that you and your family are safe."

"What's that supposed to mean? Are you calling me a coward or something?"

Jeb just shook his head and turned to talk with Frank Todd. But Kerry watched with worried eyes as Thomas Crandall and some of the other men walked away talking together and casting hostile glances back at their wagon leader.

Jeb could learn a little more tact, she decided. But after their kiss at the fire earlier that evening, she wasn't about to seek him out to tell him so. She would just head back to her own wagon with the rest of the crowd and enjoy watching her brother climb into his bed, safe and sound and alive. Morning would be time enough to try once again to give Jeb Hunter a little advice on diplomacy.

She was wrong. Morning hadn't been time enough. During the course of the night the rebellious faction had met at Thomas Crandall's wagon. They'd invited the mountain men to join them, and, after an initial reluctance, the two veterans had agreed to take over as trail guides if the association decided they no longer wanted to continue on with Jeb Hunter.

"And we'll be sure that's what they decide," Crandall had assured them.

They'd gone to rouse the wagon master from his bedroll at dawn, catching him sleepy and, Jeb noted ironically, once again without his boots.

"We're done taking orders from you, Hunter," Crandall told him. "You can ride with us as far as Fort Laramie if you like or you can just head on out of here today. But Foxy'll be taking over your job."

"Oh, really?" Jeb was remarkably calm, which surprised him. Normally he would be spitting fire about now, ready to tear Crandall's head off for risking everybody's lives in such a blamed stupid way. But suddenly he was feeling, to hell with it. It wasn't his job to save every damned fool in the world. Maybe it was something Kerry had said about his needing to punish himself by feeling responsible for everything bad that happened in the world. There was only so much that one person could do. The world would continue to be a risky place no matter how hard he kept trying. "Are you intending to call for a vote on this, Crandall?"

"Just to make it official. But I think we can be pretty sure of how it's going to turn out."

Jeb sat back down on the ground and started to pull on his boots. "Fine. Let me know when you get the results."

The men looked at each other, a little discomfited at his easy capitulation. Then Crandall said, "C'mon. Todd will have to call the vote. Let's go find him."

Eulalie woke Kerry with the news, which by then was buzzing through the train. "I think it's time for the women's party to spring into action again," the older woman told her as Kerry splashed river water on her face to wake up.

"I can't believe they're even considering this," Kerry said with disgust. "Just last night they saw again that Jeb knows what he's talking about. He said we were in Indian country, and there they were, as big as life."

"But only children," Eulalie said.

"So what? Would they have been happier if it had been a war party?"

Eulalie shook her gray head. "I know. That's why we need to get the women together again. To talk some sense into them."

"All right. I'll get Dorothy and we'll start going around to the wagons."

"We don't have much time. Crandall is insisting that the vote be taken before we leave this morning."

"It won't take us much time," Kerry said firmly.

Kerry was surprised to see Jeb sitting coolly on the lowered tailgate of the Todds' wagon, whittling a piece of wood. He didn't seem to be the least disturbed that the entire encampment was about to take a vote on whether to overthrow his leadership of the train. His bedroll and gear were still scattered near the wagon. He evidently had made no effort to get himself ready to begin to roll, even though it was already later than he usually liked the wagons to get started.

He smiled at her as she moved into the already gathered crowd and, surprised, she smiled back.

Frank was beginning to pass out tiny scraps of paper to the crowd. "I'll pass around and collect these in a few minutes. If you're voting to make Foxy our new wagon master, scratch an *x* on the paper. Otherwise leave it blank."

He handed one slip to each man until Kerry asked, "Aren't the women going to vote, too?"

Frank shook his head. "The rules say that only men vote."

"The women were included in the vote about whether Patrick and I could continue on with the train."

Frank looked apologetic. "That was a special situation. But for changing the whole contract like this, I guess it's just gotta be the men."

Kerry put her hands on her hips and turned around, looking at the rest of the women behind her with indignation. Jeb jumped down from the wagon and walked toward her, still smiling. "Don't bother yourself about it, sweetheart. Let them take their vote."

Frank finished distributing the papers, then said, "I just want to go on record saying that I stand one hundred percent behind Jeb. He's gotten us this far, ahead of schedule, without losing a wagon."

"We lost Mrs. Hamilton," Thomas Crandall said snidely.

Frank stared him down. "Yes, and we might have lost a sight more if Jeb hadn't known that it was the river that was sickening folk."

"I agree." The usually silent John Burnett surprised everyone by speaking vehemently. "And he saved my daughter's life."

"Ah, we don't know that it was the river that did the sickening," Crandall said with a wave of his hand, nodding to the men who were next to him. "C'mon, let's get this over with." And at least half of the men mumbled agreement.

Jeb stood next to her, surveying the crowd, his expression still placid. Kerry couldn't believe what she was hearing. "Just a minute," she said so loudly that even Thomas Crandall looked taken aback. "I may not get a vote, but I'm a member of this train the same as anyone else, and I at least get my say."

She pushed through the crowd to the tailgate where Jeb had been sitting and boosted herself up so she could look out over the heads of the men who were the principal dissenters.

"You men ought to be ashamed of yourselves," she said, her eyes stabbing each one in turn. "Every step of the way from Westport to this point has been made possible by Jeb Hunter. He's told us where and how to go. He's seen us safely across rivers where you know very well that other trains have lost whole wagons. He's gotten us almost to the end of Indian territory without problems, even though, as we saw last night, there definitely are Indians around, just as he said. He's cured your sick and looked after your women and children, caring about them as if they were his very own." She paused to take a deep, ragged breath. "Back at Fort Kearney we heard them say that Jeb Hunter would sooner lose his own life than the life of one of his emigrants. That's the kind of man we hired to get us to California. And that's the man who will get us there unless all of you are complete—" she sputtered a little as she searched for the word "—blockheads!"

At the edge of the crowd, Patrick began to applaud, and little by little others took up the ovation. Someone at the rear blew a piercing whistle of approval and Dorothy said fervently, "Amen to that!"

Kerry, a little embarrassed by her vehemence,

jumped down from the wagon, but she'd said her piece. Throughout the crowd, wives and mothers and sisters were busy whispering in the ears of their men, and when Frank collected the small scraps of paper, there were only two with black marks.

Jeb looked almost indifferently at the heap of crumpled paper in Frank's hands, then around at the crowd. "All right. We're getting a late start, folks," he said. "I reckon we'd better get moving."

It wasn't until later that morning that he rode back to Kerry's wagon to thank her for standing up for him.

"I can't believe I had to," she said, still indignant, holding the reins of the oxen as Jeb pulled alongside on Storm. Patrick was riding with the Burnetts. "You have a right to be furious with those men."

"I can't see that it would do much good," he said. "As I told you last night, people get the crazies along about this point in the trip."

"You seem so calm about it. Where's the Jeb Hunter who frets himself into a headache whenever anything's going wrong with his train?"

"He's learning not to fret so much."

Kerry leaned back against the seat, puzzled. "How's he doing that?"

Jeb smiled at her. He'd been smiling all day, it seemed. "Maybe by realizing that duty isn't the only thing in life, that it's all right for a man to want something more. Happiness, for example."

Now she was truly mystified. This simply did not sound like the stern wagon master she'd watched trying fiercely to take care of everyone's needs for the past several weeks. "Happiness?" she asked cautiously.

"Yes. Remember that first time I kissed you—you told me I was a wagon master, not a father." She nodded. "I've decided I'm not going to be everyone's protector anymore. I'll do my job to the best of my ability, and maybe somewhere along the line, I'll start to think about having a life of my own again, too."

"When did you decide this?" The wagon jolted into a rut. These weren't ideal conditions for a discussion that she felt was extremely important to Jeb, perhaps to them both.

Jeb looked up at her from under the brim of his hat. "It might have been while I was watching you seek comfort on Haskell's shoulder last night instead of mine."

Kerry did a quick intake of breath. This definitely was not the place for this conversation. Jeb seemed to get the same idea, because he grinned at her, then tipped his hat and said, "You'll have to excuse me, sweetheart, but I've got a wagon train to run."

Then he rode away, leaving her watching his retreating form with sweaty palms and her heart beating a heavy accompaniment to the monotonous drone of the big oak wagon wheels turning beneath her.

The sight of it had caused a cheer to be passed along the ranks of the wagons. Independence Rock—the imposing gray granite structure rising one hundred feet above the level plain. And there beyond it—their first, heart-stopping view of the Rockies. Reach Independence Rock by the Fourth of July and your passage is a success, the veterans said. And just as Jeb had predicted, the end of the prairie and the sight of the mountains rising before them, with their promise of riches beyond, gave everyone a new burst of energy and enthusiasm.

They would celebrate their country's independence as well as their own in the shadow of the rock, they decided, camping the train along its six-hundred-yard length. Jeb had declared that the day would be a holiday, and the children had already abandoned their wagons to go play in the blessedly fresh Sweetwater River.

Many of the women had banded together once again, not for a political cause this time, but to plan a feast to delight appetites sick of dried vegetables and pilot bread. Several of the men had gone hunting and had returned with rabbits and dozens of sage hens, curlews and snipe.

When the children returned from their dunking in the river, they were sent out to harvest wild onions and garlic and dandelion and mustard greens. A patch of grapes was found growing right near the rock, and while several of the young boys carved their names alongside those of the settlers who had passed through there before, the girls picked the grapes and brought them back to their mothers.

Kerry was thoroughly enjoying the camaraderie of preparing the holiday meal with the other women. Even though they had not won the right to vote with the association, joining to make a statement about their feelings had brought them together in a way that few of them had experienced back East. Kerry had a feeling that what Eulalie had said back at Fort Kearney was the truth. There were winds of change blowing in this new land they were adopting. The West would be a freer place for everyone, but especially for its women.

The holiday preparations also served to keep her busy, which was a good thing. Sitting perched on her wagon through the long, tedious days, she'd had far too much time to think and wonder. After his cryptic comments the day of the association vote, Jeb had not sought an occasion to be alone with her. He came to pick up Patrick each morning, and greeted her with a warm smile, but he'd not come to their campfire at night. He'd not called her sweetheart again.

Kerry was starting to believe that she had only imagined the comments he'd made that day. Had he really implied that he hadn't liked seeing her in Scott Haskell's arms? What had that meant, anyway? she'd asked herself impatiently. Probably nothing.

She'd been as ready as the rest of the emigrants for the morale-boosting sight of the Rock. She'd try to put Jeb Hunter out of her thoughts, she resolved. She'd enjoy the companionship of her new women friends and the celebration of the holiday. She'd think about the ranch she was going to build. And she'd do her best not to let her thoughts drift to the wagon master more than, say, four times an hour.

The women had outdone themselves. The makeshift tables were literally sagging with the weight of all the food. Fires had been stoked hot all day and the result was an endless array of goodies—pound cakes made from the precious butter that had been brought in brine-packed barrels all the way from Westport and jelly rolls made from the wild grapes the children had gathered. Dorothy had made her special Southern gingerbread. The men ate until they were groaning and discreetly loosening their trousers, and the women looked on fondly and beamed.

It was as if their eleven weeks of backbreaking journey had never been undertaken. It was as if the equally long expanse that awaited them was years in the future. They were gay and silly and, for the moment, in love with life.

Kerry thought she had never laughed so hard. Daniel and Foxy, who had been forgiven by Jeb and had decided to continue on with the train into the mountains, had entertained them with more of their tall tales. And the children had put on an Independence Day pageant that included the Burnett twins and Patrick as the inalienable rights—Life, Liberty and Happiness.

As she joined in the applause at the end of their tableau, Jeb slipped to a seat next to her. "Inalienable rights. Do you think that's what your father had in mind when he decided to take you out West?" he asked her.

She turned toward him. "I suppose so. Certainly the happiness part."

"Mmm. That's often the tough one."

Kerry nodded. "Yes. How are you doing with it?" When he gave her a questioning look, she continued, "The other day you implied that you might be interested in some of that commodity yourself."

Jeb smiled at her. "I said that?"

"Something like that."

A cricket chirped right behind where they were sitting, startling them both into a laugh. "Now there's a cheerful fellow, for example,'' Jeb said. ''Do you suppose he's happy?''

Kerry laughed again, feeling utterly happy herself. ''I don't know.''

Suddenly he was pulling her to her feet and away from the folks who were still seated around the make-shift stage where the children had presented their production. ''They're finished here. Let's go for a walk,'' he said. His voice was buoyant.

''I should help clean up the food,'' Kerry protested, but Jeb pulled her along next to him.

''Let someone else do it. You can't be responsible for everything that happens on this train,'' he said, gently mocking some of her own past comments to him.

She stopped resisting and let him lead her away from the lights and along the edge of the big monolith. When they came to the end of it, he continued right on around the corner and led her around to the other side. The narrow rock was only about twenty yards wide. ''That's better,'' he said when they had put the huge rock between themselves and the rest of the camp. He still held her hand at his side.

''What's better?'' she asked.

''This,'' he said, and then he pressed her up against the cliff and trapped her there with an arm on each side of her head. His face was totally dark. She could see nothing of his expression as he lowered his mouth to hers and kissed her. It was not a long kiss, but it was skillful and thorough. Kerry melted against the stone at her back. ''God, I've been wanting to do that for days,'' Jeb said with a small groan.

Kerry felt a smile growing from deep inside her. "Have you, now?" she asked with a touch of brogue.

"Yes."

"And what's been stoppin' you, Jeb Hunter?" The smile reached her face, turning up her already sensitive lips.

"I've been doing some considering."

She was still imprisoned against the cliff by his arms, though they weren't touching her. "Considering?"

He nodded. She could see little of his expression, but behind his head the sky stretched out in an explosion of stars. "It's going to take some getting used to, this happiness thing."

"But you're going to give it a try?"

He took a step closer to her and dropped his arms. "Yes," he whispered.

"I'm glad," she whispered back. And then neither one spoke for a long while as he pulled her into his arms and let their bodies press against each other while he kissed her again and again. After several moments he turned and braced himself against the wall behind them while he lifted her up against him so that her feet no longer touched the ground. She could feel the softest part of her body nestle against his hardness. And he continued his relentless kisses.

"How am I doing?" he asked finally.

She had trouble understanding his words. "Hmm?" she murmured.

"On the happiness. Am I starting to get the idea?"

She gave a little laugh and let herself slide down so that her feet could touch the ground again. "I think you've already gotten the idea, Jeb Hunter."

He let her go. "You're right about that. I'd give anything right now for a soft bed and several hours of privacy with you."

"You're not likely to get either, I'm afraid."

He gave a little tug to the front of his trousers. "I can see that compromise might be in order here. How about a *wagon* bed and a number of long nights between here and California?"

His words made the flush of Kerry's elation over being in his arms again begin to fade. Between here and California, he'd said. Jeb was not offering marriage. He evidently was relenting enough to admit that he wanted her, but not to believe that they had a chance at a life together. She rubbed her arms. "You forget I have a brother. And you have a train to run. I don't think that it would look very good to have you sneaking into my wagon at night."

Jeb's face was now turned toward the half moon and she could see that he was smiling. "You don't, eh?"

"No."

"Which means you're going to make me wait until after we can get to a preacher at Fort Laramie."

"A preacher?"

"Or the fort commandant. I'm not particular who marries us, as long as it means that I get to start sneaking into your wagon every night. Legitimately."

Kerry's first reaction was a surge of relief. It wasn't the most romantic proposal, but it was definitely a proposal, and now that he'd said it, she could admit that it was what she'd been wanting to hear for weeks. She put her arms around his neck and went up on her toes to kiss him, which received his immediate and full cooperation. It wasn't until long moments later that the doubts began to hammer at her. What would this mean to her plans, her promise to her father? Yes, Jeb wanted to sleep in her wagon—she wanted him there, too. But what else did he want? He'd told her that he never again wanted the kind of life he'd lost with his wife. Would he be willing to settle down and help her build her dream?

He sensed her sudden withdrawal and allowed her to pull herself away. She folded her arms and cocked her head, studying him. "So you sneak into my wagon every night, Mr. Wagon Master, but what about once the train arrives in California?" she asked. "What happens then?"

His expression turned serious as he took her cheeks in his hands and kissed her just once, softly. "Once we reach California? Now there's a question. Have you thought about children on that dream ranch of yours, sweetheart? I think we should have three."

Kerry's eyes misted. "Three? I was hoping for four," she answered him with a saucy smile.

"Four then. You see what a pushover I've become?" He lifted her off her feet and sank with her in his arms to the soft grass at the foot of the rock. "Would you mind very much if we got started right away?"

She kissed the end of his chin. "I wouldn't mind at all."

His hands had moved to her already hardened breasts and he was caressing them through the thin material of her dress. The tall grass blew around them as he began to unfasten her buttons. "One of these days we *are* going to do this in a bed,'' he said ruefully.

"I don't care," she said with a sigh, then gave a little gasp as his mouth found one sensitive nipple.

"Nor do I." He chuckled. "At least not at this particular moment." Then he made a little gasp of his own as her hand caressed him through his soft buckskin trousers. "That's so nice, sweetheart," he encouraged, which emboldened her to open the pants entirely and seek the warm hardness of him.

Jeb lay back for a minute and let her stroke him, let the waves build. This time he would give himself to her fully. There would be no withdrawal, no taking care to put limitations on his commitment. For the first time since the death of his wife he would allow himself to become one with another human being, to merge himself with her and perhaps in the process create a new life from that bond of love.

She was more than ready to receive him, and when his thrusts became more frantic she met them with strength and joy. He thought his heart would explode right along with the rest of his body as he poured himself into her. Then he held her gently, lovingly, and pressed their cheeks together as her tears mingled with his own.

"I don't deserve it," he said softly, "but I would be the happiest man in California if you would become my bride. I love you, Kerry Gallivan." The words he had never thought to say again felt like a cooling salve on deep-set burns.

She nestled into his arms beside him and sighed. "I love you, too, Wagon Master." Then they lay quietly in each other's arms and watched the star-spangled Western night.

Epilogue

Napa Valley
June 1858

"Are you sure this will be all right?" Jeb asked
with a worried frown. "I'd feel better if we had a
doctor to say you were well enough."

"I'm a pioneer woman now, darling." Kerry
pushed herself back into the pillows and put her arms
out to Jeb, who stood next to the bed, still totally
dressed. "If I could birth our baby by myself, I guess
I can decide to invite my husband back into my bed."

Tentative, Jeb put one knee up on the bed. "You
weren't totally birthing him by yourself. You did have
Patrick and me to help."

Kerry rolled her eyes. "Big help you were—Patrick running out back to get sick to his stomach at
the first sight of blood and you pacing and moaning
and wringing your hands as if I were the first woman
who'd ever had a baby. Dorothy and I did all the
work." Much to Kerry's delight, the Burnetts had de-

cided to homestead the adjoining land in the fertile valley just north of San Francisco.

Jeb leaned over and kissed her with a smile. "Well, you were the first woman who ever had *my* baby."

She met his eyes with the fond new expression that they'd each developed for discussing their son. "He's beautiful, isn't he?" she said for perhaps the dozenth time that day.

Jeb gave up his reticence and eased himself down on the bed beside her. "Sean Hunter. The most beautiful baby in California."

"Or the world maybe," Kerry agreed happily. "Is he all right, do you think?"

Jeb glanced over at the crib where his son lay sleeping soundly. "He's fine. You worry too much, Mrs. Hunter."

Kerry giggled. "Now that's an interesting charge coming from you, Mr. Wagon Master."

He inched himself toward her on the bed. "I'm not a master of wagon trains anymore. I'm only the master of my household."

Kerry drew herself up to spit out an indignant protest, but he leaned over and captured her lips before she had a chance. "And of my lovely, enticing wife," he murmured between kisses, "who has these new, alluring curves that have been driving me crazy for the past few weeks." He began to explore her fuller breasts and hips through the thin cloth of her muslin nightgown as he spoke. Then he stopped and raised his head. "Are you sure this is all right?" he asked again.

"Now who's the worrier?" she asked, pulling his head back toward her.

He let her bring it to rest on her chest and gave a sigh of contentment. "My worrying days are over. I'm completely happy with you, sweetheart, and with Sean. This land is as rich as anything your father could ever have dreamed, and we're going to have a good life here."

"I wish Patrick was happier about it," she said with a small frown.

Jeb lifted his head. "I've told you before, your brother's fourteen now—the age of adventure. It'll do him a world of good to spend the summer in the gold fields with Haskell."

Kerry still found it ironic that following her rough frontier wedding last year at Fort Laramie, Jeb and Scott had proceeded to become great friends. It appeared that once the question of rivalry for her affections was settled, the two men were able to look deeper and discover kindred spirits.

"It was good of Scott to agree to take him," she agreed.

"My prediction is that he'll find that the glamorous life of a prospector is mostly sweat and hard work. He'll be happy to come back to us in the fall."

"And in the meantime, we get to have a little of the privacy you once told me you wanted. A soft bed and hours of privacy, I believe was the way you phrased it."

"We've managed to do well enough without it," Jeb noted with a grin and a wave at little Sean's cradle.

"But I was promised four of those critters, Captain. I believe it was in my contract."

Jeb laughed and, giving up any pretense at resisting

her efforts to seduce him back into her bed, sat on the edge of the bed, pulled off his boots and then dived for her, carefully rolling her over on top of him in his arms, making a tangle of the blankets. "New items keep creeping into that contract. I thought it was finished when I delivered you to California soil."

"No, that was the first contract. I'm talking about the one when you made me your bride." She looked down at him. Her milk-heavy breasts had hardened against his chest. But Sean had just been fed. The tingling she was feeling now was due to a different stimulation.

"Ah, that one. That's the one that says I get to have you to myself every night for the rest of our lives." One of his hands gently sculpted a breast through her nightgown. He was being so careful, so slow. It had been so long. Kerry thought she would go crazy with the waiting.

"Yes, the rest of our lives," she agreed, growing breathless as he eased her to one side and finally reached for the buttons of his shirt.

"Kerry, Jeb?"

Jeb sat up abruptly, banging his head on the back-board of the bed. Around the corner of the open bed-room door two identical blond heads were peering.

Kerry pulled the neck of her nightgown together and sat up beside Jeb. "Polly, Molly," she acknowl-edged, a little self-consciously.

The girls moved around the door and into the room, unaware of what they had interrupted. "Are you busy?" Molly asked innocently.

Kerry looked at Jeb, who was trying to keep the annoyance off his face. She gave him a sympathetic smile, then turned back to the girls. "No, sweeties, we're not busy. Did you want something?"

"Molly was missing Patrick," Polly explained.

"Polly is, too," her sister added.

"Well, I miss him, too," Kerry agreed. "But I expect he's having a good time with Scott."

"Do you think he's going to find a fortune?" Polly asked with wide eyes.

Kerry shook her head, aware of Jeb's hand inching up her thigh under cover of the blanket. "I...ah... don't really know."

Polly scuffled her feet, then said. "We thought you might be missing him, too, so we came to give you some company. Mama said you might be feeling lonely."

Kerry gave a helpless glance at Jeb, who winked at her and took over. He smiled over at the girls. "Now, that was very nice of you girls. But right now, little Sean is sleeping and Kerry was just about to take a nap herself. New mothers need lots of rest, you know."

Both girls nodded. "Maybe we should come back later," Molly suggested.

Jeb smiled his approval. "Tomorrow would be good," he told them. His hand had reached the very top of Kerry's thigh and she lay back against the pillows, closing her eyes and biting her lip to keep from moaning. "See, girls," he said, lowering his voice. "She's already going to sleep."

"We'll come back tomorrow morning," Polly said, grabbing her sister's hand and turning to tiptoe out of the room.

"Not too early," Jeb called softly after them.

"Scoundrel," Kerry said, opening her eyes. But her smile was deep. Under the blanket his fingers continued their exploration.

"Will you tell me if anything's uncomfortable?" The frown furrowed his forehead again.

"Darling husband, the only thing that's uncomfortable is waiting to feel you inside me again."

The remark had him instantly aroused. He rolled to his feet, carefully closing and latching the door this time, then stripped off his clothes and joined her in bed, where she'd already pulled off her gown. "Ah," he breathed with satisfaction as their naked bodies met.

"It's nice to have you back, husband," she murmured between kisses.

His eyes took on a look of deep contentment. He held her gaze as he ever so gently eased himself into her. "Remember how your father used to have you freeze your favorite moment?" he asked. Kerry nodded, her heart too full for words. "My love," Jeb said. "This one is mine."

* * * * *